South
of
Sideways

Jeff
Zwagerman

BLACK🌹ROSE
writing

The final approval for this literary material is granted by the author.

First printing

This is a work of fiction. Names, characters, businesses, places, events and incidents are either the products of the author's imagination or used in a fictitious manner. Any resemblance to actual persons, living or dead, or actual events is purely coincidental.

ISBN: 978-1-61296-811-7
PUBLISHED BY BLACK ROSE WRITING
www.blackrosewriting.com

Printed in the United States of America
Suggested retail price $19.95

South of Sideways is printed in Book Antiqua

I dedicate this book to my childhood and lifelong friend, Hugs. While poles apart in interests and life experiences, the influence of this friendship on both our lives is yet to be discovered and understood. Thanks for the ride my friend.

South of Sideways

Prologue

De duivel schijt altijd op de grootste hoop
The devil always shits on the biggest pile.
—Dutch Proverb

The trucker was looking forward to stopping at Story City, Iowa. It was hot. People used to say, after the week of the 4th of July, summer was over. Nobody told the weatherman in Iowa. The gauge in his truck read 99 degrees, hot by anybody's standard.

He was ready for a late lunch. He always tried to time his stop to coincide lunch or dinner at his favorite chain restaurant in Story City, the Happy Chef. A man of simple tastes, he loved the huge white statue of a fat chef, complete with a checkered apron, near the entrance. The trucker was a man of simple tastes. He had stopped at various restaurants in the chain while he moved from highway to highway. Story City was his favorite, although, he didn't mind the one in North Mankato, Minnesota. It was a close second.

He saw his exit and slowed the eighteen-wheeler enough to make the curve safely. The Happy Chef was just on his left, but he always parked in the lot of the outlet mall across the street. It was an easy in and easy out for him. His little mutt, Mr. Peabody, was sitting up on the passenger seat, panting in anticipation.

The trucker was always amazed that the dog behaved the same way when they made this particular stop. Mr. Peabody was a smart dog, for a mutt, but he never quite got this routine down.

"Mr. Peabody, you better go back and lay down in the sleeper. You know you don't get out here."

Mr. Peabody did as he was told. He always did. He was a good dog.

The trucker locked up his rig, making sure the big diesel was running, so the air conditioning would be functioning for Mr. Peabody. He checked the gauges on his "reefer" to make sure his cargo of *Blue Bunny* ice cream stayed frozen. He had been pulling a refrigeration unit for more years than he could remember. The "reefer" unit was an amazing piece of trucking marvel. He could run things that needed to stay warm all the way down to things that needed to stay frozen. There was versatility in running a rig like that. He still preferred ice cream, however.

Everyone knew him in the restaurant. His route from Le Mars, Iowa to Minneapolis, Minnesota and back to Des Moines usually put him at the Happy Chef once a week. All the waitresses loved him. He always left a big tip on his rather small check. He knew they needed the money.

They teased him when he walked in, and he teased them back. The trucker had a good sense of humor and was always upbeat. The servers always flipped a coin to see who got to wait on him. One of his favorites won the toss, and sauntered over to his table.

"Hey hon, back in town again?"

They all called him hon because that's what they called everyone.

"Just blew in to see your pretty face, Thursday."

Thursday was the day of the week he had met her, so that became her nickname.

"Aw, I believe you say that to all the girls."

"Why yes, I believe I do." The trucker winked and agreed.

Thursday was a cute little blue-eyed blonde, who could speak to anyone. She was too young for the trucker, and anyway, she was married to a nice guy. The trucker had even met him once. He liked him right away because he had a successful company that made side-dump trailers. That gave them both a lot to talk about.

"Will it be the usual, or do you need a menu?"

The trucker had been trying to keep his weight down. His "usual" lunch was generally some kind of salad with a low calorie dressing. He always let one of the servers choose it for him, but he was tired of salad.

"Better give me a menu, beautiful."

He called all the waitresses "beautiful".

"You got it. We've got some pretty good iced tea today. It's not sweetened."

"Bring it on."

Most of the lunch crowd had left, and he was alone at his table in the corner. He watched the traffic go by. He wondered if he would ever settle down in a small community like this one.

The waitress brought over the iced tea and menu, and left the trucker alone to make his lunch choice.

It didn't take him long at all. He noticed the hamburger steak and he decided on that. He got two sides with it, so he chose the light cottage cheese and the green beans.

The waitress took his order, refilled his ice tea, and was gone. It gave the trucker time to contemplate his "creature of habit" existence. He figured he needed a change, but change was something way out of his comfort zone.

Change had happened to the trucker only when it was forced upon him. He was still thinking about change when his food arrived. The server put everything in front of him, and included his usual "doggy bag" with two plain hamburgers with no buns. It was for Mr. Peabody, and it truly was a "doggy bag". The staff loved the dog and would have let him bring him in the restaurant, but it was against management's policy.

When he was almost finished with lunch, most of the staff came out and sat at his table. Thursday was her usual spunky self, and everyone always felt better when she was around. It was a fine way to spend an hour. These people may have been the closest thing he had to call friends.

Just when the trucker thought he should get moving, Thursday spoke.

"There's a woman over there hanging around your truck," she said motioning toward the front window. "I think she's been there for over a half-hour."

The trucker stood up and looked over at his rig. A woman was standing on the passenger side running board.

He didn't like anyone messing with his truck.

1

The trucker's name was Herbert Schutt. It was a Dutch name, and the last name was pronounced "Skut". He had grown up in the small northwest Iowa town of Hospers. His parents had a farm northeast of town, where the family eked out a marginal existence. Everyone called him Herbie. He had always been a big kid. By modern standards, he might even been labeled borderline obese.

Herbie went to Hospers Public School until they merged with the surrounding communities of Alton and Newkirk to form the Floyd Valley School District, so called because of their proximity to the Floyd River. Rumor was that Lewis and Clark named it after Sergeant Floyd, who was the only casualty on their trek in search of the Northwest Passage.

Herbie didn't like the river. It was muddy from all the black soil run-off, and he thought it smelled like hog shit. It wasn't much of a river at all. In the summer, there would be places where it completely dried up. The few remaining fish would find the standing pools of black water. When they used up the oxygen, they died. That was one of the reasons Herbie hated the river. He didn't like seeing death, and he certainly didn't like the smell of it.

Herbie wasn't a typical farm boy. His interests involved listening to the radio and watching television. He seldom went outside unless his parents forced him. Luckily, he had other siblings to help with the farm chores. Television was a hit-and-miss project back then. There were three Sioux City stations to choose from, and they almost always were "snowy". The radio was limited to AM stations, but after dark, the transistors could dial in the megawatt channels like KOMA in Oklahoma City, KAYL in Little Rock, and WLS in Chicago. All would be great unless there was a thunderstorm, then there was nothing but static.

By the time Herbie reached high school, he had an uncanny ability to name all the songs and every artist who sang them. He could name the members of all the groups, and he knew the names of every daytime and nighttime DJ. Herbie had always wondered why he had that particular talent. It wouldn't help him in school and it did nothing to further his net worth, which was as close to nothing as anyone could get.

Herbie couldn't remember when he and Sander Van Zee became friends. They had attended the same church and went to Sunday school together, but that, and early school days, proved to be just acquaintanceship rather than a full-blown friendship. As he thought about it, Herbie figured they became close friends while riding the bus from Hospers to Alton where they attended high school.

At some point during those four years, Sander became "Zander" and Herbie earned the nickname of "Beached Whale Boy". It was due to his form in physical education class. The boys and girls were separated back then, and all the guys always stopped whatever they were doing to watch him try to do sit-ups. It was good that Herbie had the ability to laugh at himself. It took the sting out of the nastiness of trying to fit in, during those awkward teen years. Kids were cruel, and the adults did little to stop the bullying back then. It didn't matter to Herbie, and soon the guys in his grade accepted him for his cheerful disposition and his ability to make them laugh. He never had the same luck with the females, however.

Try as he might, he couldn't get one girl to give him as much as a second look. It frustrated him. He even started writing anonymous letters to a few of the girls in the class below him. He always got caught, and then the humiliation would be relentless. That pissed him off worse than anything else. Other than his family, no one knew that he had a terrible temper. He had done an excellent job of burying it along with all the hurt he experienced over the years.

The morning bus rides were always crowded. Not many students had access to cars back then, and everyone rode the bus. The afternoon return trips were much less crowded. The after school activities took many of the students, and they had to ride the later bus home.

It was on one of those early March afternoon bus rides, that Zander and Herbie cemented their friendship. It was unusual for Zander to be riding the regular bus home in the afternoons, but he had jammed his knee at basketball practice the day before. The coaches were looking toward the upcoming tournament schedule and needed Zander to be healthy. They called his parents and convinced them to take him to the doctor that afternoon.

There weren't many on the bus, and a few of the guys were bored. Someone brought out a permanent marker, and suggested they all write their names on the seat backs. Of course, nicknames were to be used. Herbie was writing "Beached Whale Boy" when Zander noticed the bus driver squinting into the mirror. He was trying to watch what was going on. Zander passed the word along quietly.

One of the girls had an ink eraser and with a bunch of elbow grease, most everyone got rid of the evidence. It took Herbie quite a while to get rid of what he wrote. At sometime during the process, he looked over at Zander.

"Why couldn't you assholes just call me Al?"

The whole bus erupted.

Zander pitched in and by the time they reached the bus stop, the lettering was gone. The bus driver stopped the bus and told everyone to stay seated. He went down the row checking for writing and seemed perplexed at not finding anything.

"I know you did something, and I'm not going to put up with any more of your nonsense." The bus driver was always saying stuff like that, and the kids never paid much attention.

Zander would get off the bus at that point, and Herbie would continue on the rural route. Zander gave Herbie "five" before he left the bus. Herbie thought that might have been the best day ever. Zander's gesture of friendship increased his coolness factor one hundred percent.

Herbie had one thing that Zander lacked, and that was access to wheels. It made for a dependent relationship during the junior and senior class plays.

Herbie had the use of an old 1956 Ford Fairlane. The muffler housing still existed, but there was nothing inside of it. The radio didn't work but that didn't matter, because it was so loud going down the highway, no one could have heard anything anyway. The passenger side floorboard had rusted out, and Zander freaked out the first time he rode down the highway with Herbie. He could see the highway below his feet. Herbie had a good laugh at Zander's expense, but he found a piece of plywood that he fitted over the hole and threw an old floor-mat over it. Zander never seemed very comfortable riding with Herbie after that, however.

When Herbie was a senior, he got some money from an aunt, who had passed away, and he bought himself a used Volkswagen Beetle. It was hard to tell what year it was, because they all looked the same. There was no heater to speak of, so Herbie bought a cheap portable catalytic heater. They had to crack the windows to keep from getting asphyxiated; still it was a huge step up from the Ford.

Both Herbie and Zander had the leads in the senior production of *Silas Marner*. They had read the book in English class and were familiar with the story. Herbie played the part of Silas and Zander was Godfrey. It always puzzled Herbie why the writer called herself George Eliot instead of using her real name. Zander tried to explain that just maybe she wouldn't have been published because she was a woman. Times were much different then. That type of thinking was totally foreign to the both of them.

After graduation, Herbie enrolled in Nettleton Business School in Sioux City. Zander went off to Northwestern College. They got together once, the first year, at a party in Sioux City. Many of the old classmates were there, but goals and interests were changing. That was the last real reunion of the guys.

Herbie never took to business school. That reality became even more evident when he received his first semester grades. He needed to do something. The draft was taking the dropouts and failures as quickly as the county draft boards got their hands on the information. Everyone was drafted into the army, and almost all of the draftees went to Viet Nam. Herbie knew he was a lover, not a fighter. In truth, he was neither.

The Navy looked to be about as good a choice as any, so Herbie enlisted. They put him on what they called the "fat farm". He became a total transformation. He lost over a hundred pounds in his first year.

When he returned home on furlough, Zander didn't recognize him. If it hadn't been for that same old blue "bug" he drove, Zander would have just driven right on by when he met him on the street.

They had some good laughs together, but Zander noticed Herbie seemed more serious. Sometimes when people experienced a lifestyle change, their personalities changed right along with it.

2

Herbie walked from The Happy Chef toward his truck, intent on finding out what the woman thought she was doing climbing all over his rig.

"Can I help you with something?" Herbie asked, trying not to show any irritation.

"Is this your truck?" The woman had a strident voice that Herbie didn't like very much.

"Yes, that's my rig, and I was wondering what you were doing climbing all over it." He tried to make his voice sound as grating as hers.

"I don't know if you had noticed, but it's close to a hundred degrees out here today." Herbie thought she must have had quite a bit of practice trying to patronize people.

Herbie smiled at her.

"It would be difficult not to notice, especially with all of the humidity," Herbie said, and smiled broadly once more.

"You have an animal in there," she said, and jerked her right thumb at the cab.

"That's my dog, Mr. Peabody. Do you want to meet him? He's a good dog."

Herbie moved around to the driver's door and unlocked it.

"No, I don't want to meet him. Are you dim-witted or just an ass?"

Herbie stopped and looked at her.

"Well answer me," she said, raising her voice.

"Apparently a little of both." He smiled again, hoping he

wouldn't lose his temper.

She was getting angry.

"You should never keep animals in a vehicle when it is this hot outside. They can die in less than five minutes. You should be ashamed of yourself."

"I am, for a lot of reasons. This doesn't happen to be one of them, however."

Herbie thought it looked like she was ready to explode. Her face was beet red.

"Before you give yourself a stroke, let me inform you about this truck. It is a refrigeration unit and I'm hauling ice cream. As you pointed out so astutely, it is hot out today. I keep the engine running to make sure I don't lose my load. I keep the air conditioning on, in the truck, so the dog remains comfortable as well. I love my dog and wouldn't do anything to hurt him."

"That's not good enough! What if the truck would stall or something happens to the cooling system? That animal would be dead!" The woman's face was even redder and the veins were sticking out along her neck.

Herbie hoped she wasn't going to stroke out.

"Lady, this is a Kenworth. It's American-owned. I bought it because of the company's reputation. They were the first to put fuel consumption and emissions as priorities. It's a totally reliable tractor or I wouldn't be driving it."

"I wonder if that would impress animal control when I call them."

Herbie pulled off his cap and wiped his forehead. He was almost at the end of reason.

"Butt cracks and opinions. Everyone's got one. I'm not much interested in either of yours." It was a variation on an old joke, but Herbie had always liked it anyway. Herbie liked things the way they were, and there was quite a bit of truth in it.

Herbie got into the cab. Mr. Peabody came over and licked his ear. It made Herbie smile, and that broke the tension.

"At least someone still likes me," he said, and roughed up the dog's fur.

In one fluid movement, Herbie put the rig into gear and started rolling through the parking lot toward the stop sign.

He looked into his side mirror and saw the woman staring at the truck with her hands on her hips. He shook his head and turned up the radio.

Soon he was on I-35 heading south for Des Moines. He didn't notice the dark gray Buick following closely behind.

3

Sander Van Zee, a.k.a. Zander, sat on a stool in the bar he owned with his good friend, Fats. The bar was called the Branchwater, and it looked suspiciously like the Long Branch from the old TV show *Gunsmoke*.

He was pondering how life had a funny way of slipping past when a guy wasn't looking. It had been almost five years since he buried his parents, and he never felt the need to share the truth of their death with anyone. His father's decision to end his sick mother's life, along with his own, seemed to be a private decision between the two of them. Zander wished his father wouldn't have shared it in a letter to him. A letter he destroyed on the spot. Zander wondered why that particular memory kept coming to the surface so often.

Lately, he was feeling a bit restless. The bar was doing extremely well. Better, than either of them had hoped when they bought it. Zander had footed the entire purchase, with Fats making payments for his half. Fats had made his last payment a year earlier. They respected their agreement not to steal from each other, and their employees never had a chance, because one or both were always on duty when the bar was open.

It was a great place for both locals and tourists. Zander had his share of "hits," with a variety of women coming into the Branchwater. Nothing seemed to stick, however. Zander figured it was his fault. He hadn't had much luck with long-term relationships. The women he was attracted to carried huge amounts of baggage or they had a history of dreadful happenstance that left them broken.

Even worse were the women with a flair for drama. Zander always enjoyed the theatre, but he drew the line with personal comedies and tragedies playing out in everyday life. Most of these women lasted one night, and he put them on their way the very next day. So, something was lacking in his life.

If he had believed in psychologists, they might have told him he had a mild case of depression. He would never hear those words, however, because he came from a "Dutch" background. No "shrinks" allowed. They believed in picking yourself up and getting on with "it," whatever "it" might be.

Zander and Ingrid had kept their long-term relationship intact for a few years. She would visit him a few times during the winter, and Zander would spend a few weeks with her in the summer. Sometime during the third year, Zander's old high school friend and Ingrid's neighbor, Danny, lost his wife. It was some kind of farm accident involving the power takeoff on a tractor. It was sad, and Danny didn't handle it very well.

Zander attended the funeral, and he and Ingrid spent as much time with Danny as possible. Zander noticed that Ingrid had a gift for making people feel better. She had overcome so much herself. Losing her husband to the hand of Stryker helped her develop a soft and easy empathy for people with similar experiences. Most people could never understand that sort of quality. Zander knew, however. He thought they were called "rainy day people."

If Zander was surprised when Danny showed up at the Branchwater a year later, he didn't show it. Danny didn't have to say anything. Zander could read everything in his face.

"So have you asked Ingrid to marry you?"

Danny seemed shocked at Zander's bluntness. But he just looked away.

"Danny, this isn't anything I wasn't expecting," Zander said, quietly.

Danny turned back to Zander and looked him in the eyes.

"But how could you know?"

"I saw the way she looked at you when you lost your wife. It was like you were kindred spirits. You both lost so much."

"But you two, you were…." His voice trailed off.

"If it was meant to be, it would have happened three years ago. Ingrid knew we were two different people and told me so. I happened to agree."

"But you were happy together. I could see it." Danny was clearly miserable.

"But we both knew it wouldn't work. She is tied to the land, and I could never go back there. We are broken, but broken in totally different ways. Your misery can be healed by each other, because you both have the same needs and wants. I hope you don't take this wrong, because I thought the world of you and your family, but this might be the best thing to happen to you both."

Danny stared at Zander for an uncomfortably long time.

"I don't know how to respond to that."

"No one wants to think about destiny. Mostly it's better to just to live your life and let it happen. But, now and again, life throws you a knockdown punch. Sometimes you have to lie there and think about what the future will be if you get up. Then you get up anyway."

"I came here to try and convince you to let Ingrid go and now I see you already have."

Zander smiled.

"Not so fast. I still have some memories," he said, and pointed to his head. "She's pretty good in the old sack-a-roo, isn't she?"

Danny gave him a good-natured punch in the arm.

"You're talking about my future wife," he said, smiling.

"Well, be careful. She's taller and outweighs you by a bunch. Don't do anything to piss her off or I'll be attending your funeral." Zander meant to be glib, but was sorry after he said it.

Danny didn't seem to mind. He was relieved that his friend would remain his friend.

"She's out in the car. Do you want to see her?"

"Of course. Go get her."

Before Danny could move and get Ingrid, Zander put a hand on his shoulder.

"Danny, I'm very happy for the both of you. I mean that, but I am also pleased that you had the guts to come all the way up here to be upfront with me."

Danny nodded and headed for the door.

Ingrid was nervous when she walked into the bar. Zander smiled broadly and went over and hugged her gently. Then he kissed her on the cheek. He couldn't help but think that of all the places he had kissed her, he couldn't ever remember just kissing her on the cheek. Maybe because all the other kisses had been in the throes of passion. A kiss on the cheek signaled friendship only. He would miss the passion.

They spent the day together in the bar. It was a celebration, and it was on Zander's tab. But it was bittersweet.

• • •

So Zander continued to sit on the bar stool thinking about his life, and the chain of events that led to all of this. He and Lilly remained good friends, but they seldom saw each other. She was in Aspen, and he lived between Frisco and Breckenridge. Neither had reason to leave their confines. They both had different lives, and Lilly seemed happy. Zander was pleased that she could find some peace after her experiences with Rooster. The thought of that name made him shudder. Then it made him angry, because it brought Sara Jane to mind. She was a user, and he figured she didn't care who she hurt. She had hurt him. If he would have examined it further, he might have realized the experience with her was causing his restlessness.

Zander thought about his three serious relationships. Well, two out of three weren't bad and ended positively. The one that should have been of little, or no consequence still haunted him even if he wouldn't admit it.

Little did he know.

• • •

Fats watched his friend's contortions. He knew he was hurting inside even though he wouldn't show much on the outside. He made an arbitrary decision right there and then to help out his friend. He had set the wheels in motion a good deal earlier, just in case. It looked like it might have been the right thing to do. He would try to explain it to Zander when the time was right. He hoped Zander would accept it in the spirit it was intended.

4

Herbie traveled south on I-35 in his Kenworth. He was still unaware of the gray Buick following closely behind his trailer. He was concentrating on the mile markers. Actually he was looking for mile marker 119 that signaled a rest area. It was south of Story City. It was about five or six miles, but if he missed it, there would be no more rest areas until Des Moines.

He usually stopped there and fed Mr. Peabody his two plain hamburgers. It was a good place to let him run and do his business. Herbie always took him to the pet area on a leash before he freed him. Herbie was a rule follower.

Mr. Peabody ate the two burgers without much use for table manners. Since there was no table and he ate off the paper they were packed in, there wasn't much need for the finer graces.

After a fifteen-minute romp on the grass smelling every place where a dog had urinated before him, Mr. Peabody worked his way back to the picnic table where Herbie was sitting. He knew instinctively that it was time to go. Herbie always wondered if it was the repetitive movements of their lives, or if Mr. Peabody just sensed things. He would never know. Mr. Peabody wasn't talking. As he was putting on his leash, Herbie thought it might be what he liked most about his pet. He couldn't talk.

Herbie had rescued Mr. Peabody from an animal shelter in Sioux City. He didn't know how old he was, but he was still playful. They told him the dog was mostly terrier but Herbie could see Pekingese in the face. It didn't matter; the dog loved Herbie and Herbie loved the dog.

When he turned around and started heading back to the truck, he saw the same woman with her hands on her hips staring at him.

"Aw, shit," he muttered.

"I heard that," the woman answered.

"Did I say that out loud?"

"You're a funny man," she said, without facial expression.

"Well, I try to be. It doesn't look like it's having much effect on you."

"Maybe if you changed your ways, people might look at you more favorably."

"What's your excuse? Seems to me, it's better to stop trying to change the world and just focus on changing yourself."

"Such insight from a trucker. I'll have to remember to put that quote in my editorial next week."

From her sarcasm, Herbie hoped she wasn't serious. He was concerned about her editorial remark.

"So, do you work for a paper somewhere?" he asked.

"Owner and editor of the Story City Herald Tribune." she said, with just a little bit of arrogance.

Herbie winced. His Navy CO had drilled into his head this slogan: "Never get into a pissing match with people who buy their ink by the barrel." The armed forces were always careful around the media. It was a good motto, and it had served Herbie quite well over the years. He wasn't about to change his luck now.

"Maybe we got off on the wrong foot back there," he said, referring to the parking lot at Happy Chef.

"So now you want to make all nice because you found out what I can do to you in my paper?"

"What can you do?" Herbie wanted to know.

"I've taken your license number and your truck and trailer information, and I'll publish it. The Des Moines Register loves stories about animal abuse. They'll pick it up, and eventually it will get to people you know. Probably even your employer."

Herbie knew this was going downhill fast. He needed to get away from her. He started walking away with Mr. Peabody in tow. When he got close to his truck, he noticed she had parked her Buick sideways in front of his grille.

He wondered if the old "bag" thought he didn't have reverse. He was getting very close to the quick temper he knew as an adolescent.

"If you leave, I'm calling the Highway Patrol." The "bag" was whistling like a teapot.

Herbie opened the driver's door, and put Mr. Peabody gently inside. Mr. Peabody turned, and looked at the woman who had been following them. He snarled at the woman. It took Herbie completely by surprise. Mr. Peabody never growled at anyone, and here was an out-and-out snarl.

"He doesn't like you either." Herbie liked his comment.

He reached in the storage area behind the cab, and pulled out a heavy hammer that truckers used to check their tires. He hadn't needed to check the tires, but he thought it might be fun to have the "bag" see a little show of force. Herbie pulled the hammer out and held it up for the "bag" to see. He wasn't quite prepared for what happened next.

The woman took a step back and clasped both hands to her chest. Herbie just looked at her, puzzled. What was her game now? Was she making fun of him? Maybe he'd use the hammer on her to get her attention, after all.

He wouldn't have to worry about that. The woman went down suddenly and just crumpled to the blacktop. Herbie thought it looked pretty graceful. Nothing like when someone went down in the movies or on television. She hardly made a sound.

Herbie put the hammer back into the storage area and approached the "bag." He smiled at the thought because she did look a lot like a "bag" now.

He didn't know anything about CPR. He felt her neck for a pulse. He couldn't find any. He looked around. There was no one in the truck parking area besides his Kenworth and the woman's Buick. There were a few cars parked near the restrooms, but no one was looking his way.

He thought about going up and using the payphone and calling 911, but that would attract attention, and he wanted out of there as soon as possible. He walked over to her car and noticed the notebook she had been using to write down all the items she said was going into her editorial. Herbie ripped out the pages and folded them neatly and stuck them in his front pocket. He would destroy them later.

Without even glancing back, Herbie got back into his truck and backed up just enough to miss the car and the body. He put it into first gear and inched out of the parking area. Soon he was gaining enough speed and began merging onto I-35.

All in all, Herbie thought he had been pretty lucky. It looked like he would escape this incident without damage. That's what he was still thinking when he started shaking just outside of Ames. The realization that he may have caused the "bag's" death was having its way with his emotions. He needed to stop calling her the "bag." It only made it worse.

Mr. Peabody sensed something was wrong with his master. He tried to lick his ear and then settled for curling up in Herbie's lap. Herbie felt bad. He hadn't needed to show the woman the hammer. What was he trying to do?

But Herbie knew what he was trying to do, and he should never have done it. This was something that wasn't going to be easy to forget. He knew one thing for sure; he would avoid that rest stop in the future.

• • •

The woman stirred just a bit. Then she opened her eyes. It was hot. She would die if someone didn't come to help her. Her chest felt like someone had put a stone planter on it.

She tried to call out a few times at the cars above her near the restrooms, but she had no voice, other than a whisper.

Then by luck, or what Zander might have called nemesis, a big Freightliner pulled right into the space next to her Buick. The driver in the eighteen-wheeler made an emergency call on his CB before he even got out of his truck. When he was positive the right people got the message, he tried to make woman comfortable before the ambulance arrived. He was just a little pissed off. He was on a tight schedule, and he didn't need this shit today.

He wasn't sure she would make it. He was happy he didn't need to give her mouth-to-mouth, however.

5

Zander went through the motions, but he wasn't finding much satisfaction with his current state of affairs. He hadn't worked at The Bridge for a number of years. His own bar took all of his time. Sometimes he missed the carefree life of the vagabond bartender. Having responsibility for a business wasn't something he had planned. It made him feel confined and trapped.

Fats had taken to his role as owner/operator much better than Zander. People liked him. He had a gift of dealing with the customers. The locals enjoyed playing pool with him, and he let them win enough so they would come back. When Zander was on duty, customers would ask when Fats was coming in. That just added to Zander's restlessness.

Fats found himself a woman, and it seemed like a serious relationship. They had hired her as a server and part-time bartender. When the relationship started to heat up, Zander suggested that she find another position. At first Fats was offended, but he relented when Zander explained the possible conflict of interest with other employees. Zander found her a similar position at The Bridge. They were happy to have her.

Zander wasn't sure how he felt about it all. Fran was nice. She was almost as skinny as Fats. Zander liked her immediately. Fats was happier than he had ever been, and that made Zander feel good. He wasn't sure about losing his friend, however.

He hated that thought. He wasn't losing a friend. It was just another change in his life. The older he became, the faster the changes seemed to happen. He just wanted everything to slow down.

That's about the time he realized he needed a break. Routine was a good thing until it wasn't. It was doing nothing for his peace of mind at the present. He decided to talk to Fats about it one slow afternoon near the end of July.

Fats was washing glasses in the double stainless steel sink.

"Fats, I've got something I want to talk about with you."

Fats stopped and dropped the glass back into the sink.

"This doesn't sound good," he said, as he wiped his wet hands on a bar towel.

"Let's sit," Zander said, and poured them two coffees.

They took a table near the back and drank the coffee. Fats waited patiently for Zander to speak.

"I've been doing a lot of soul searching lately."

"Is that what you call it? We've been thinking it's something else."

"We've?"

"Well, Jo thought you might be depressed."

"So, I'm the subject of your private scrutiny?"

"You didn't give us much choice, dude. You haven't been yourself. Face it; you've had a lot going on lately. Most of it not very copasetic."

"Doubtful." Zander wasn't ready to agree.

"OK, so what's the beef?"

"No beef. I was just thinking that I might need a break."

Fats said nothing.

"So, I was thinking, that maybe I needed some time to myself."

Fats just looked at him.

"You know. Maybe a vacation."

"We're not just talking a week or two here, are we buddy."

"I guess not."

"So, Jo was right. You're depressed, and now you think you need to go find yourself."

"I suppose so."

"Well, just be sure you aren't going to go looking for old whatever-her-name-is."

It was Zander's turn to stare. That thought had never crossed his mind. At least he didn't think it did. He wouldn't have any idea about where to start looking for Sara Jane. He wondered what she was calling herself these days, and then he was angry about even thinking about her.

"I hadn't even thought about her until this very minute." Zander was agitated.

"I think you're just fooling yourself. You've never stopped thinking about her."

Zander said nothing.

"And another thing, if you think this depression shit is something you can fix all by yourself, you are an asshole. Running away never solved anything. Stand up and face the cosmic universe, and it will back itself down. Trust me."

Zander had to smile. Fats was on his cosmic universe kick again and it always amused him.

"Trust you? That's a tall order for anyone."

"You know what I mean. If you don't believe me, go over and talk to Jo. She'll straighten you out."

Zander decided to pass on that suggestion. He had enough talk about depression for one day. Besides, he knew he wasn't depressed; he just needed to get away.

"I'm not thinking of leaving right away. I thought maybe I'd take off during January and February."

"That's our busiest time," Fats said, with concern.

"I know and I hate to leave you then, but I've got to get out of the gray skies and into some sunshine."

"Depression," Fats said, quickly.

"No, not depression. I'm just tired of the snow and the cold. I need some warmth and sun."

"Where will you go?"

"South someplace. I'll drive until I find a place I like."

"Never took you for the hippie lifestyle. You'll be back in a week."

"Don't think so. I need to sort out some things, and I need to do it alone."

Fats just shook his head and brought the coffee cups to the sink.

"We'll have time to hire someone good to help you," Zander said, trying to soften the blow.

"Already thought about it. I think I'll hire Fran back."

Zander instantly was pissed.

"We talked about that, and I thought we were in agreement. If this is just a way to get back at me for leaving, it's not going to work."

"Oh don't flatter yourself. I've been thinking about this for quite a while. She's a good worker, and she knows the business. She'll be an asset not a liability."

"Well, there is a way it could work."

"OK, I'm biting. How do you think it will work?"

"Marry the girl. Then she'll be a partner in your business."

"Whoa! Back that horse up. I ain't the marrying type. Couldn't we just live together?"

"You already are. Not the same thing at all."

"Well, there's got to be a better way than throwing the marriage ball and chain at me."

Suddenly, Zander had another idea. It was like it was there all along and just needed something to spring it loose.

"Make her a partner."

"I just can't follow you when you're depressed."

"Look in that mirror, I'll show you depression," Zander said. He couldn't help himself. Fats was such an easy target.

"Don't get all pissy with me. I'm just following your karma."

"She can buy out my share of the business, or you can, and just call her your new partner."

Fats stroked his chin.

"It's got some possibilities, I'll have to admit, but I would be nervous having her own half this place. What if it didn't work out?"

Zander was impressed. Fats was forward thinking and it was something he didn't do very often.

"I think you are right. You buy me out and then you are free to do anything you want. You can tell everyone she is your partner, and no one will be the wiser."

Fats sat down on the bar stool closest to him. He put his head in his hands, as he did often, when he was thinking.

"How would we work out the deal?"

"It's already worked out. It's all in the original contract. Fifty grand will buy me out."

"But you know it's worth way more than that," Fats said.

"It doesn't matter. Those were the terms of the agreement, and I'm good with it."

"Sounds like you want out bad."

"Not really. I just want to experience life before more of it slips away."

"You know, I just paid you off. I don't have fifty grand just laying around."

"We'll work the same deal as before. Only this time, you'll be the sole owner, so you'll be able to make the final payment a lot quicker."

"What if I start stealing from myself, and I tell you I can't afford to pay you back?"

"Fats, I know you. If I thought for a minute you would try to screw me, I wouldn't have offered you my half."

"Dang trusting, if you ask me."

"Who's asking you about anything?"

Fats stood, paused for a moment, and walked over and grabbed Zander's hand.

"We've got a deal. I hate to lose you as a partner, but I think I can handle another new business venture," he said, pumping Zander's arm up and down.

"Easy there skinny, I'm no pump handle."

Fats let go of Zander's hand.

"So, do you think it's a sagacious move to hire Fran?"

"Hell, I don't even know what that means. But, if you were asking me if it's a wise decision, I would have to say no. You'll be the boss, so you'll have to live with the consequences. I would suggest you have some sort of agreement before you make the move."

Zander knew Fats had already decided. He was just trying to think it through.

"Oral or written?"

"Written would be better. Remember, you're the one who said he didn't want to marry. You'd better be protected if you start telling everyone she's your partner."

"Maybe I should let her buy into the bar business, and I keep the controlling interest."

"Get a lawyer and write it up if that's what you want."

Zander could see Fats torn between what his heart wanted and what the business would need to survive.

It was time to let him stew for a bit. Zander had no doubts that Fats would hit him with a dozen different scenarios before he made up his mind. No matter. They would have time to hash it all out before Zander made his exit.

The pieces seemed to be falling.

6

Herbie was still shaking over the death of the woman. He reached his delivery point in Des Moines and dropped off the last of the ice cream. He checked in with the dispatcher and found there wasn't anything to pick up for the return trip, so he deadheaded west on I-80 for Le Mars.

He would follow 80 until it split into 680, taking the right split and exit bound for I-29 north. He hated to go through Sioux City with the truck. There was always construction, and there were stop-and-goes along that route. But it was the easiest drive for a big rig, and once through Sioux City, he would pick up highway 75. In twenty-seven miles he would be in Le Mars.

Herbie found that I-80 west of Des Moines was an easier drive than the same road east. There was less traffic. Much of the truck traffic split off on other roads in Des Moines. Western Iowa had less population than the eastern side.

Eastern Iowa's border was formed by the Mississippi River, and that part of the state was older, having been settled decades before the rest of the state. Western Iowa was flatter and had better farm ground. Small towns were getting smaller, people were having a lot fewer children, and the farms were getting larger. It all added up to less population. Herbie thought that there was no addition involved. It was a steady subtraction of the population.

The stretch of interstate always relaxed Herbie as he drove it. But it wasn't doing much for him today. The woman's face kept creeping into his mind. He tried everything to keep it out. He turned up the music, switched to talk radio, and even tried counting cars. That didn't work at all; there were so few cars on the road.

When Herbie saw the sign advertising the town of Avoca, something flashed in his mind. He had been getting little electrical bumps in his head ever since he left Des Moines. They were the kind of bumps that signaled something forgotten that one meant to do. Herbie had ignored them.

It was more difficult to ignore a huge flash, however. He tried hard to think what it meant. Certainly it had something to do with the woman.

Then his phone rang, and it all became quite clear.

The Shuster Company supplied all its drivers with a TracFone to use exclusively for communication with the dispatcher. They were desirable for the company, because service was paid for when the phone was used. There were no contracts and no monthly plans. The phones were to be used only for business purposes and were checked frequently. Herbie was a rule follower and never used the phone for any other reason. In fact, he had his own TracFone. He seldom used it. He had no one to call.

The phone rang again. Herbie picked it up. It was one of the dispatchers.

"Herbie where are you?" Like usual the dispatcher was brief and to the point.

"Just east of Avoca." Herbie could also be brief and to the point.

"Take the Avoca exit and head up highway 59."

"What's up?" Herbie was confused.

"Steve will be calling you shortly."

The dispatcher hung up.

That's when it hit Herbie. He was driving his own tractor, but he was hauling a Shuster Company trailer, and it had the name plastered all over the front and sides. Had someone noticed the name?

He didn't have much time to think about it. His phone rang again. But this time it was his personal phone.

"Hello?" Herbie answered quietly.

"This is Steve. What going on Herbie?"

"You tell me."

I just got a phone call from the Story County sheriff's department. Someone there questioned me about one of our rigs heading down I-35 around Story City earlier today."

"What did you tell him?" Herbie's mouth was dry.

"Well, I didn't lie. I told him none of our tractors were in that area but it might be an independent contractor pulling one of our reefers."

Herbie felt some relief.

"What else did he say?"

"He wanted to know who was pulling the trailer. I told him I would have to check, but it wouldn't be until later in the afternoon before I could get back to him."

Herbie let out a sigh of relief.

"Now, you tell me what's going on," Steve said.

Herbie relayed the whole story, not leaving out anything, including his feeling about the woman before and after the incident.

"Are you on 59?"

"Somewhere between Harlan and Denison."

"Good. When you get to Cherokee, take highway 3 into Le Mars. Go directly to the old truck stop and leave the trailer. Tell the guys at the truck stop to check the electrical. Tell them you had some lights flashing. It might be a short. I'll have one of the guys go down and haul it back to the shop later."

"You've got me worried. Did someone see the name of the trailer?"

"The woman's not dead, but her memory's kind of sketchy. It was the one thing she could remember, however."

Herbie didn't know how he felt about the news. On one hand, he was relieved that the "bag" didn't die, but he was confused about what it might mean.

"So, what's the problem?"

"Attempted murder, that's what. She is saying you tried to kill her."

"Bullshit!"

"Maybe so, but I have to give them your truck plates sometime later today, and the sheriff will call the highway patrol to stop you."

Herbie instantly had a sick feeling in the pit of his stomach.

"I don't need this shit," Herbie said, forcefully.

"Neither do we. You're going to have to lay low someplace for a while. I'll tell them you're coming in through Sioux City, and then up highway 75. They'll be looking for you that way. It's the best I can do."

"Thanks Steve. I'm sorry to put you through this shit."

"Just take care of yourself. Don't do anything stupid. Is there someplace you can hide out for a while?"

"I was thinking I could go..."

"Don't tell me. The less I know, the better for both of us. Give me a call in a few months, after all of this dies down, and let me know where I can send the remaining money I owe you."

"Will do, and Steve, thanks for sticking your neck out for me. I'd like to clear my name with this woman, but I'm afraid my word against hers wouldn't have much credibility."

"I wouldn't do this for everyone, but you've been a good employee. Zander always said you were a good guy, and that was enough for me."

Steve clicked off.

Zander had put in a good word for Herbie with Orville Shuster, Steve's father. He was the founder/owner until Steve slowly took over the daily operations. It was a good company. They treated their drivers well.

When Zander was a teacher in Le Mars, he had the Shuster children in school. He built a friendly relationship with the family. He had even helped out around the shop one summer. It had been a good source of summer employment, and Zander had made many friends. That hadn't gone unnoticed with the Shuster men, so Herbie got the job because of Zander.

At the time, working for Shuster was just the change Herbie needed. Now, he wasn't sure he was ready for the changes that were coming. Of course, who was ever ready for any type of change in life? As he pulled into the truck stop in Le Mars, he realized it was the last time he would pull a load for the Shuster Company. It made him depressed. He would have to vanish. His life, and the lives of those he had worked for, wouldn't be wasted on litigation. It might be impossible to defend himself against the word of the "bag." He remembered the "ink by the barrel" adage. He wasn't about to take the risk.

Herbie unhooked the trailer from his tractor, and explained what Steve had told him to tell the mechanic on duty. He got back into his truck and headed up highway 75. He would wind his way over to Sioux Falls and try to figure out where life would take him now.

7

She had visited the panhandle of Florida from Pensacola to Tallahassee, but realized it was still too cold that far north during the winter months. Panama City was a cluster of concrete hotels and condos. She got out of there as quickly as possible. Tampa and St. Pete were too big. Besides, it was still too chilly in January and February to suit her.

So she kept traveling south. Eventually she ended her journey in Key West. It was her kind of place, both wild and anonymous. She took her new name from the two south Florida communities of Bonita Springs and Marco Island. She was now Bonita Marco. Bonnie was a little less formal, and it was a name she could remember for some odd reason.

"Bonnie Marco," she rolled it off her tongue a few times.

She liked the way it sounded. It was so much better than Sara Jane De Graff. It had been her name a lifetime ago, but it was dead to her now. Of course she had to keep her identity in order to gain access to her accounts in the Caymans, but those documents were locked away and hidden in a case with a shitload of money. She didn't know how much, but it had to be over a million.

She thought about looking for Zander's card somewhere at the bottom of her purse, but it always seemed to be too much work. Knowing it was there was enough.

She had no idea that someone had been following her from the time she left Colorado. The tail had been too good. Each place she stopped, the tail would change rental cars. Every day there would be a new make and model. Sometimes the tail even had a hotel room next door to hers. Bonnie had no idea anyone was in her shadow.

She found someone, who knew someone, and got a new set of documents with her new identity. It was all there, a driver's license, birth certificate, and passport. From that point, it was easy to get credit cards and bank accounts. She had three of each.

The tail saw everything and decided to get some new identity as well. Waiting a few weeks would be a good idea. There was no sense jeopardizing all the secrecy with lack of good judgment. It wouldn't be in anyone's best interest to tip off the woman too early.

Bonnie wasn't in any hurry to do much of anything. She found a two-bedroom condo overlooking Duval Street and rented it for a month. In the mornings, she would have breakfast somewhere on Duval Street, always in a different place. She was exploring the island, taking in everything.

In the afternoon, she would wander around, looking at all the historic places. She liked the Ernest Hemingway home the best. The six-toed cats fascinated her. She even read a few of his books but found them too tedious.

She was surprised that Harry Truman had a place he called the "Little White House." The Butterfly Conservatory was a relaxing place to listen to music and let the many varieties of butterflies land on your head and shoulders.

Bonnie's favorite place was the northwest part of Duval Street. Everything happened there. In the evenings people wandered over to Mallory Square to watch the sunset and, if it was a clear day, hopefully see the "Green Flash." Almost everyone would be surprised at the circus that ensued.

After a few weeks had passed, Bonnie felt she had experienced everything she needed to know about Key West. She decided to rent another month. She needed some business venture to occupy her time.

In the meantime, she spent most of her days sitting in various bars on Duval. She tried Sloppy Joes, but found it was far too full of drunken tourists. The Hog's Breath wasn't much better.

She was content to sit at some of the smaller, less-trafficked places. She even sat in some that sported a multi-colored flag. Bonnie didn't care what sexual preferences people enjoyed. She had even experienced a woman or two back in the Skip The Light Fantastic days. Mostly, that had to do with the business. Marty had wanted to make sure the girls knew all the tricks of his trade, and that fell on the shoulders of Sara Jane's alter ego, Jayne. All in all, they hadn't been unpleasant experiences. Life was too short not to try all of its delicacies.

Bonnie realized early on that Key West was a place where many people vacationed from the colder winter states. She knew she would probably see people she'd recognize from her past. That was something she didn't want or need.

Over the years, her sandy hair color had become mousy-looking. She decided to go completely blonde. That meant not only her hair but her eyebrows as well. She didn't think areas south of that would be important enough to worry about.

She never went out without a huge hat and sunglasses and seldom removed either when in public. Her dress was of island flair. There were countless little shops that sold all kinds of Key West garb, and Bonnie had trashed all her wardrobe from her past. She particularly liked to wear sundresses that had nothing on her shoulders and sported a plunging neckline. They turned more than a few heads when she walked down the street.

It seemed ironic that someone who didn't want to be recognized would dress quite so provocatively. Bonnie had a method to this madness, however. She knew that if people were focusing on other parts of her body, they wouldn't be looking at her face.

One lovely afternoon, Bonnie was at a small table at an outdoor café, having a late lunch. It was a particularly busy day on Duval, and she was content watching the people drift by.

As she was finishing a red snapper salad, her server came by and sat in the empty chair facing her.

"Hi. I hope you don't mind but I like to find out about the people I serve."

Of course, Bonnie did mind, but she didn't want to draw attention to that fact.

"And what have you found out about me?" she asked, fishing.

"Nothing really. I have seen you around almost every day for the past month. Sometimes here and sometimes in other places."

"What does that tell you?"

"Either you are coming off a bad relationship and trying to hide out here, or you are looking for something."

"What if both were true?"

"Then you'd be like almost eighty per cent of the people here."

"Are you always this perceptive?" Bonnie was trying to humor her.

"I like to study people. It's a pastime of mine. My name's Avon Bartow, by the way."

She stuck out her hand. Bonnie paused a bit and looked at her outstretched hand. Something told her not to get involved with anyone. But she was a bit lonely and needed a friend.

"Bonnie Marco," she said, and grabbed her hand.

She smiled as she said her name. It was the first time she had said it out loud to anyone.

Avon looked at Bonnie when she said her name but didn't say anything.

"Avon? Do you sell cosmetics as well?" Bonnie asked, trying to sound light.

"Maybe. Have you ever been to the Snook Inn?" she asked.

"I don't know what that is." Bonnie was a bit confused.

"You must not watch television."

"I'm afraid not," Bonnie was tiring of the conversation that seemed to be going nowhere.

"Oh, it doesn't matter. It's just a place. I'll tell you about it sometime."

"You can bring the check at any time," Bonnie said, trying to dismiss her.

It wasn't working. Avon wasn't going anywhere.

"Would you like to go out some evening? We could join the bar crawls that come over from the ships."

Key West was an ending destination for the cruise ships coming out of Fort Lauderdale and doing the Caribbean circuit. It was the last night out for many of the tourists, and they were all ready to party.

Bonnie was trying to sum up the woman who called herself Avon. She couldn't get a read.

"So would this be a date, or would we just be going out to have some fun?"

"It can be whatever you'd like it to be."

"I'm just going to come out and ask you. Are you gay or straight?"

"I can be whatever you'd like me to be."

The answer took Bonnie by surprise. She didn't like to be surprised.

"I'd have to think about an offer like that." Bonnie smiled at Avon.

"Well, just let me know. I'm here working most days except Sunday."

She got up and went over to the bar leaving Bonnie to her own thoughts.

Bonnie was thinking about the offer when Avon returned with her bill. Bonnie decided to pay with a credit card. She hadn't used it enough to establish any kind of credit score.

When the transaction was completed, Bonnie noticed that Avon had written her address on the bottom of the customer copy. Bonnie looked up at Avon.

"Just in case you get curious." She winked and was gone.

Bonnie sat quietly for almost ten minutes. Avon never came back, which was a provocative act in itself.

When Bonnie left the café, she didn't quite know what to do. She stood on a street corner for a while just watching people come and go. Finally, she decided to go shopping.

If she was going to pursue whatever relationship this would turn out to be, she would need something to wear to make her look good in all the right places.

8

Herbie went to Sioux Falls to stay with his sister until the heat died down. He soon realized he had to something about his Kenworth. It pained him to think about getting rid of his old friend, but it would only serve to draw unwanted attention.

There were a number of truck dealers in the Sioux Falls area. He found one that specialized in used tractors. They didn't seem to be overly concerned with paperwork. Herbie liked that. He would have to take less than what he thought the thing was worth, but in the long run, it would be worth it.

Things weren't going quite as smoothly at his sister's house, however. Herbie had never gotten along with his siblings, but his relationship with his sister, Lola, was the worst. She was a few years older and had always been the boss. When they were kids, Herbie used to sing the old Hit Parade song, "Whatever Lola wants, Lola gets" as a way of getting back at her. It worked just fine.

When Herbie showed up without warning, she was less than pleased.

"Why are you here?" Lola asked, not mincing words. She never did.

"Can't I just stop and visit my sister without getting the third degree?"

"I haven't heard from you in almost three years, and then you just show up on my doorstep."

"When was the last time you heard from Bill?"

Bill was her husband, until he couldn't take it any longer, and headed for the hills. Literally, he headed for the Black Hills. Herbie ran into him randomly at a truck stop in Rapid City a year before.

Herbie found out that Bill had moved in with a woman and was pretty happy. Herbie always liked Bill, maybe because Bill didn't like his sister either.

"With any luck, I'll never hear from Bill again."

"That's funny. That's exactly what he said."

"I figure you're in some kind of trouble, and you're using me to hide out."

"Maybe. So what?"

"I won't have it. I want you out of here, or I'll start calling around and find out what's going on."

Herbie knew she would do it, too.

"I'm selling my truck, and as soon as that's done, I'll be gone."

"I don't think so. I want you gone now. I don't need your shit, and I'm not going to cover anything up."

"So much for family love and caring. I'll tell you what, I'll leave right now, but I'm going to take the tags off Bill's old pickup he left out back."

"Tags? What tags?"

"License plates."

"That's my pickup now."

"That figures. Anyway, I need those plates for awhile."

"Why?"

Herbie was getting frustrated.

"I need to buy some wheels to get me out of here. You told me I couldn't stay. So, until I get settled somewhere else, I'll need those plates until I can get a new set. Otherwise, I can stay here until the DMV gets the paperwork done. But that means they'll have to contact Iowa's DMV, and that could take a week or two. Is that what you want?"

"Take the plates," Lola said, and went into the house. She came back out with Mr. Peabody in tow.

"Take this flea-bag with you." She gave Mr. Peabody a kick down the steps. That pissed Herbie off, but Mr. Peabody was nobody's doormat. He turned around, ran back up the steps, and bit Lola in the back of her foot.

She was screaming something Herbie couldn't understand, so he decided not to waste any more time or effort on his sister. He got the plates, and put them, and Mr. Peabody in his truck.

• • •

The deal with the truck went smoothly. He opened an account at the Wells Fargo Bank and deposited the check. Herbie knew wherever he ended up; there would be a Wells Fargo Bank close by. It would be convenient.

He went to a used car lot to find some transportation for his trip to nowhere. It was a tough decision. He wanted to buy a pickup, but he needed something with a little better mileage. Besides, the less attention his vehicle received, the better.

He settled on an older Buick Le Sabre. The color was called champagne, and it was as big as a boat. Herbie hated every inch of it, but he thought it might be a good thing. If he hated it that much, then most people wouldn't give it a second look. Sometimes, one had to trade style for function. Mr. Peabody didn't seem to share his dark feeling for the car. He found a comfortable spot on the back seat and went to sleep.

Herbie paid for the car with a check from the new account he had just opened. While the salesman went inside the office to call the bank to make sure there were sufficient funds, Herbie slapped the plates on the Le Sabre. He couldn't help remembering the car the "bag" was driving. It looked a lot like the car he had just purchased. Maybe that was why he disliked it so much.

He went back to his sister's place to get his belongings. He traveled light, because he didn't have much. Lola wasn't home, and Herbie was happy for small favors. Soon he was heading south down I-29 to parts unknown.

He didn't realize it would be the last time he would see his sister.

• • •

Unbeknown to Herbie, Bill had come back to Sioux Falls a few months later to reclaim his pickup. Lola was having none of it. There was much screaming and swearing. One of the neighbors called the police. By the time they got there, Bill had beaten her senseless. She died later in the Sioux Valley Hospital.

South Dakota called first-degree murder a capital crime. Luckily for Bill, he was charged with a crime of passion. It was an irony to be sure. There was never much passion between Lola and Bill. Mostly, it was just out-and-out hatred. There didn't seem to be any premeditation on Bill's part, and the police department had some past experiences dealing with Lola. Perhaps, they had some sympathy for Bill.

So, Bill got life in prison. Many years later, when Herbie found out, he felt bad for Bill. He always liked him and could understand how he had gotten himself into the situation with no escape. If the truth were told, Herbie had contemplated killing his sister on more than one occasion.

Herbie wondered what happened to the plates he had sent back to Lola. He thought about writing to Bill in prison but trashed the idea. He didn't need anyone knowing his whereabouts.

9

Bonnie Marco had settled into her new name quite well. It was a mystery how someone could gain an alias, and then, actually become that entity.

Avon Bartow had somehow wormed her way into her life. Bonnie was confused about her feelings. She had always been attracted to men and never thought much about relationships with women. She never had any close friendships with females over the years. She was always too busy with men, or maybe, she was just trying to get the better of them.

She didn't have any of those emotions with Avon. There was no pressure, and she was totally at ease around her. They went out a few times. Bonnie didn't know if they could be called dates. She just viewed it as two friends spending time together.

She was very cautious. If someone came on too strong, it made her nervous. But she was also inquisitive and ready to try new things. Now that she had a new identity, it would even be easier to become a totally different woman.

Exactly four weeks to the day that Bonnie first met Avon, she showed up at her door with all of her things in tow.

"I need a place to stay," Avon said, barging past Bonnie. "They jacked up my rent. Screw 'em."

"Come in." Bonnie couldn't remember asking her to move in. It wouldn't be a problem, because the condo had two bedrooms. Avon could help with the expenses.

"Where's the bedroom?"

"The guest bedroom is here." Bonnie led her down the hall.

Avon peered in and turned around.

"That's an office, not a bedroom. Where's yours?"

"The master is down the hall, but I'm afraid..."

"Good. I'll stay there with you then."

With that, Avon went back outside to get her things, and began moving them into the condo.

Bonnie was confused. She wasn't used to being dominated by any woman. She was the one in charge. She was the one who made others follow direction. And yet, something about Avon fascinated her. She needed to see how this relationship would play out. There would have to be some basic ground rules, however.

Bonnie went to the deck that overlooked Duval Street and took a seat. The place was equipped with bar stools, so people on the deck could see over the railing and watch the people walking below. She had decided not to help Avon move her things into the condo. She needed to mark her territory, and that would be her first little theatrical show of who was in charge.

"Hey, I could use a little help down here." Avon yelled.

"Sorry, you're on your own." Bonnie smiled to herself.

The condo was a three-story affair. The first story was the parking garage under the units. The second floor contained the kitchen, living room, and deck. The bedrooms were on the third floor. There were a lot of steps. Bonnie thought it might be good for Avon to navigate them by herself.

Bonnie went back into the kitchen and found a half-bottle of some white wine and poured a glass. She liked red wine better, but it was hot, and red wine made her face flush. She returned to the deck and looked out at Duval.

It amazed her to see all the different people walking. It looked like the Key West Express had just arrived from Fort Meyers. People were pulling their suitcases toward their hotels a few blocks up the street. Everybody walked once they got to Key West. It was just easier, and there wasn't anyplace on the island that couldn't be reached by walking. It was always easier to take the boat to Key West. Driving down Route 1 was a horrible experience. It took forever because of all the traffic and the absurd and counterproductive speed limits.

Bonnie took the road when she first came to Key West and found it to be a fascinating drive. There was history in the keys, and if one wasn't in a hurry, there was much to be learned. Most people were in a hurry, however.

Bonnie didn't see a need to travel the road a second time. If she needed to go anywhere, it would be by boat or plane. For some variety, she did travel up the road as far as Marathon a few times. There were a number of smaller keys that were just right for exploration, but that was when she needed a change of scenery. Some of the locals said they went that direction when they became bored with Key West. Bonnie couldn't imagine anyone becoming bored in Key West.

She was just finishing her last swallow of wine, when Avon popped her head through the slider from the living room.

"Starting a little early today, aren't we?" she asked, pointing at the wine glass.

"It's after lunch. This is Key West. Drinking is permitted everywhere at any time."

"I'm still getting used to that."

"Why don't you pour yourself some wine, and pour me another glass while you're at it." Bonnie handed her wine glass to Avon.

Avon looked at the wine glass.

"All right, but don't think I'm going to be your permanent server. I get enough of that at my day job."

"I'm sure you do. We need to have a conversation about how this roommate thing is going to work. I think it's best if we both have some wine to help us through it."

Avon frowned but turned and walked back to the refrigerator. Bonnie noticed the frown and smiled. She liked being in charge.

Soon the two were sitting together on the bar stools looking out over Duval. Neither said anything. Bonnie was enjoying the sounds coming from the street below. Avon seemed somewhat uncomfortable, which suited Bonnie just fine.

"I'm not used to drinking this early in the day." Avon looked at

Bonnie.

"I've never seen you drink much of anything at all," Bonnie stated. "Why is that?"

Avon just continued to look out over the street.

"Some little secret?" Bonnie asked.

"We all have them, don't we?" It wasn't a question, and it took away some of Bonnie's smugness for just a beat.

"What's that supposed to mean?"

"I don't know. You tell me."

"I have trouble with people being obtuse. If you have something to say, just say it."

"Obtuse? Really? Who are you trying to impress?"

That comment made Bonnie angry, but she tried not to show it. She didn't do a very good job, because Avon noticed it right away.

"OK, let's start with your name."

"What about it?"

"Oh come on, Bonita Marco? Are you kidding me? Remember when I asked if you'd ever been to the Snook Inn?"

"Not really."

"Well, I did. The Snook Inn is on Marco Island. It's a big tourist place."

"I'm not following."

"Marco Island is south of Bonita Springs. It doesn't take a genius to see you made up your name by looking at the map. You actually should visit those places before you take them on as your name. Wouldn't it be less suspicious to have visited those places, just out of curiosity?"

"Pretty damn smart, aren't you?" Bonnie was pissed again.

"Hey, don't get mad. Look at the map. Do you think you're the only one who came up with that idea?"

"I'm not following."

"The center of Florida has a place called Avon Park and another called Bartow."

Bonnie looked at her for a time.

"So, you're saying you took your name from two towns in

Florida?" She was still trying to act confused.

"All I'm saying is everyone has secrets. Sometimes it's best to leave them alone. They are secrets for a reason."

"So, you don't want anyone to find out your secrets?"

"Do you?"

Bonnie didn't answer. Her job had always been to know people's secrets while keeping her own. It was unnerving to have someone break down her new name that easily.

Avon softened her tone just a little.

"Florida's a big state. There's room for lots of secrets."

Bonnie nodded in agreement. She would find out more about his woman. She hoped she hadn't done anything rash. Keeping her close might be the right thing, however. She couldn't put her finger on why there was an attraction between them, but it could be that they both mirrored each other. That was just a little bit unnerving.

"So, what do you want to talk about?" Avon asked, trying to change the subject.

"I need to know your expectations."

"I suppose since this is your place, you should tell me yours first."

"We'll share the rent equally."

Avon nodded in agreement.

"We'll share the grocery bill equally."

Avon nodded again.

"If we need our space, we'll respect that."

Avon was in agreement.

"No visitors or parties unless we are both in agreement."

"I wouldn't have it any other way."

"If anything is bothering either one of us, we'll mention it right away."

"OK. Is that all?"

"One more thing. From this moment on, there will be no secrets. The past is the past."

"If you say so."

"I do say so," Bonnie said, but she was thinking about how she could open Avon's secret past. "Now what are your expectations?"

Avon stood up, took both empty wine glasses, and set them on the patio table. Then she took Bonnie's hand and led her up to the master bedroom. She pulled of one of her bags off the bed and turned to face Bonnie. She kissed her with an open mouth.

Avon undressed Bonnie and slipped out of her own clothes effortlessly. She turned back the blankets and sheet and pushed Bonnie into the bed.

If it surprised Bonnie, she didn't let it show. She was already showing too much.

10

When Herbie reached Omaha, he made a conscious decision to make a detour. He had lost track of Zander, but he remembered visiting him at the Glass Onion when he first came back from the Navy. Maybe he had moved on, but someone might know of his whereabouts.

It took him some time, and some convenience store directions, to find the place. The bar was almost deserted when he walked in. The woman behind the bar had a nametag that said Donna.

"Hi Donna. How are you?" Herbie pretended to remember her.

"Hi yourself. Do I know you?"

"I'm a friend of Zander. I visited him here a few times."

"Well, buy a drink and then we'll talk." Donna was a good salesperson.

Herbie ordered a vodka and cranberry. He paid her on the spot, and waited for her to return from the cash register.

"What can I do for you, hon?"

"I was hoping you could tell me where Zander is hiding out these days."

Donna looked at him peculiarly.

"I thought you were his friend."

"I am. It's just that our paths haven't crossed in a while, and I'd like to see him again." Herbie didn't think this was going particularly well. He could see that Donna was protective. He remembered the owner's name was Jasper.

"Maybe I could talk to Jasper?"

He could see Donna relax.

"He's not here. The old fart is probably home taking a nap."

Herbie smiled his most disarming smile.

Donna reached under the bar and rummaged around for a moment. She came up with a card that she handed to Herbie.

It was Zander's card with his answering service number.

"It's the best I can do. I haven't seen him in a while. He's somewhere in Colorado, so if you call that number, he'll get back to you, if he wants.

Herbie thought she might know more than she was letting on but decided not to pursue it. He liked the fact that she was trustworthy and protecting Zander. There weren't many qualities like that left in people anymore. Herbie thanked Donna and finished his drink.

As he was leaving, Donna yelled at him, "Tell him hello from Donna."

Herbie nodded and smiled. When he got to his Buick, he could tell that Mr. Peabody needed a bathroom break. Herbie grabbed his phone and walked his dog around the grassy area behind the bar.

He called Zander's number and got his answering service. He left his phone number and a message. It was short and to the point. Herbie said he was headed to Colorado and would like to get together, if they could work it out.

When he hung up, he realized it irritated him that Zander didn't have a phone. It didn't surprise him, but it irritated him just the same. Zander was always just a bit left of center. He always thought differently than most people. Herbie knew that was why he liked him. He felt bad that time had slipped away, and they had slipped away with it.

When Mr. Peabody was satisfied, Herbie headed for I-80, and nosed the big boat Buick toward Colorado.

He drove for the better part of the afternoon, and as he was nearing Sterling, Colorado, he was beginning to feel just a bit nervous. What if Zander didn't call? How in the hell could he find him in a state that was mostly mountains?

Just before he reached the first Sterling exit, the phone rang.

It was Zander. Relieved, Herbie pulled off the interstate and stopped on the shoulder. He hated driving while he was on the phone. He saw too many accidents from distracted drivers, and he swore he would never be one.

"Herbert Schutt, you old sonofabitch, what rock did you crawl out from under?"

"You're not far off." Herbie thought of his recent "between a rock and hard place" situation.

"Well, where are you?"

"Just outside of Sterling. Where are you?"

"I've got a little bar business in Frisco."

"Where the hell is that?" Herbie had never heard of it and was hoping it wasn't short for San Francisco.

"About an hour west of Denver, just off I-70."

Herbie was happy to hear it was in Colorado instead of California. He needed to get out more and see the country. His American geographical knowledge was sorely lacking.

"I'm coming to see you."

"Bring it on. It will be good to get together with the world's biggest asshole."

"I think I'll wait until tomorrow. It's been a long day, and I don't want to drive the mountains in the dark. Besides, this big asshole is tired out. I'll find some motel and spend the night here."

"Sound thinking from someone as dense as you."

"Still espousing those left of center ideas and having them go south on you?" Herbie didn't wait for him to answer. "I'm glad some things don't change."

"How about you? Everything you touch still going sideways for you?"

"Pretty much."

"Then we'll get along fine, like always."

"Like always. Me going sideways, you south." Herbie suddenly felt good.

"I should be working the bar by 10:00. It's right on the main drag."

"What's the name?" Herbie was writing things down.

"It's called the Branchwater. You can't miss it."

"We will see you tomorrow, then. Is there a decent place to stay up there?"

"Oh, bullshit. You stay with me." Zander hung up, and Herbie had to smile.

When everything around him was changing, it was comforting to know that some things, like Zander, hadn't changed at all.

Zander was thinking the same thing. He remembered thinking how he liked Jasper, because he never changed. Now Herbie shows up, and he was about to enjoy his stability as well.

Of course, nothing could have been further from the truth.

11

Herbie slept at the old Motor Inn Motel. For an extra five bucks, Mr. Peabody was allowed in the room. Herbie was still sound asleep when Mr. Peabody gave one sharp bark, while he waited at the door. It was his way of telling Herbie he had to go out. Herbie had to get up and do his thing as well.

"You'll have to wait, Mr. Peabody. Me first." He bounced out of bed and hit the bathroom in two steps. Mr. Peabody sat down and waited patiently.

After both nature calls had been answered, Herbie hooked Mr. Peabody up to his leash, and they walked across the street to a little coffee shop that had outside seating. It was a nice morning, and he enjoyed Mr. Peabody's company while dining whenever he could. Eating alone was a lonesome business. Herbie tied the leash around a chair and went inside to order breakfast. There was the usual side order of sausage links for Mr. Peabody, as well.

The waitress brought out a carafe of coffee and a bowl of water for Mr. Peabody. Herbie thanked her for her thoughtfulness.

"It's no trouble," she said, "I lost my dog last Christmas. Been with me for almost fifteen years."

"Mr. Peabody was a rescue dog. You could do something like that," Herbie said, trying to be helpful.

"Can't. I'm still grieving. It's too quick. Besides, they won't let me have a pet in my apartment anymore."

"That's sad." Herbie didn't know what else to say.

The waitress was scratching Mr. Peabody's back just above the tail. Mr. Peabody was in heaven, and Herbie could see she knew her way around dogs.

"What kind of dog did you have?"

"It was a Pomeranian, and I miss him every day." She hung her head.

Herbie hoped she wouldn't cry.

"What was his name?"

"He had such a bright orange coat, I had to call him Sunkist. You know, like the name of the orange soda."

"Sure. I used to drink that when I was a kid."

"Me too. I'll go see if your order is ready." She got up and went back into the café.

Herbie wondered about her backstory. She seemed to be about his age, but it looked like she might have had a hard life. She wasn't unattractive, and she seemed nice enough. Herbie always liked people who liked dogs.

She came back with the breakfast and put it in front of Herbie.

Herbie motioned toward the side order of sausages.

"Mr. Peabody always likes to eat with friends, especially when they feed him his breakfast. Do you think it would be all right with your manager if you joined us?"

She looked at Herbie strangely for a moment. "I own this place, so I guess it's fine."

"Sorry. You just don't see owners waiting tables very often."

"I'm a better waitress than a cook, so I hire that part and do the rest. It's hard to make it in a small place like this otherwise."

"Have you been here long?"

"Lived here since I was fourteen. Got married young and lost him in the Viet Nam thing. I guess they didn't call it a war, but a lot of good people died anyway."

"I know. I enlisted in the Navy, so I didn't have to grunt it out over there."

"That was smart. My parents owned this place. I just worked here until they died and then just sort of took it over."

"My name is Herbert Schutt by the way, but everyone calls me Herbie."

Gail paused for a moment and looked right at Herbie. Herbie thought she had something on her mind, because it looked like she was looking right past him. He could have sworn her eyes glazed over. But then she spoke lightly.

"Happy to meet you Herbie. Mine is Gail Roberts." She stuck out her hand.

Herbie grabbed it and shook it softly a few times.

"That's a good name," Herbie said, trying to keep the conversation going.

"Pretty common. There are a lot of "Roberts" in the world. What is it you do, Herbie?"

"I'm a trucker. Trucked for a company that hauled ice cream around the country. I mainly drove the upper Midwest. Blue Bunny ice cream; have you heard of it?"

"Well, sure. We carry it here. Always have a flavor of the week."

"That's it. It's pretty good stuff."

"So, it sounds like you used to do that. What are you doing now?"

"I'm going out to see my old high school buddy in a town called Frisco."

"That's nice country. Copper Mountain is right down the road from there. It's one of my favorite places to hike in the summer. Don't get there much anymore. This place takes all my time and energy."

"That's what I was thinking. That's why I came out here. I needed a change before my life flew right by me." The statement was a partial truth, and Herbie thought if he kept repeating it, eventually it would be the real truth.

Gail sighed. "I know what you mean. It seems my life is going nowhere, and there just aren't any prospects for it to get any better."

Herbie finished his breakfast, while Gail fed the remaining sausage to Mr. Peabody.

"Mr. Peabody likes you, and he's a good judge of character."

Gail laughed. "I think he's a judge of good sausage."

Herbie liked her. She wore no make-up, but she had a kind of earthy beauty about her. Herbie thought if she could relax, and maybe not work so hard, she wouldn't look so tired. There was pretty woman underneath all that.

Herbie pushed his plate away. "That was excellent. Thank you for a great breakfast and some wonderful conversation. Mr. Peabody never says much."

"It was nice to talk to somebody who's a nice guy." Gail dropped her eyes, and Herbie thought he could see some pink creep into her pale cheeks. It was now or never.

"Gail, I was wondering, after I go out and see my friend, would it be all right if I stopped back and took you to dinner."

Gail looked Herbie right in the eyes again. "I would love that. As long as it's not here."

"You would have to choose the place, since I don't know the area."

"It's a date." She handed Herbie a card. "Give me call when you're headed back this way."

Herbie stuck the card in his billfold. He would be sure not to lose it. This was turning out better than he could have hoped.

Gail got up and as she leaned over to clear the table, she put her hand on Herbie's shoulder. It felt a bit suggestive and didn't go unnoticed by Herbie. He turned and took her hand in both of his.

"At the risk of sounding too corny, there is a line from an old movie, and it fits this very moment." Herbie continued, "*I think this could be the beginning of a beautiful friendship.*"

Gail blushed, but she didn't pull back her hand. Herbie thought it was a good sign.

"I'll bet you say that to all the girls up and down your route." She smiled when she said it.

"No, I can truthfully say, you are the very first."

"Well, thank you for that. It made my day, but I've had so many disappointments in my life. I hope this doesn't turn out to be another one."

"Me either." Herbie was serious when he said it.

"Well, I'd better go before my cook quits. He doesn't like to wait on people, and I've stayed here longer than I had planned."

"I'm happy you did. We'll see you soon, Gail. I'll call you when I decide to return," he said, and patted his billfold.

"I'll get your ticket," Gail said, and slowly removed her hand from Herbie's clasp.

"No need." He handed her a twenty for what looked to be a six-dollar breakfast. "Keep the change."

Herbie always liked to say that, but he especially liked telling it to Gail.

"Don't be a stranger," Gail blurted out, because she didn't know what else to say. After she said it, it sounded stupid to her.

"I was one before I came to your place of business, but I believe I won't be one any longer."

Gail was impressed by his comment. He was a nice guy. She hadn't found many over the years, but she wasn't about to get her hopes too high. She had been burned before.

"Goodbye Herbie."

"Goodbye Gail. We'll see you soon."

Herbie took Mr. Peabody and walked back to the motel.

Gail watched him walk back to the motel and hoped she would see him soon.

She hadn't said anything, but Herbie had looked familiar when he first came into the place. In her formative years, she had lived in the Hospers area. Her dad ran a corn sheller business and kept busy servicing the farmers in the area. Her mother waited tables in one of the cafés. Together they made a livable wage.

Times were changing then, however. Farmers were buying combines to replace their corn pickers. Her parents bought and ran a small grocery store and made enough to pay the bills. That business started to dry up and at age eleven, Gail's parents picked up and left Hospers. They left their rented acreage looking for a better life. Her father had no marketable skills, and her mother only knew the food and grocery business.

They bought the place in Sterling, on contract, from an older couple. It was a life with long hours, but the profits were sufficient because it was a family-run business. Besides, they worked constantly and didn't have time to spend much of anything. They lived above the business, so they never got away. Gail had felt trapped, and she married the first nice guy who treated her with respect. That turned out just like everything else in her life.

And now this face from the past happens into her life. She took it as a sign. She remembered Herbie as a fat kid who was always smiling. He was still smiling, but the fat kid was gone.

She had been a skinny little thing and painfully shy. She was sure Herbie wouldn't remember her. Boys didn't pay much attention to girls until after 7th or 8th grade. She was long gone before that. Besides,

Roberts was her married name. She had been Gail Klein when she lived in Hospers so many years before.

Gail thought it might be wise not sharing any more personal information than necessary. She needed to find out more about this Herbert Schutt character.

12

Herbie found the business district shortly after he arrived in Frisco. It wasn't a big place, and he liked that mountains surrounded it. He rode west up the main drag just taking in the scenery. There was a huge mountain erupting right out of the end of the street, or at least that's how it appeared.

It was a nice place, a bit touristy, but small enough to make it livable. He could see how this would appeal to Zander.

He made a U-turn and returned east on the street. He spotted the Branchwater a block and a half later. It looked like a nice place, and Herbie pulled into an empty, angle parking spot, near the front door.

The sun was bright, and it took a few moments for Herbie's eyes to get used to the darkened interior.

"Hey, are you Herbie?" It was a voice that appeared to come from behind the bar.

Herbie shaded his eyes for a moment. "Yeah."

"Zander told me to look for you. He had to go to the post office. He should be back shortly."

"Thanks." Herbie looked around.

"Come on over and have a seat. My name is Fats. In the short term, I'm Zander's collaborator in this little intercourse. Soon to be the paramount, notwithstanding."

Herbie was sure he didn't understand anything the guy had just said, but he went over and took a seat anyway.

Fats stuck his hand over the bar, and Herbie shook it.

"Any comrade of Zander automatically becomes a confrere of mine," Fats said, and grinned at Herbie.

"Nice to know." Herbie was unsure how to take this hippie-looking character. He didn't understand him.

Just then the back door slammed.

"Sounds like your consort is back," he said to Herbie. Then Fats yelled toward the back. "Zander, your little compeer is here."

Herbie couldn't ever remember anyone ever calling him "little". Suddenly, he liked this skinny hippie character. He didn't have much time to ponder it, however.

Zander bounded into the bar and almost knocked Herbie off his bar stool with his huge bear hug. Herbie had forgotten how big 6'7" was when it was hovering and almost flinging you to the ground.

Fats just looked at them.

"Get a room," he said, finally.

"I wouldn't have let you hug me like that in high school," Herbie said.

"Hell, I couldn't even get my arms around you when you were in high school." Zander laughed.

"True, but keep that to yourself." Herbie returned the laugh.

"Sounds like a good story," Fats chimed in.

"You just get the coffee," Zander told Fats.

The next half-hour was filled with "remember whens" and other superfluous reminiscences. When they started to run out of stories, Zander decided to show Herbie the way to his cabin. Fats showed some disappointment. He was enjoying the anecdotes even though they smacked of legend and that being mostly fiction. Tales of the past always seemed to become allegorical. He even had a few of his own. Some even involved Zander, but he kept most of those to himself for self-preservation.

The duo went to Zander's cabin in Herbie's big boat Buick.

"Seriously, Herbie, this is your car?"

"What's wrong with it?" Herbie pretended to be hurt.

"Well, nothing if you're an old man. I don't think I'll ever be old enough to drive a Buick."

Herbie shrugged his shoulders. Zander thought there was something he wanted to say, but he let it go. He showed Herbie the small spare bedroom and gave him some time to get situated.

Zander had expanded his cabin over the past few winters. He didn't get any building permits or ask anyone's permission. He just did it. The first year he added a bedroom. The second year he added another bathroom and expanded the master. The third year was the most complicated. He had to expand the footprint of the cabin to make a nice sized living room. He was careful to do most of the work at night, and no one paid much attention. He was proud of how everything turned out. It was a comfortable place to live, and Zander thought it had some style as well, even if he did say so himself.

Herbie came out of the bedroom and put his shaving kit in the guest bathroom. Zander had two beers waiting on the table near the fireplace. It was too hot for a fire, but it was a nice place for conversation.

Herbie saw the beers. "Seems a little early to start drinking."

"If you don't start drinking in the morning, you can't say you've drank all day." Zander liked the old joke.

Herbie liked it as well, took the beer, and sat in the recliner next to the couch.

"I think we both have some things to tell each other to catch us up," Zander said.

"Maybe." Herbie wasn't ready to share anything until Zander took the lead.

Zander looked at him for a moment. He wondered why Herbie had just showed up out of the blue. It wasn't like him. He was a creature of habit.

"I think you should start first," Herbie said, and sat back.

Zander started telling Herbie the highlights of his life since coming to the mountains. He didn't stop with Sara Jane but went right on with Lilly and Ingrid as well. When he was finished they were on their third Coors.

Herbie had been careful not to bring up Sara Jane. He knew the whole story about her death and how it affected Zander when they were in school. He was shocked to learn she was still alive. Zander's life story made his seem trivial.

He told it to Zander anyway. He felt he owed him something. He started from the last time they had seen each other and finished with his experience with the woman at the rest stop. He stopped short of including meeting Gail Roberts. After all, nothing would probably come of it. He hadn't had much luck with romance in the past.

63

Zander enjoyed sharing the stories. It made him feel better knowing others had some similar bad experiences. His mother always said, "Misery loves company." He knew that to be true.

Herbie found the Sara Jane tale to be fascinating. He wanted more but realized if there was anything else, Zander wasn't sharing. Secrets were something he could accept. He had a few of his own.

Zander spent a few days showing Herbie around. He pointed out the highlights and shared the local history. Herbie was appreciative, and as soon as he got his bearings, he told Zander to get back to work. He didn't want to strain their friendship, and he liked being by himself. He was used to it.

He experienced all he could, took the local tours, drove to the area communities, and tried most of the local eateries. One nice morning he decided to go to Copper Mountain. He remembered that Gail had said it was her favorite place to hike.

Copper Mountain was a series of ski slopes with hotels and restaurants at the base. There was even a golf course. Herbie didn't have much use for anything involving a ball. Sports were a bad memory of his overweight youth.

He decided to ride up the ski lift and hike down the mountain. He knew going down was the easy part. He wasn't in terrible shape, but he wasn't anywhere close to his Navy days.

The ride up stopped at the first slope. The lift to the top of the mountain was closed in the summer because of the possibility of lightning storms. Storms seemed to pop up indiscriminately. At least that was what the lift operator told him.

He decided to take the access road to the top. It was easier than trying to take the path along the lift towers. The view was spectacular. He could see why Gail said this was her favorite hiking place. Along the way up, Herbie spotted something red in the small trees just below the road he was hiking. He slipped over the edge of the road and went into the trees. He found a red ski pole. It looked like someone had dropped it from the ski lift that intersected the road at that spot. Herbie wondered how long it had been there. It looked like it was still in pretty good shape.

He was ready to return to the road when he stumbled on another ski pole. This one was purple and a little more beat up. They would make two good hiking sticks. The red one still had the wrist strap intact. The purple stick's was missing. No matter, it was fun sticking the sharp ends into the sandy road.

Herbie spent most of the day hiking up the last leg and then hiking back down. He was amazed at the views. He was sorry he didn't have a good camera. That was something to remedy if he was going to continue to travel the country.

There wasn't much open in Copper Mountain Village during the summer. Herbie found a restaurant with a big bar that stayed open, because it was owned by one of the hotels that catered to both the summer and winter vacationers. Herbie ordered a big dark tap beer and sat outside on their veranda. He liked to watch people but there were very few around, so he looked out over the golf course and the mountains on the other side of the valley.

It was time to take stock of his life. He was going nowhere. It was bothering him more and more. He decided right there, at that minute, that he would return to Sterling and see Gail Roberts.

13

Bonnie and Avon were an item. At least that was how it appeared to Bonnie. She had to admit, it wasn't an unpleasant relationship. It still was somewhat confusing to Bonnie to have been attracted to a woman, but she tried not to dwell on it.

The end of summer was near, and soon the winter tourists would start to arrive, many for a just a short time. The snowbirds, however, would arrive and stay for the entire winter.

Avon was complaining about working at restaurants. She kept telling Bonnie that they needed to start a business.

"Nobody ever makes any money working for someone else," Avon said, one afternoon after a bad lunch hour shift.

"I would agree. You've been saying that quite some time. What did you have in mind?" Bonnie was getting tired of just taking up space. There was no justification in her slothful existence. Her Dutch upbringing was weighing heavily on her conscience, such as it was.

"If you are serious, come with me." Avon took her by the hand and pulled her out onto Duval Street.

It was a nice day and people were moving about. They walked toward Front Street and rounded the corner. Bonnie was looking toward the ocean and noticed a huge cruise ship that had just docked.

Avon stopped suddenly and was looking at an entrance to one of the many shops. Bonnie noticed a "For Sale" sign in the window.

"What's this?" She asked Avon.

"Something we could do. We could even do a lot more."

Bonnie was puzzled, but interested.

Then she saw the window displays. It was a sex shop. There were all kinds of items. Some Bonnie had seen before, some she had not.

Some she recognized from her past with Marty. Zander had called him Rooster. That made her smile, and then just as quickly, put the thought out of her mind.

"What is this?" Bonnie tried to sound perturbed.

"What does it look like?"

"It looks like something I don't want to get myself involved in."

It was Avon's turn to be agitated.

"You don't seem to mind when I use some of these things on you."

Bonnie realized Avon was right. Why she was acting so puritanical with Avon was bewildering.

"Is there a point to all this?"

"I've done the research. I've talked to the owners. There is money to be made selling this stuff."

Bonnie realized that Key West was wide open. There were all kinds of people who walked to different kinds of lifestyles. Tourists did things they would never do when they went back home. They might have dreamt about using sex toys, but it took being away from home to build up the courage to experiment.

"OK. Let's find out some details," Bonnie said, and took the lead into the building.

Bonnie was Jayne again and totally in charge. Avon could not help but to notice the transformation. It surprised her. She had been the dominating one. At least that's what she had thought.

Bonnie spent the remainder of the afternoon talking to the owners and going over their financials. She was pretty thorough but wished she could have had the help of Lilly who had been excellent at financials. She may have been too good as Bonnie remembered.

The owners owned the business and not the building. They leased that from someone who lived in Indiana. The yearly lease was reasonable for something as close to the waterfront. Bonnie liked the location.

The asking price was a hundred and fifty thousand. It was way too much for what was offered. The stock came to somewhere between 20 and 30 thousand. It was true; there were living quarters above the shop. After Bonnie saw what they had done with the space, she felt better. The price was still high, however. There was entirely too much blue sky built into the asking price.

After some intense negotiations, they settled on ninety thousand. Bonnie could see they wanted to sell badly. Sex businesses weren't for most people. It appeared there weren't very many buyers for that type of retail. She tipped the sale when she told them she would give them cash in hundred dollar increments. Cash opened many doors. Apparently, sex shops were no different.

Avon had been silent during the negotiations.

As they were leaving the shop, Avon asked Bonnie:

"Where are you going to get all that cash?"

"Don't worry about that."

"Well, I am just a little worried. What's my role going to be in this business?"

"Day-to-day operations."

"Well, what are you going to do?"

"I'll be the general manager, since it's my money that's going to finance everything. Or were you planning on coming up with half? If you did, then we could be partners."

Avon didn't say anything.

"I didn't think so. After we get this thing off the ground, I may have a way for you to become a partner. But we'll talk about that later."

Avon looked at her, while Bonnie led them back to the condo. There were some secrets that Avon knew nothing about and she didn't like that. Maybe she'd better make another phone call soon.

14

It had been two weeks, and Herbie was becoming restless. Zander had been a great host, but he could tell that his presence was weighing on him just a bit. Guests and fish begin to stink after three days, and it had been fifteen days since he drove into Frisco.

He liked this place, but he knew he wouldn't much care for it in the winter. Besides, he had to figure out what he was going to do. All he understood was trucking. He couldn't be spending everything he got from selling his tractor before he bought something in its place.

Zander had gone down to the bar, and as Herbie sat on the porch with his cup of coffee, he made a decision. He would leave for Sterling today, find Gail Roberts, and see if he could make something work for once in his life. He threw his remaining coffee into the pine needles surrounding the cabin and went back inside.

He packed up his things and loaded them into the Buick. He made sure everything was cleaned and straightened. Then he stripped his bed and threw everything into the washer. He would try and remember to tell Zander to put them in the dryer when he got home. Then he thought better, found some paper, and left him a note on the kitchen table. Other than the note, he was satisfied that his presence at the cabin would only be a memory.

It took him five minutes to get to the Branchwater. He decided to make a short detour and visit the Wal-Mart that was just a block from the interstate. He brought some flavored water and snacks for his trip to Sterling. In the electronics section, he found a TracFone similar to the one he owned. He paid for everything, and drove back to the bar.

Zander was cutting limes when he walked in

"Herbie, you're actually up for the day?" Zander asked it

seriously, but Herbie knew him well enough to see he was joking.

"Nobody to screw at your place. Way too quiet."

Zander was going to tell him that he never had a piece of ass in his life, but then thought better of it. Herbie probably never was with a woman unless he paid for one. He didn't want to hurt his feelings.

"So, what's your plan for the day?" Zander kept cutting limes.

"I'm taking off. Just stopped in to say goodbye and thank you for your hospitality."

Zander missed the lime and cut his finger.

"Damn it."

He turned around and ran some cold water on it. It wasn't a deep cut, and Zander wrapped a paper towel around it until it would stop bleeding.

"I didn't realize my leaving would have such an impact."

"Oh, you are a funny boy."

Zander poured two cups of coffee and slid one to Herbie. Herbie had enough coffee but took a sip to be polite.

"Ew. You need someone to come in here and make your coffee. This stuff is terrible."

"Why don't you stay and do it. We're looking for someone to help out around here. After I leave, Fats will need someone he can trust. Besides, he likes you."

For a moment, Herbie considered the proposition. Then he reconsidered. He had already made up his mind. He couldn't change now; no matter how much it appealed to him.

"It would never work. I hardly understand anything that comes out of his mouth."

Zander smiled. "I have to admit, it takes some time and a lot of listening before you can actually communicate. But it's worth it in the long run. He's a great guy."

"I have no doubt. You've always been a good judge of character."

But that wasn't true at all.

"So, if I can't get you to stay, why don't you tell me what you're going to do?"

"I've been thinking a lot about Florida, lately."

Zander was interested.

"That's interesting, so have I. You know, if you would take me up

70

on my offer until January, we could go down together."

"Nice idea, but no. I've got something to do, and I don't know how long it's going to take." Herbie was enjoying the mystery he was creating for Zander.

"Whoa. Back this horse up. You'd better explain that last comment."

Herbie took a sip of coffee and spit back into the cup.

"You got anything else? How about some iced tea?"

Zander took away his cup and came back with a large glass of ice. He opened a can and poured it in.

"Fresh huh?" Herbie asked.

"Just made it myself. Sugar and lemon?"

"Certainly. If this is anything like the coffee, I'll need something to mask the taste."

"Enough dancing around. Spill it."

"I met someone in Sterling on the way over here."

"Male or female?"

"Female, you asshole."

"Hey, I'm just trying to get past this tight-lipped shit."

"Well all right then." Herbie took a drink from his glass. Zander waited. Finally he just came out and asked.

"Is this a romantic thing or some kind of business deal?'

"I'm hoping it will become romantic, but I don't know. She seemed interested."

"Good God, Herbie, why are you still sitting here?"

"I guess I'm trying to get up enough nerve."

Zander looked at his friend for a few moments before he spoke.

"Herbie, I'm going to give you some advice. You need to put every ounce of effort into making this thing work with…"

Herbie interjected, "Gail."

"With Gail. Look at the both of us. Neither of us have any meaningful relationships. In our forties and alone."

"Different circumstances. You made your choices. I had none." Herbie was just a bit annoyed. He and Zander weren't at all alike.

"Maybe so, but the end result is the same. Maybe too many things have happened to me and not enough happened to you. But here is your chance. If you don't go after it with everything you've got, you'll wonder what could have been for the rest of your life."

"I know that. I've always had a comfort zone, and it's hard break out of that."

"The only person who can change your life is you."

"I might say the same thing about you, Zander."

The comment took Zander off guard for a moment. Herbie was right, however. What right had he to give Herbie a big fat lecture on living, when his own life was in such disarray?

"You know that I was married once," Herbie said, quietly.

"No, I didn't know that. What happened?"

"She was one of those base girls who followed the enlisted men. I met her in in a bar on leave, after I had lost all the weight. I looked pretty good for the first time in my life, and I was confident back then. Didn't know any better. It was a short romance, and we got married by a justice of the peace off base one weekend. I had to ship out shortly after that for six weeks. When I got back, she was gone."

"Did you look for her?"

"I asked around. Some of her friends were still around, but they didn't know anything. At least that's what they said."

"I don't know what to say, Herbie."

"I don't think I had time to even know what I was doing. Looking back, I don't think that I even loved her. The sex was good though." Herbie smiled at the thought.

"Well then, it wasn't a total waste," Zander joked.

"I'm sure I wasn't very good at it. It was my first go-round."

"Why do you think she left?"

"She probably found out I didn't have any money. Most of those camp girls were trying to get out of their own hopeless situations. I suppose someone else came along with better prospects." Herbie sighed.

"What was her name? Zander asked.

Herbie stopped and looked at the counter.

"It was Trixie something or other. I forget her last name."

"Trixie? Is that short for something?"

Herbie thought some more. "Hooker, I think."

They both laughed.

"Zander, I'm going to give this thing with Gail all I've got."

"Good. Tell me about her."

Herbie explained how he met Gail and shared their conversation almost word for word. He had no trouble explaining what she looked like, because it was burned into his memory.

Zander felt good for his friend. He hoped things would work out for the two of them. He also was thinking about himself. He needed to find a woman who wasn't broken, or maybe he needed to unravel his own life before he could rectify his past.

Just as Herbie was finishing his story, Fats burst in.

"Greetings and salutations on this picturesque and symmetrical ante meridiem."

"Where does he come up with that shit?" Herbie asked.

"Pulls it out of his ass, I think."

"I hear you both. I am standing right here, after all." Fats didn't seem bothered in the least.

"Herbie is leaving us, Fats."

"Well you horse's ass, did you offer him the job like we discussed?"

"He turned me down."

Fats sat right down next to Herbie.

"If it's my rhetoric that bothers you, I could try and tone that down."

Herbie laughed. "I'm starting to get used to it. Don't do that. It's who you are. I just have something else I need to do right now."

"Would you come back after you complete whatever task you are contemplating?"

"Hopefully not. But if it doesn't turn out as expected, I might be persuaded." Herbie smiled, and he realized he was even starting to talk like Fats.

"He's not coming back," Zander said, forcefully.

He turned to Herbie. "Try to be positive. You will make this work."

"I will."

"Well, are we at least going to have one last blow-out before you go?" Fats was already planning a party in his mind.

"As tempting as that might be, I'm heading out at the end of this conversation," Herbie said, and finished his iced tea.

Zander handed him one of his cards. "If you need to get in touch."

"I've got a better idea." Herbie reached into his pocket, pulled out the TracFone he purchased at Wal-Mart and handed it to Zander.

"What am I supposed to do with this?" Zander was slightly irritated.

"Praise the Lord and pass the ammunition. We're going to get Zander into the twentieth century." Fats was almost yelling.

"Before you get all pissy with me, you need to know this is just a basic phone. You can store the numbers of those you want to call, and those names will come up on the screen when they call you. If you don't recognize the number, you don't have to answer it. The most important thing is, you don't have to give out your number to anyone if you so choose."

"What if I call someone's number who's not in my phone?"

"Then they'll have your number if they choose to save it. But why would you do that, when you're so paranoid the way it is?'

"I'm just trying to understand this crazy technology."

"Well, it will make your life a lot simpler than it is now," Fats broke in.

"Who asked you?"

Fats left abruptly and headed for the back room.

"Now I'm going to show you how to program this thing, and you can choose to use it or not. It's up to you. But it is a gift from me, and I hope you take it in the spirit it is intended."

Zander was screwed and he knew it. "OK. Show me. But I'm not making any promises."

Herbie was good with technology and even a better teacher. It took about twenty minutes for Zander to get comfortable with the functions. After Herbie was sure he understood everything, he gave him his phone number to put into the TracFone.

Fats snuck back in to watch the whole process.

"Hey, put my number in there, too."

Zander just glared at him. "If I do that, you're going to have to promise me that you won't give my number to anyone unless I agree."

"No problimo, dude."

"I'm serious. You will call me and ask me for permission before you give it out to anyone. Understood?"

"Anything to get you into the here and now, compatriot. What about Lilly and Ingrid?"

"What about them?"

"You should put their numbers in as well."

"We'll see." It was the best Zander could do at the moment. Too much information coming at him made him crazy.

The two were busy putting in Fats' number, when Herbie made a quick exit unnoticed by either one. He hated goodbyes. He seldom used the word. It had such finality to it.

He would give Zander a call on his new phone, when he felt the time was right. He hoped it would be the good news he was anticipating.

15

Bonnie and Avon closed the shop for a week when the sale was finalized. They moved their personal belongings to the loft above the business. It was a nice space, and they hadn't needed to do much to spruce it up.

The store was another matter. The former owners had lost interest in maintenance and cleaning. So they had to move all the merchandise to a storage facility. Bonnie hired plumbers, electricians, and painters to make the necessary repairs. She got their attention when she said she would pay cash. She was sure she was paying above premium, but the work was getting finished. The locals had a saying, "Bend over and welcome to the island, man" which was pretty much true.

The planned week closure lasted almost three. Bonnie and Avon finally felt the exhaustion kick in, as they put the remaining stock in place. They decided to celebrate by going out for wine and dinner. It was early afternoon. They decided to drive up to Marathon to get away from Key West for an evening.

Bonnie hadn't used her Camaro for some time and thought it needed to be driven. She hadn't moved it from the parking garage under the condo, and it needed to be moved before the owner would have it towed. There was ample parking in the space behind the shop, but she had just been too busy to think about it.

Bonnie carried the conversation as they walked over to retrieve the car.

"There are a few things we need to discuss concerning the business. The first needs to be decided by tomorrow."

"What's that?" Avon wondered.

"What are we going to name it?" Bonnie responded, with her own question.

"That's a good question. I hadn't even thought about it."

All the way to Marathon, they tried to brainstorm a catchy name. They laughed at some of the bizarre titles. As wide open as Key West was, they would still be unacceptable. They were still discussing names as they walked into Porky's Bayside Barbecue Restaurant. Bonnie had suggested the place. She had stopped on her way to Key West, and found the pulled pork to be some of the best she ever tasted. It was a funky little place right on the water. Avon liked it the moment she walked in.

They had some blue concoction that was the drink of the day. Neither had any idea what was in it, but it was sweet and seemed appropriate for the keys. By the second drink, they were amused with the alcohol-induced names.

Avon offered: "Nymphomaniac," "Climax," "Coitus," "Debauchery," "Copulated," "Gigolo," "Fornicated," and she was especially fond of "Lickerish". That one got them both laughing.

Bonnie thought they should tame it down just a bit and try to appeal to all the deviations generally. She suggested: "Sexual Desire," " Courtesan," "Libido," "Erotica," "Sexual Deviations," and "Carnal Knowledge." They were serious about the last one, until they realized it was the title of an old movie. They decided against using it because it seemed like a dated reference to that old movie.

After a few more drinks and dinner, they settled on two titles: "The Libertine" and "The Aphrodisiac." Avon thought "The Libertine" sounded too literary. Bonnie didn't want to lose clientele, because they might think the place was a bit too highbrow. So it became The Aphrodisiac, by default. They both liked the name. Bonnie would see to the signage in the morning.

They were back on the road and heading back to Key West after dinner. They had four drinks each. Bonnie felt fine to drive. Dinner had helped to calm the giggles. Avon was looking out the window at the various keys they passed. She thought it was a marvel the way the highway appeared to come right out of the ocean.

Bonnie had something else on her mind, and thought the time to brooch the subject might be right.

"Avon, have you kept in touch with some of your server friends from the various places you worked?"

"I haven't had a lot of time lately, but yeah, I still have quite a few friends on the island. Why?" Avon thought it was a strange question, and she was just a bit wary.

Bonnie assumed she had spent quite a bit of time on Key West. She didn't realize that Avon had followed her to the island. That was a little secret Avon didn't want to share.

"I've been doing quite a bit of thinking about the business."

"The Aphrodisiac," Avon added.

Bonnie smiled. "Yes. I don't think we're going to make much of an impact on the bottom line by just selling sex toys."

"So what are you thinking?" Avon was still alert and somewhat cautious.

"We need to diversify. We need to add a full line of provocative clothing for both men and women."

"That sounds like a great idea. We could have a full line of leather."

"Oh, we need to carry way more than that. We should stock swimwear, sleepwear, underwear, sexy everyday wear and evening wear. It would be heavy on stock for women, but we could carry things that appeal to the men as well. We certainly have enough room."

"I think it could work. We should check with some of the boys at a few of the bars to see what they think we should stock."

"I hadn't thought of that. It's a great idea Avon."

Avon smiled and sat back in her seat.

Bonnie paused for a few minutes trying to sort through how she would present her next idea in the best possible light.

"I asked you before about your friends in the serving business. I was wondering if you could speak to the ones who you feel would be agreeable to earning extra money."

"Doing what? I don't think we're in a position of hiring extra help just yet."

"You're right, but this is a perfect setting to offer our customers something more."

Avon wasn't sure liked the way the conversation was heading.

"I think you better just come out and say what's on your mind."

"I think we could run an escort service right from The Aphrodisiac."

Avon looked out the side window. She was trying to think about how to answer.

"I wouldn't be interested in something like that."

"Well, it wouldn't be you directly involved. We would just be the booking agent."

"So how would it work?" Avon seemed unsure.

"I think we would have a separate phone line or maybe just a cell phone dedicated to that side of the business. We could have a set of cards displayed at the cash register. It would be like an independent contractor doing business off premises."

"So, nothing would happen at The Aphrodisiac?"

"Absolutely not. We aren't running a brothel. We're just hooking people up. It would be totally voluntary."

They pulled into the Key West city limits as they were speaking. Both remained quiet, until Bonnie parked the Camaro behind the shop. She turned to Avon.

"I just want you to think about it. Sleep on it. We'll talk some more tomorrow."

Avon didn't get much sleep the rest of the night.

16

Herbert Schutt made his way down the mountains on his way to Sterling. He pulled off I-70, at Golden, for gas. He decided to have lunch at Wendy's just across the street. Before he went in to order, he stopped and sat on the hood of his big boat Buick, and took out his phone. He found Gail's card and programmed her number into the phone. He thought he was being practical, but he knew he was just stalling for time.

When he was finished, he slipped the phone back into his front pants pocket. Then he stopped, pulled it back out and before he could change his mind, dialed the number.

"Coffee Cup." It was Gail's voice. He didn't know if he had even remembered the place was called the Coffee Cup. He wasn't surprised. Every town had an eatery with that name.

"Hello Gail. It's Herbie."

There was a pause. Herbie wondered if Gail was trying to come up with an excuse to dismiss him. He was well prepared.

"Oh my gosh. Herbie. I wasn't sure I would ever hear from you again."

Suddenly, all the self-doubt and loathing melted away.

"I told you, I would call you when I was coming your way."

"You did."

"I always do what I say I will."

"I like that in a person." Gail's voice was as sweet sounding as anything Herbie had ever heard.

"I'm in Golden. I thought if the offer still held, I would come on down your way."

"I think that would be wonderful." Gail's voice almost danced.

"I'll see you in a few hours then. I'll check into the motel across the street before I come over. Do I need dress clothes for our dinner this evening?"

Gail stopped short of telling Herbie not to check into the motel but to stay at her place instead. It was too soon for that. She would want to know his intentions before she offered her place.

"Dress casual. We're not going anyplace that fancy."

"That's a relief. I would have needed to go out and buy something. I don't own anything that nice." They both laughed bit nervously.

Gail was impressed. If Herbie had even thought about buying something to go out on a date with her, he was already running heads and shoulders above any of the other dates she had lately. After she thought about it, she realized she hadn't even had any dates lately.

"Should I pick you up at the café?" Herbie asked.

"No. Why don't you come to my condo about 5:00? We can have a few drinks and discuss where we will go for dinner."

She gave Herbie the address and directions from the café. Sterling wasn't a big place, and the drive was an easy one from the café to her condo. She liked easy; life was too complicated as it was, without relationships gumming up the works. That's why this little tryst seemed so unusual to Gail. It wasn't something she embraced, ever. In fact, she had avoided similar situations her entire life.

"Thanks Gail." She heard Herbie say through the fog that was surrounding her. Then the line went dead. She stood looking out the window of the café losing all sense of time. The sound of a bell coming from the kitchen snapped her back to reality. Someone's order was up.

Herbie decided to go through the drive-up at Wendy's. He figured he didn't need a repeat of his experience with the "bag." Besides, it was too warm to leave Mr. Peabody in the car. He got enough food for both of them, and drove toward the interstate. Just before he saw the I-70 sign, he saw a little park with picnic tables shaded by small roofs. It was a perfect place to stop for both of them. He wasn't in any hurry. Nothing much was going to happen until 5:00 anyway.

17

The Aphrodisiac was open for business. Avon had made a temporary sign and put it in the window. She made it out of tag board. It was bright and colorful, and Bonnie was impressed with her artwork. She had no talent in that arena.

Neither of the women had brought up the discussion from the night before. Bonnie knew Avon would talk about it when she was ready. She didn't know Avon wouldn't be ready until she made a call.

Bonnie hadn't let any grass grow under her feet waiting for Avon's decision, however. She had made a few contacts of her own, both male and female, and had spoken with them about the escort idea. She had a number of interested parties.

When she had business card made up for The Aphrodisiac, she had the same number of cards made for the escort business as well. She would do this, with or without, Avon's blessing. She still liked the name Libertine, so the card read Libertine Escort Service. She thought it sounded sophisticated. She didn't want to pull herself back into the massage world, and this just felt right. The business should be quite profitable, and the escorts themselves would dictate what their limits of service would be.

Bonnie still hadn't come up with a plan of what to charge. She knew she couldn't trust the escorts to share their actual take. People always lied when it came to dealing with money.

There had to be various charges for various services. If someone wanted a person for a business dinner, it would be cheaper than someone who wanted to have sex. Everyone had different tastes, so the billing had to reflect it as well.

She would collect from the customers and share the proceeds with the escorts. What the customer wanted, and what the escort would actually fulfill, would determine who would be paired. It was going to take some work to get the proper data from each escort. She hoped she would have a number at her disposal.

Avon's voice broke into Bonnie's thoughts:

"I'm going over and get some breakfast. Can I bring you anything?"

"Bring me some coffee." Bonnie said.

"I'm going to the Hog's Breath."

"Never mind," Bonnie said, quickly.

"That's what I thought." Avon laughed and was out the door.

As she walked over to the restaurant, she wondered how she had gotten herself so involved with this woman. Lilly had said her name was Jayne but Fats had called her Sara Jane. She wondered about all of her secrets and how she would be able to keep it straight in her mind. It was hard enough for her just to keep this one.

Avon had walked away from The Aphrodisiac as Avon, but she entered the Hog's Breath as Mona Kane. She walked right through the busy restaurant and headed right for the phones in the back on the wall near the restrooms.

Mona picked up the phone and dialed the operator. She gave the operator Fats' phone number, and then reversed the charges.

Mona was a friend of Lilly. She had been looking for a job and was lucky to meet Lilly before Rooster or Jayne had the chance. Lilly had steered her away from the massage business. She found her some honest work helping a private detective with some of his surveillance work.

Mona was good at it. She didn't fit the "private dick" persona, so she wouldn't arouse suspicion like a man would. Lilly liked her "private dick" terminology and the two of them had a few laughs over it.

When Zander left to take care of his parents' funeral, Fats started to get worried about Sara Jane. He could feel the distance she was trying to create between herself and everyone else. That's when he called Lilly and asked for her help. Lilly didn't hesitate. Zander was her good friend, and she didn't want to see him hurt again. Besides, Lilly didn't give a damn about Jayne.

Lilly contacted Mona and asked for her help. Together they hatched the plan for Mona to follow Jayne and report back to Lilly. Lilly, in turn, would report to Fats. At first Fats and Lilly shared Mona's costs. Neither had any idea it would last as long as it had.

When Lilly moved on and took up residence in Aspen, she decided that Fats should be the contact. It was no longer appropriate for her to be involved, especially since she had found her new life with Roger, the man she now loved.

At first Fats panicked. How would he pay for the expenses? He couldn't bill them to the bar. Lilly decided she could finance everything as a third party. She had talked with Roger, and he gave her his approval. That made everything much easier.

Roger had met Zander one Christmas and decided he liked him. He loved Lilly and wanted her to be happy. He wouldn't drive a wedge into their relationship with something as trivial as this. He could see Zander's friends were trying to keep his best interests at heart. He liked that.

From then on, Fats received weekly phone messages on his cell phone from Mona. Of course, she was Avon now, and he tried to remember that when he took her calls.

On the fourth ring, Fats picked up the phone.

"This is Fats. State your concern."

"Fats, this is Mona."

Fats went out the back of the bar, so he wouldn't be overheard.

"Well, Avon, it's been a long time. How can I help you?" Fats liked the intrigue, and enjoyed playing the game.

Mona told her latest saga involving Bonnie as quickly as she could. Fats liked what he heard.

"Sounds like she's up to her old tricks. I mean that quite literally."

"So, what do you think I should do?"

"It might be a good time to make an exit. You've given me what I need. I don't think she'll be leaving anytime soon. I just need to cogitate about what I'm going to do with all this intelligence."

"I don't think I should leave right now. It might make this Bonnie character suspicious."

"Maybe so, but you need to be diligent. She's one treacherous freak. Worst I've ever seen."

"I'm able to handle myself," Mona said, testily.

"Then you would be the best I've ever seen."

"So, what are you going to do with this information?"

"Reflect, contemplate, and deliberate. How I involve Zander will be a quandary, for sure."

"I like you Fats, but you're very odd."

"Correct. Take good care of yourself around her. If you feel, at any time, that your cover is blown, flee quickly and quietly. Your very life will depend upon it."

Mona thought Fats was enjoying the cloak and dagger stuff a little too much. It was time for her to go.

"I'll be careful, Fats. My biggest concern is this escort business she is determined to get us into."

"I'd let you escort me Mona, I mean Avon."

"Hey, aren't you living with someone?"

"Ah, variety! Bane of my existence." He hung up.

Mona had to smile. He was a weird dude, for certain. But you just couldn't help but like the duck fart.

Mona left the Hog's Breath and as she stepped onto the street, she became Avon Bartow once again.

18

Herbie settled back into the old motel with Mr. Peabody. His dog had always been his companion because there had always been just the two of them. Now someone new had entered into his dual existence, and Herbie had to think about what was to happen with his best friend. He couldn't take the dog along on their dinner engagement, but he didn't want to leave Mr. Peabody in the motel room. He decided to walk over to the Coffee Cup and ask Gail what she recommended.

Mr. Peabody was always up for a walk, and after many unnecessary steps and out-of- the-way explorations, they reached the café. Herbie was surprised to see that it was closed. It was 3:30. When he looked at the door he found out the reason. The hours of operation were from 6:00 a.m. until 2:00 p.m.

The café was a breakfast and lunch place. He could see why Gail had looked tired. To have the place open by 6:00, he was sure she had to be there by 4:00. It was a hectic schedule, to be sure, but at least she didn't have to be open during dinner. Herbie realized that would have been an impossible schedule.

Still, Herbie thought that someone should be around getting ready for the following day. He looked into the window trying to see if there was any movement in the kitchen. What he saw made him step back for a moment. Chairs were strewn around the dining area. Tables were overturned everywhere. Then, out of the corner of his eye, he saw someone move. Someone in a dew rag moved in front of the server window. Herbie ducked back behind the wall. For a moment, he panicked. What if Gail was still there?

Herbie gathered his thoughts, and then ambled back to the motel with Mr. Peabody just like they were on their usual walk. He put Mr. Peabody into the room and turned on the TV to keep him company. Then he got into the Buick and intentionally drove past the Coffee Cup. He went around the block and noticed an alley in the back. There were three motorcycles parked near the café's back door. They looked like crotch rockets.

Herbie hated motorcycles. They were hard to see on the road. He was always concerned that he might hit one with his truck. He hadn't always felt that way, however. When he got out of the service, he bought a used Harley and enjoyed the heck out of it. He even made a few trips to Sturgis for the rally. Mostly he went to see the women in various states of undress. He was seldom disappointed.

When he started trucking he sold the bike, and decided to dislike all bikers. He especially hated the crotch rockets. They would swerve in and out of traffic going like a bat out of hell. Not only were the bikes dangerous, the riders were assholes.

Herbie drove halfway down the alley and then stopped. He pushed the trunk button and got out. He had a huge red toolbox in the trunk filled with Snap On Tools. He had taken it from his Kenworth when he sold the truck.

The toolbox didn't contain anything he could use as a weapon, but Herbie had an old axe handle lying in the trunk next to it. He had forgotten where he had picked it up, but it was a handy thing to keep with him in the sleeper to ward off intruders. The weight was good and fit Herbie's hand.

He grabbed the axe handle and went over to the back door of the Coffee Cup. The door was partway open, and Herbie could see into the kitchen. He saw someone lying on the floor. He assumed it was the cook. It looked like he had been beaned pretty hard. He wasn't moving, anyway.

Herbie pushed the door open so he could get a better view. That's when he saw Gail. She was tied up and had a strip of tape over her mouth. She had a gash over her left eyebrow, and there was blood down the side of her face. Suddenly Herbie felt a rage boiling inside of him. He was shaking with anger.

Gail saw him and tried to get up. He motioned for her to stay where she was. He put a finger to his lips. Then he went back toward his car, took out his phone and dialed 911.

When the operator had sufficient information, she told Herbie to remain outside and not to confront the intruders. Herbie agreed, while walking back to the open door and entering the café.

He heard some noise in the basement. It sounded like they were trying to destroy everything. Herbie went over to Gail, picked her up, and carried her back to the Buick. He carefully placed her in the front seat and removed the tape.

"Don't say anything. Save it for the police. I called them, they should be here any minute."

He stood back up and started walking back to the café with his axe handle.

"Stay here with me until the police come," she pleaded.

"Can't take the chance. They might get away. They'll be spooked if they see you're gone." Herbie was on a mission, and nothing was going to get in his way.

He walked up to the three bikes and pushed the first one over, and all three went down like dominos. Then he took his axe handle and started to beat on anything that would break. His goal was to make a lot of racket and get the assholes to the back door.

Herbie took a spot next to the door, where he couldn't be seen, but would have a full swing arc toward the open door. He knew he had to take control of the situation. There would be no second chances. He didn't know if they had any firearms. He hoped not. He wasn't equipped to fight anyone with guns.

The first asshole came out of the door and looked over at the bikes. That's the last thing he saw. Herbie's handle came streaking parallel with the guy's neck. Herbie caught him on the throat. The guy made a gagging sound as he put his hands to his neck. Herbie wound up again and hit him hard on the side of the head. As he was going down, blood was already coming out of his ear.

"Concussion," Herbie said, out loud.

Herbie looked down at the guy. He couldn't have been more than twenty. He was a big kid and wearing some kind of biker leather. He belonged to some gang by the look of things.

"Just a bunch of gang bangers," Herbie said, again out loud.

"What the hell is all the racket, Boxer?" One of the guys hollered from the dining area.

"Your buddy is taking a little powder. I've called 911. The cops should be here shortly. If I were you, I'd come out peacefully and wait for them."

"Fat chance."

Then, the two stormed out together. Herbie hadn't planned on that. The fact was he hadn't planned on anything. He had just reacted.

Both stormed out the door with two huge knives drawn. Herbie connected with the one closest to him. The handle caught the kid right between the eyes. He didn't go down right away, but he was stunned and looked like he just got off a tilt-a-whirl.

Herbie raised the handle to bear down on the third guy when the knife caught his arm. He looked down and thought he could see the bone just before the wound filled with blood. He almost dropped the handle.

The kid was smiling.

"You're dead, old man."

Herbie didn't like that at all. Hell, he was hardly into his forties. Who was this punk, telling him he was old?

"The kid outweighed Herbie by at least eighty pounds. Herbie thought most of that was flab. But he could see the axe handle wasn't going to be stout enough to take the monster down. He concentrated on the knife hand. When the time was right, he would break the hand with the handle, and retrieve the knife.

Herbie moved into the center of the alley. The second guy was still wobbly, so Herbie cracked him another blow to the head. He went down like a sandbag.

The last guy was circling around Herbie, looking for his chance to plunge the knife into his gut. Herbie had no doubt the kid meant to kill him. He needed to be coy and wait for his chance. His training in the Navy kicked in.

Herbie had put both hands on the axe handle to help steady it. He didn't have enough power in his right arm because of the gash. He thought he might need to get that repaired.

Herbie decided to make his move. He turned his back on the guy for a split second, and when he lunged at Herbie to bury the knife, Herbie came around with the handle and caught the banger's knife hand with his full force. Coming around in a full arc gave Herbie more momentum. When the handle hit the banger's hand, Herbie could hear the entire hand crunch. His hand was mush. The knife dropped to the ground. Herbie came around again and hit him in that sweet spot right between the legs. He went down on all fours.

The guy was finished, but Herbie wasn't. He picked up the knife and with both hands jammed it right up the banger's ass. He drove the knife up until the hilt stopped it. The guy was squealing like a pig. Herbie thought he might have looked a lot like a pig. He didn't think the guy would die, but he wasn't going to be taking a shit the normal way anytime soon. Maybe he'd have to wear a bag the rest of his life. Herbie didn't care. Then he noticed the handle of a pistol sticking out of the banger's belt in the back where the leather jacket had ridden up.

Herbie pulled it out and saw it was a nickel-plated Colt 45 with pearl handles. It was a beautiful gun. All Herbie's darkness started to pass away. He stuck the gun into his belt.

Suddenly, he remembered Gail sitting in his car and ran over. She had freed herself from the electrical cords they had used to tie her up. When she saw Herbie's arm, she gasped.

"Your arm. What happened? Are you all right?"

Herbie thought he was all right, but he was feeling a little light headed so he sat down. Actually, it was more of a fall down.

Gail was hovering over him, almost instantly.

"There's a first aid kit in the trunk. It's in the red toolbox. I think we should get this bleeding stopped before I pass out," Herbie said, sounding like he had just ordered breakfast. Gail went to the trunk, and Herbie threw the gun under the passenger's seat of his car. He couldn't wrap his mind around why the guy didn't use the pistol on him. Maybe he didn't think Herbie was that much of a threat. Regardless, Herbie thought he was pretty lucky to be alive.

Gail went to work, and by the time the police arrived; Herbie was starting to feel a little better. The bleeding had stopped, but he would need stiches. Herbie sat on the ground leaning against his Buick. He heard Gail tell the police officer what happened.

"I kicked these boys out of my place last week. They were causing all kinds of trouble and making my customers uncomfortable."

"Did they threaten you?" The police officer asked.

"Sure. But I don't pay much attention to threats. They're just some punk wannabes."

"Maybe not. We've had our eyes on them for quite some time. They belong to a gang called Los Pistoled Animas. They should be avoided."

"What are they doing around here?"

"Trying to expand their drug business. They are pretty ruthless. You're lucky to be alive. So is your cook. What I can't figure is why they didn't use their pistols. We found two of them with the guns stuck in their belts, but the guy with the knife up his ass didn't have one." He looked at Herbie. Herbie avoided his stare.

The alley was full of emergency vehicles and police cars in addition to Herbie's Buick. No one had bothered to talk to Herbie, and that was just fine with him. He looked worse than he felt.

When one of the emergency workers tried to get him into the vehicle, Herbie balked.

"I'll have Gail take me to the hospital." I want to make sure she's okay."

The guy just shrugged. He didn't care. They were busy enough with all the other bodies scattered about.

Gail walked over to Herbie, after she was finished talking to the police. The officer followed her.

"I think everyone was pretty lucky that you were around today," the officer said to Herbie.

Herbie just shrugged. He didn't like it when his blackness took over. He didn't want to relive it again.

"You'll need to come down to the department and give a statement, after you get patched up."

Herbie nodded, and the officer moved on.

"How's your cook?" Herbie asked Gail.

"They hit him pretty hard. The EMTs said he had a concussion but he should recover. He might be out of commission for a few weeks."

"Looks like the Coffee Cup will be too." Herbie looked at the back door.

"No way. I'm going to open just as soon as I can. These jackasses aren't going to beat me."

Herbie liked her spunk. He might have an idea for her.

"Do you suppose we could go to the hospital, get me patched up and have that forehead of yours looked at?" Herbie asked.

"It's a scratch. Head wounds always look worse than they really are, because they bleed so much."

"Humor me," was all Herbie said.

On the way to the emergency room, they talked about what would happen to the café. By the time Herbie got stitched up, and Gail had a butterfly bandage put over her eyebrow, they had come up with an idea.

Herbie would take the orders, and Gail would be the cook. Gail wanted Herbie to cook, but Herbie had to explain he had absolutely no knowledge in that area. If Gail wanted to keep customers, the food would have to be edible.

On the way back to the Coffee Cup, both were silent. Finally, Herbie broke the quiet.

"There's going to be quite a bit of work getting the café back into shape."

"I think so. I guess this puts a damper on our dinner date."

"Just a rain check, I'm thinking."

Gail smiled at that.

The place was a mess, but there wasn't as much damage as Herbie had thought. They picked up the chairs, righted the tables in the dining area, and found few other problems. A picture of eastern Colorado lay in pieces on the floor. There was broken glass all around it.

"No matter," Gail said, "I always hated that picture. Who wants to look at sage and sand, when the state has such beautiful mountains?"

"Maybe we can find something more appropriate," Herbie said, trying to be helpful, as he swept up the remaining pieces of broken glass.

Gail looked at him. She decided she liked this guy.

The kitchen hadn't been touched. It was going to be the last place the bikers destroyed. The basement storage area was another matter.

The walk-in refrigerator had been emptied. Flour, eggs, sugar, lettuce, tomatoes, fruit and everything else was mixed together and thrown all over the floor and walls.

The freezer's door was open, but it didn't look like they had the time to do any damage there. Herbie's run-in with the gangbangers' bikes must have cut short the destruction.

Gail looked into the freezer, and satisfied that everything seemed to be in place, closed the door.

"Now what?" Herbie asked.

"I think I need to call up my suppliers and explain what happened. They usually are pretty good about helping us out in emergencies."

"Good, you get going on that, and I'll try to clean up the mess down here."

Gail bounced up the steps two at a time. She was on a mission. So was Herbie, but looking around, he wondered where he should start. He decided to get Mr. Peabody before he forgot all about him. Besides, Mr. Peabody could help with the clean up. He would find some delicacies hidden somewhere in the mess on the floor.

The three of them worked long into the night. Mr. Peabody supervised, while Gail and Herbie did the grunt work. The walk-in had been restocked by midnight, and by two o'clock, one would hardly have known that anything had happened almost eleven hours before.

Herbie and Gail were exhausted.

"You know, we could get things ready for opening at 6:00, and then get a few hours of sleep." Herbie suggested.

"That might be a good idea. We wouldn't have to be back until 5:45, if we're ready to go."

"We could go back to the motel. Might be easier than trying to get you back to the condo for such a short time."

Gail looked at him. Herbie realized how it must have sounded.

"Wait. No! I didn't mean anything. Just sleep." Herbie was panicked.

Gail smiled.

"I've got a king, but I could request two doubles." He was still rattling on.

"A king would be just fine."

It worked out quite well. The two slept soundly for a few hours, with Mr. Peabody inserting himself strategically in between.

19

Summer was over. Avon and Bonnie could see the numbers picking up by the amount of traffic in their shop. Avon was always surprised by the number of women who came in, looked at the items and giggled over what seemed so far out of their comfort zone. These same women seldom walked out without buying something. People on holiday were less inhibited, it seemed.

Avon hadn't had much luck finding anyone who wanted to be part of the Libertine side business. She didn't try that hard. Bonnie thought she knew a lot of people on the island, but the truth was that Avon hadn't been here any longer than Bonnie.

Bonnie, on the other hand, was a master at recruitment. She combed the bars and restaurants looking for women and a few men. There was always call for more women in the escort business than men. Now and then, there would be a man who wanted another man, as well as women wanting other women. This was Key West, after all.

Avon had visited with a few of her server pals, who she thought were more open to special arrangements. She found a few of the younger girls who thought it was an adventure. Avon introduced them to Bonnie, who immediately put them on the roster. Avon hoped they knew what they were getting themselves into. She would try to keep her eyes wide open. Sexy clothing and toys were one thing, but this other side smacked of prostitution. It was fairly high class, but she couldn't help but feel like a pimp.

Bonnie could sense that something was wrong. Avon had been distant since she introduced The Libertine. She had always been the aggressor in the bedroom, but they hadn't had sex since they opened.

Not that it was a huge deal either way, but it puzzled Bonnie. Avon had always seemed insatiable. Bonnie liked that in her. She had thought, just maybe, she would want to participate in the escort service. She had badly misread that idea, however.

There was a panhandler that had come into the shop a few times looking for odd jobs to make some money. Bonnie had turned him down. Now she was having a change of heart.

"Avon, go find that guy with the limp and tell him I have some work for him."

"Are you sure? That guy is totally weird."

"I thought we could have him sweep up outside, and maybe do some floor work in the shop before we open in the mornings."

"As long as I don't have to deal with him. He gives me the creeps."

Bonnie smiled. "Just go find him, and tell him to come see me."

Avon left the shop and moved toward Duval Street. She had seen the Gimp begging on various street corners but usually tried to hang out around the busier places. She didn't have to go far. He was parked on his butt near the World's Smallest Bar. The place was set up in a small pathway between two buildings. It was open sporadically, and today it hadn't opened. It was a great tourist place for pictures. The Gimp had a cup in front of him with a few bills sticking out. He was playing something on a harmonica that Avon didn't recognize.

• • •

Everyone called him the Gimp. It was more his name than the one he was given at birth. His father wanted to name him Rocky, but his mother was having none of it. She called him Fabiano. It would be Fabiano Farnum. Partly to honor her Italian roots, but also because she liked the name. It was different from every other Anglo name in America. His father called him Rocky, anyway. He thought Stallone was Italian after all.

He was just a few months old, when his parents were killed in a car accident. Fabiano was in the back seat in his carrier. It was before car seats were the law. It took the rescue workers two hours to extract him from the crumpled mass of steel.

Fabiano had appeared to have severe brain damage. The doctors hadn't given him much hope. After some time in the hospital, he was released to an aunt on his mother's side. She took him because it was the right thing to do, not because she wanted to. Fabiano's left side had paralysis. He had limited use of his left hand, and he drug his right foot along behind him. The aunt had become widowed early, so Fabiano became her companion. They lived a spartan life on Key West. She had a little shack she called home in the middle of the island. When he was old enough to understand what was going on, the aunt started to abuse him sexually. It wasn't all together unpleasant for Fabiano. It was about the only time he got to experience love, no matter how perverted it might be.

Fabiano went to school and got the name Gimp. It stuck. No one meant anything cruel by it. But it was cruel nevertheless. When Fabiano went to high school, his actual surname was lost. It was partly due to the very nature of the school culture, but also his aunt bailed out of their lives.

A hotel developer offered Gimp's aunt more money for her piece of property than she had ever seen in her life. She took the money and ran. She was the only person in the world to call him Fabiano, other than his parents. He had no memory of them.

His aunt went and fled north. The Gimp didn't know where. He didn't care. He just knew that sex would be harder to come by with her absence.

He was relegated to living on the streets, but Key West wasn't the worst place to do that. There were an abundance of beach showers that he used after dark. He wore shorts and t-shirts. When they got beyond wearing, he procured another set. Mostly he stole them, but sometimes if he begged enough, he could purchase something. It was a hard life, but it was all he knew. A few businesses felt sorry for him and gave him some odd job work. He hadn't finished high school, but he was adept with his hands. It surprised most people after they saw his handicap.

The pickings in the restaurant's dumpster were spectacular. He never went hungry. In fact, some would say he was thriving. His six-foot frame filled out. He was strong from living the hard life. He lifted things heavier than he should have and did work no one else wanted. His strength also made him frightening too many.

• • •

Avon waited until the Gimp was finished playing his harmonica, out of courtesy.

When he put down the mouth harp, he looked up.

"Hello Avon. What can I do for you?"

Avon was instantly afraid. She had never talked to the Gimp in her life until now. She couldn't understand how he knew her name. It threw her off for a moment.

"Bonnie, over at The Aphrodisiac, wants you to drop over and have a talk."

"When?"

"Right now."

"Okay, but you have to walk with me."

Avon was instantly repulsed. She hated the feeling, and the short hairs on the back of her neck told her something was not right with this guy.

"Sorry, I've got other things to do. Don't wait too long. It might be worth your while."

Avon started walking away as quickly as possible. The Gimp tried to call after her, but she paid no attention. She knew he couldn't catch her.

She decided to head over to the Hog's Breath and use one of the pay phones to make her weekly contact. When she got there, the phones were all in use.

She decided to get back to the shop before the Gimp. She wondered what Bonnie had in store for him. She didn't fear him as much when she was with Bonnie.

When she walked into the shop, the Gimp was already there. He and Bonnie were sitting in the office. Avon couldn't hear what they were saying, but the Gimp was listening intently and nodding his head from time to time.

When Bonnie saw Avon, she stood up and shook the Gimp's hand, and ushered him out the back door. When she came back, Avon looked at her.

"We've got a new employee. He starts tomorrow. He'll be cleaning the sidewalks by eight each morning. He'll hose down the puke, if there is any, from the night before."

Someone was always getting sick wandering from the bars late at night. The sidewalks were usually the recipients.

"So, he will be just doing outside things?' Avon asked.

"No. At nine he'll come in through the back and vacuum and clean the floors. He has an hour to do the work, and he'll be gone by ten when we open."

"Good. He gives me the creeps."

"Is that why you ran away from him today?"

"Well, yeah. He knew my name, and it freaked me out."

"You told him you had other business. I was wondering what that might have been."

Suddenly, Avon's little voice of caution was speaking in her ear. Bonnie was prying into her comings and goings, and that might be dangerous. She would need to be extra careful from now on.

"Just trying to make some distance between the Gimp and me. I went to the Hog's Breath and got a coffee. Is that all right with you?" Avon said, putting some sarcasm into her voice.

"Just wondered where you went. I'm concerned about you, Avon, that's all.

Avon knew that it wasn't all.

"I'm not in the habit of checking with anyone every time I decide to do something, and I'm not about to start now. I think there is something wrong with the Gimp. I don't like the way he looks at me."

"Let's start by calling him by his name. I found out it is Fabiano. Isn't that a fabulous name?"

"Oh, it's great. Maybe you could get him to be one of your escorts." Avon said, pushing the subject to the edge.

Bonnie sat down in her office chair. Avon could see she was trying very hard to control her temper.

"That's enough on this subject," she said, smiling. But the smile on her face wasn't a smile at all.

Avon realized she had pushed her far enough.

"Whatever you say. Just don't think that he's going to be my best buddy."

"I don't expect that at all. I just think we can be civil to someone who's had a tough life. A little human kindness never hurt anyone."

"Something's wrong with that guy. I can feel it, and I don't mean his physical stuff, either."

"We can start by calling him by his name, Fabiano. We won't be using the Gimp around here any longer. Is that understood?'

There it was, that undercurrent of telling her "or else." Avon didn't like it one bit.

"I won't call him anything. He's your hire, and you can deal with him. I won't disrespect him by calling him the Gimp, but I won't let him get familiar, either."

Avon stomped out of the room for effect. She hadn't wanted to piss off Bonnie, but she wanted her to know she wasn't going to be her doormat either.

She went upstairs to their quarters and went to the fridge looking for something to drink. When she passed the counter, she noticed her Coach purse on the counter. She stopped. Her purse had been in the bedroom. She was sure of it.

Avon opened the bag and looked inside. The first thing she noticed was that her clutch purse was out of place. She kept it on the left side pocket. Her license was upside down in the little plastic window. Everything was out of place, including her passports. She panicked immediately. The purse had a false bottom where she kept her real license, passport, and credit cards. She moved into the bedroom and dumped the contents on the bed. Then she carefully pried up the false bottom. Everything seemed intact. Everything was banded in place and nothing looked disturbed. Bonnie hadn't found them. Avon was instantly relieved.

She put the contents back into her purse in order. She noticed her phone was on. She seldom used it, and kept if off to preserve the battery. The screen showed the numbers of recent calls. There it was. Bonnie was suspicious and wondering who she was contacting.

It seemed uncharacteristic for Bonnie to be this brazen and not cover her tracks. Then she realized that it was no accident. Bonnie wanted her to know she was suspicious. The game was getting too complicated. But Avon couldn't let Bonnie get by with this type of intimidation.

She bounded down the stairs two at a time with her purse over her shoulder. No one was in the shop, so Bonnie went right into the office.

"If you need anything from my purse, just ask. You don't need to rifle through it. There should be some things that are off limits between us."

"Sorry. You weren't here, and I needed some information for some paperwork," she lied. "Our jobbers need phone numbers and social security numbers."

Bonnie was smooth. She could make the biggest lie seem inconsequential. Avon couldn't decide who she feared the most, the Gimp or Bonnie.

Avon would need to contact Fats very soon.

20

It couldn't have gone any better at the Coffee Cup for both Gail and Herbie. People heard about how Herbie had stood up to the bikers, and they paid their respect by coming to the café. The business was booming. Some of the guys thumped Herbie on the back. Most said they wished he had taken the bastards out. Apparently the biker gang had worn out their welcome. Others told their own tales. Herbie wondered if they were all true or just "could'a, would'a, should'a" responses.

No matter. They were local heroes. Everything was pretty good for a few weeks. Then it started.

The three bikers had been recuperating at some prison hospital before they would stand trial. Someone had allowed them visitors against orders. After that visit, the rest of the organization was up to speed.

That's when the drive-bys started. Usually between 2:00 and 3:00 in the afternoon, a group of 15 to 20 bikers would drive by the café slowly and point in their direction.

Gail called the police, and they made a show of presence for a few days, but there wasn't anything they could do. The assholes weren't breaking any laws.

Herbie was starting to get concerned. These idiots were crazy and didn't behave like normal people. They would do anything for revenge. It was a matter of principle with them. The consequences didn't matter.

People like that were dangerous. The worst part was they had huge numbers. They were more than Herbie could handle. It would take a small army, with a great deal of firepower, to subdue this gang.

Herbie didn't want that kind of involvement.

Lately, they were becoming more brazen. They parked over at the motel's parking lot and gave the Coffee Cup a number of hand gestures. The motel owner finally called the police, and they rousted them out of the lot.

Gail was livid. She was having none of it. One day she went out the front door and gave the entire gang the finger. Herbie pulled her back inside.

"You need to stop this," Herbie said, forcefully.

Gail was perturbed. "These animals need to be stopped."

"I agree. But giving them a reason to go after you doesn't make any sense."

"I'm not following."

"They don't care about you. It's me they are after. I'm the one that hurt three of their bikers. They have to make an example of me. Besides, they already got back at you, but if you add more fuel to the fire, they will make it their goal to involve you."

"I don't care. They can't intimidate people and get away with it."

"Looks like they've been doing a pretty good job around here lately."

"Until you came around. Now they know, we've taken enough."

"That's what makes them so dangerous. They will do whatever it takes to make consequences of us, and they won't care what happens."

Gail stopped talking. The gravity of the situation had hit home.

"So, what are we going to do?"

Herbie liked the sound of "we." He never had been a part of "we" before. He led her to a table, and they sat.

"I want you to consider for a moment that you might have to make a major change in your life."

Gail just looked at him, puzzled.

Herbie continued. "This may seem sudden to you, but have you ever thought of selling out and moving on?"

Gail looked out of the window before she spoke. "All the time. But where would I go? This is all I know. I'm not an adventurous person. Not like you."

Herbie started to laugh. Gail stopped and looked at him.

Herbie stopped laughing. "Maybe you have the wrong impression of me. I'm not adventurous at all. I'm here because of an event that forced my hand. Otherwise, I would still be hauling ice cream in Iowa."

Gail looked back out the window and paused for what seemed to Herbie like an eternity. When she turned back, she looked into Herbie's eyes. It was an action that always made him uncomfortable.

"So, what you are telling me is that this is an event that is forcing my hand?"

Herbie thought she had grasped the situation far quicker than he had.

"I guess that's what I'm saying."

"So, what's my solution? I'm at a loss at how to proceed."

Herbie knew the next part would be tricky, and he had to tread lightly.

"Well, you know what I've done. Do you think you could do something like that?"

"Not alone." Gail responded, quickly.

"Could you do it with me?" Herbie asked, quietly.

"Yes." It was as if Gail was waiting for the invitation.

"Well, here's what I think, you, I mean we, should do. We need to sell the business and get out." Herbie was starting to formulate his plans.

"Sounds like a lot of work. How long will it take?"

"We leave tonight. We pack up your stuff, and we're down the road in my big boat Buick." Herbie smiled.

Gail looked panic-stricken. "How can I leave when there's so much to do?"

"Let me make a few phone calls, and we'll get everything in order. I promise you, if you aren't comfortable with anything, we'll wait until you are. But remember, the longer we wait, the bigger the danger.

Gail nodded. She had a lot to think about.

Herbie had quite a bit to do if they were going to leave by 3:00 a.m. Stealth always required perfect timing. Leaving at 3:00 would bridge the time between the night owls and bar crowd, with the early morning work crowd. Most everyone would be in their beds after their comings and goings.

Gail decided to make sure everything was in order for what she thought would be vacation mode. Of course, she had never taken one, but she had dreamed about it, and had run through this kind of scenario in her mind countless times. She knew what had to be done.

Herbie went outside to make his phone calls. His first call was to Steve Shuster in Le Mars. He told him he wanted to get down to Florida and wondered if he had any contacts where he could get a job driving truck. Steve gave him the address of a produce company based in Immokalee. He said he knew the owner and would put in a good word, but Herbie might want to consider having his own refrigerated straight truck. It would help to put him in a favorable employment status. It would also mean better pay. Herbie was planning to buy another truck anyway, so this was welcome news, and he wouldn't have to put money out for a new tractor. He wasn't sure he wanted to drive an eighteen-wheeler in a state as populated as Florida, anyway. He thanked Steve and told him he would be in contact when he got settled.

Herbie was almost ready to hang up, when Steve stopped him.

"I'm glad you called. I was hoping to get in contact with you. I think the heat is off that other thing at Story City."

"That's great news," Herbie said, relief in his voice.

"I got a few follow-up calls from the patrol, but they didn't seem all that excited to make this a high priority. It sounds like that woman had been writing articles, taking their department to task on some issues in the past. I got the feeling they thought this just might be some just retribution. Anyway, they aren't taking anything any further. As far as they are concerned, you've dropped off the face of the earth."

"Thanks Steve. I owe you."

"I always want people to owe me. Take care." He was gone.

Finally, a bit of good news; now for the other call.

Herbie called Zander on his new cell phone, and he hoped he would pick up.

He listened to six rings and still nothing. It was apparent Zander hadn't set up the answering system. Herbie was about to give up, when he heard Zander answer, weakly.

"What the hell? Were you in bed boinking somebody?" Herbie asked.

"Smart ass. Don't I wish? I was in the back. Couldn't hear the phone."

"Gees, you are a dumb ass. You're supposed to keep it with you. Put it in your pocket, you stupid shit."

"Yeah, Yeah, Yeah. What the hell do you want anyway? Wedding plans?"

"No, I'm afraid I need some advice."

"Why didn't you say so? I'm full of that."

"Full of something, I agree. Just listen."

Herbie told Zander everything that happened and tried to keep it as short as possible. Zander wasn't yelling about his used phone minutes, however.

"Okay Herbie, do you want me to get Fats and come up there and kick some ass?"

"I'm afraid it's way beyond that. There are just too many of them. We'd be on the short side of the stick."

"What can I do? Tell me how I can help?"

Herbie knew in that instant, why he considered Zander his best friend. He had always been there for him, and it hadn't changed in the least.

"Gail needs to sell the business, but I can't use anyone here. It's just too risky. I'm afraid they would beat out our location from any realtor we would use here. So, I was wondering if you knew someone we could trust up there to do the job?"

"Sure. You met Bert and Jo. That's what they do. I'll go over and talk to them right now. You couldn't be in better hands."

"We'll need an attorney to handle the closing, don't you think?"

"Maybe. If you do, they've got a guy they work with right here in Frisco. We'll let them handle the details. Agreed?"

"Agreed. Thanks Zander, I owe you."

"I always like it when my friends owe me." Zander hung up.

Herbie had to laugh. It was the second time he heard the phrase in just two phone calls. Apparently, he was in debt to two of his only friends. He didn't mind. He was happy to be in their service.

By 9:00 that evening, Gail and Herbie were closing up the Coffee Cup forever. There was a "For Sale" sign in the window. The number they listed on it was Zander's.

After talking with Jo and Bert, Zander thought it was better for everyone concerned if he would be the go-between. He could screen the calls and give Bert and Jo the ones he felt were legitimate.

Gail had called her cook, who was convalescing at home, with the news of the pending sale. He was surprised to hear about the sudden changes. He also expressed some interest in the business. Gail gave him Zander's number, and told him she would cut him a better deal if he wanted to take it over. They agreed that it was better to wait a few weeks until after the biker gang lost interest. He promised to keep an eye on the place, making sure all the refrigeration units were working and nothing was out of order.

The back door handle had a combination lock that could be dialed to open the door. Gail put in a new sequence and made sure Zander had the numbers. He would give it to Jo and Bert, who would pass it on to the other multiple listing realtors. That way, they could show the business without having to deal directly with Gail. All correspondence would be handled through Bert and Jo.

It sounded like a plan everyone could live with, and that was important, especially with the "Los Assholes" looking to make life miserable.

Gail talked to her neighbor in the condos. She agreed to return the key to the landlord at the end of the month. Gail told her she could keep whatever furnishing she wanted and sell the rest. The place was spartan, and there wasn't much Gail wanted to keep anyway.

They packed the clothes they thought she needed and put everything else in the dumpster. No need for winter clothing where they were going.

Gail had more things than Herbie. Everything he had fit into a camping bag. Gail took the rest of the trunk and the entire back seat. There were things she just couldn't leave behind.

Herbie didn't mind. There was room for Mr. Peabody, Gail and himself. He just wanted Gail to be happy. If little things would help, he was all for it.

At precisely 3:00 a.m., the unlikely trio began their journey. Herbie decided to go east on highway 6. From there, he took highway 385 until he reached I-70 east at Burlington. Eventually he would reach I-35 south and make his way to Texas. Then he would take I-10 all the way to Florida.

Herbie thought it might be an unusual route, but he didn't care. He was with his favorite girl and dog. He wasn't in any hurry.

21

Zander's morning ritual included having coffee with Bert and Jo at their little office down the street from the Branchwater. As soon as he realized he was leaving, he decided to spend as much time with the couple as possible. They were his friends and other than Fats, his best friends in Frisco.

It had been a week since he fielded Herbie's phone call. There had been some interest in the Coffee Cup but nothing solid. Herbie had told him that Gail wanted her cook to have the place if he was interested. So Zander wasn't very concerned about the sale. It would get done. Bert and Jo would see to it, even if they had to go down there. At least that's what they told him. Zander wasn't going to let that happen, however, at least not at the moment. They would have to wait until the los frickin' losers situation played out. Zander made them promise to check with him before they did anything stupid.

Bert reached into his desk drawer and pulled out a file. He was ready to change the subject.

"Here, look at this," he said, as he threw the file over the desk at Zander.

Zander opened the file folder. It contained information about *The Villages* in central Florida.

"What's this?" Zander wondered.

"It's a retirement village in Florida. It's fifty-five plus to qualify."

"Looks like they've got a lot of activities." Zander held up the booklet. It had everything from bridge to polo.

"They bill it as a golf community," Jo said.

"Do you two golf?" Zander asked.

"That's where we met," Bert said.

"We were on the golf teams in college," Jo added.

"Man, those overnight trips were something weren't they, Jo?"

"Oh, be quiet. Zander doesn't need to hear any of that."

"I don't know, maybe I do," Zander replied, with a twinkle in his eye.

"Trust me, you don't," Jo said, ending the conversation.

"So, what brought this on?" Zander asked.

"We were talking about how you are making changes in your life. Well, we're getting older and maybe it's time for our own changes," Jo said.

"I thought you were Coloradans forever."

"Getting tired of the cold," Bert said, simply.

"I hear you."

"Well, anyway, it's just something we've been considering down the line."

"Right, you're too young right now."

"You always know the right thing to say." Jo mussed up Zander's hair.

As Zander walked to the Branchwater, he decided he would truly miss these two.

He didn't have much time to ruminate. Before he could even put the key into the lock on the front door, he saw Fats sitting at the bar. It was unusual for him to be anywhere before mid to late afternoon.

Zander opened the door.

"What do we owe the pleasure of your company this early in the morning?"

Fats looked at him trying to find some words. It apparently was very early for him.

"Couldn't sleep."

Zander noticed that he looked terrible. His eyes looked hollow, and the wrinkles around his eyes were more pronounced.

"What's up?"

"I don't know where to start."

"Try the beginning."

"Wherever I begin, you're not going to like it." Fats had such a hangdog look about him; Zander couldn't help but smile.

"Let's get some coffee. It always helps." Zander was always

amazed at the change that took place in Fats when something was bothering him. He lost all that hippie philosophy and affected dialogue.

"I made it a few minutes ago, it should be ready," Fats offered.

Zander grabbed two mugs with the bar's name on them.

When they were situated, Zander started.

"You'd better get this out in the open, especially since it apparently involves me."

"I realize all that, but you're not going to like it."

"Spill it," was all Zander had to say.

Fats spilled everything. He told him about how Mona was hired to follow Sara Jane. He even told him about Lilly's involvement. Zander was surprised to learn that her husband was helping with the financing.

"If I told you I was less than pleased, would it be a surprise?"

"No," was all Fats could get out.

"So, I'm thinking you wouldn't be sharing your little secret with me unless something forced this disclosure."

"I haven't heard from her in over two weeks."

"Who?"

"Mona. I guess she's going by the name of Avon down there."

"Down where?"

"Key West."

"What the hell are they doing down there?"

"Sara Jane is going by the name of Bonnie Marco now. They opened a sex shop called the Aphrodisiac."

"I suppose I shouldn't be surprised."

"Everything was going like clockwork, and then Mona quit calling. I'm concerned. It was because of me that she was involved with this whole thing anyway."

"So, why are you telling me all this now?" Zander asked, but deep down he knew what Fats wanted.

"Well, you talked about going to Florida. I thought maybe you could go down there and find out what's going on."

"I always like it when you put me in the middle of things."

Zander tried to be forceful.

Fats caught the change in Zander's voice and immediately his demeanor changed.

"So will you go?" Fats asked.

"It's something I'd have to think about. You took me off guard with all this. I'm not sure I want to open the Sara Jane chapter again."

Fats looked him. "Who are you trying to jape?"

Zander realized his friend Fats was back.

"I'm not sure I understand."

"You've had the Sara Jane chapter open all along. You have had neither preexistence nor post-existence since your lethal symbiosis with that harlot. Unless you put some finality into your jaded dependency, you'll never be emancipated." Fats was back on his hippie soapbox.

On one hand, Zander was happy that his friend was back. On the other, he wasn't appreciating what he had to say. He knew in his mind however, that what he was saying was the truth.

"How often was Mona supposed to check in with you?" Zander asked.

"She usually called once a week with an update and how much expense money she needed to have put into her account."

"And you haven't heard anything for over two weeks?"

"Correct. So your departure for the sunshine state is paramount."

"Let me ask you this, have you considered that something bad has already happened to her?"

Fats looked down. "That's all I can even think about."

"Well, I'm not going to be ready to leave for at least a week. I've got a lot of loose ends to tie up."

"Don't worry about Branchwater. I will mobilize whatever resources conceivable to see that the saloon continues to flourish."

"I'm not worried about that, I've got personal things to take care of before I leave. Besides, if something bad has happened to Mona, it will already be too late. So rushing blindly into the unknown has no attraction for me."

Fats shook his head in agreement.

"Not knowing is suffocating me. So, I'm in your debt in that regard."

"Fats, if I find that harm has come to Mona or Avon or whatever she calls herself, by the hand of Sara Jane, what do you want me to do?"

"Do us both a favor. Kill the bitch."

22

Avon was becoming more and more concerned with Bonnie's behavior toward her. She was constantly watching, asking where Avon had been and what she was doing. A few times she thought she had seen the Gimp following her. When she would try to check it out, he was gone. It unnerved her. She kept her purse with her constantly. There was no reason for Bonnie to stumble onto the hidden bottom.

It had been time to check in with Fats, and she changed her usual phone spot from the Hog's Breath to a little place called Rick's across the street from Sloppy Joe's. She had decided that maybe she was becoming too predictable.

There were phones between the restrooms, and Avon felt she could keep an eye on things easier. She hadn't noticed Fabiano enter and quickly head to the men's room. He stood next to the closed door and kept it open just a crack with an ink pen he always carried. He was close enough to the phone to hear, if he kept his ear pressed to the crack.

The problem became quite clear. Avon was keeping her voice so low that he could only make out a few words. He thought he heard a name, Sara Jane. It was confusing but something worth passing along to Bonnie. It wasn't long and the conversation ended. He decided to use the restroom as long as he was waiting.

When he was finished, he opened the restroom door and peered over at the phones. Avon was gone. He decided to talk to Bonnie immediately. This might be something she would want to hear. He would have to be careful not to let Avon see him, so he would walk by the shop a few times to make sure she wasn't there. He walked out quickly.

Fabiano didn't notice that Avon was sitting at the bar opposite the phone. She had felt something wasn't right after her call. When she had looked over at the men's room, she saw something wedged in the door holding it open. She decided to wait to see what came of it. She ordered some "drink of the day." They all tasted the same. The contents were usually rum and some variety of juices in a slushy mixture that you had to suck out with a straw. She managed to get her usual "brain freeze" before the bathroom door opened.

She almost fell off her chair. It was the Gimp. She had no doubt he was following her, but she was unclear about how much he had heard. For the first time since she came to Florida, she was afraid.

She took a pull from her drink. Then it hit her. She had to be proactive. If she hurried she could easily catch the Gimp before he could talk to Bonnie. She threw down some money for the drink and took it with her.

Avon hurried through the throngs of people keeping her eyes peeled for the little creep. Then she saw him dragging his foot and moving as fast as he could. It looked like he was headed for the Aphrodisiac.

Avon moved quickly and skirted around him without being noticed. She decided to wait around the corner of Duval and Front Street. There was a two-level touristy shop that was right on the corner. She could surprise him there.

Avon took her position and a few minutes later the Gimp rounded the corner. She was looking across the street sucking on the straw of her drink.

Fabiano saw her and stopped. Avon looked over at him.

"So, why are you following me?" she asked, as sweetly as she could.

"I'm…. not." He stumbled.

"You got a thing for me?"

He smiled at that. Avon didn't care for his smile.

"I suppose so," Fabiano said, playing along.

"I saw you at Rick's."

That bit of news made him lose his smile.

"Using the john."

"With something stuck in the door? I doubt it."

"Don't know what you're talking about." He tried to push past Avon. She was having none of it and blocked his way. Then she stepped on his bad foot.

"Jesus. That hurt. Why did you do that?"

"I'm trying to get your attention. But, I suppose you calling out for Jesus might work just as well."

She stepped on his foot again. This time just a little harder.

This time he squawked. Avon had to smile. He actually squawked. She grabbed him by the shirt trying not to touch his skin. He stunk horribly. It was all she could do to stay this close to him.

"Let me go or…"

"Or what?" she asked, as she slammed him into the wall.

Fabiano just looked at her. Avon thought she could see hatred behind his milky eyes. He was reaching for his side, and Avon caught his hand. She patted his left side and pulled out a long knife. It looked like the kind the fishermen used to fillet fish.

"She pulled it out and put it to his throat. "Is this what you had in mind?"

He shook his head no.

"I don't know what you heard, but if I were you, I'd keep it to myself."

He nodded, but Avon could see he had no intention of keeping quiet.

They were starting to draw attention so she had let him go. She wanted to wash her hands after touching him.

She found a spot in the brick wall where there was a crack and she could insert the knife. She bent it until the blade snapped in half. Then she gave the pieces back to the Gimp.

"You ever try pull a knife on me again, I won't be putting into a brick wall."

Avon was puzzled by the Gimp's refusal to fight back. She was sure he could have put her down easily. Instead he allowed her to push him around. What the hell was going on?

She walked back to the shop. It was time to confront Bonnie.

23

It was a long way from Colorado to Florida. Herbie decided to take his time. He wanted to see some of the southernmost part of the United States.

Texas was huge. It took forever. He liked San Antonio but decided they could keep the rest of it. They would stop when they got tired and about six to seven hours was enough for Gail and Mr. Peabody each day.

Louisiana was an interesting state. Of course, Herbie was only seeing the southernmost part of it. They spent a few days in New Orleans. They would see the sights by horse-drawn carriage during the day and experience the music and nightlife in the French Quarter, on Bourbon Street, during the evenings.

It was a wide open city, where almost anything was available. Hookers, drug dealers, and Jesus Freaks approached them. Gail's head was spinning. She turned to Herbie.

"I feel like such a Christian here."

Herbie laughed until he cried.

They both loved the music, however. That Dixieland sound couldn't be reproduced like it was in New Orleans. Maybe it was just the location that made it all seem so perfect. They would sit in front of some of the halls with their drinks in hand and listen to the music until it quit. Herbie would have liked to go in, but Mr. Peabody was a problem. So they were content to listen from the street. Besides, what other place could you drink right on the sidewalk while looking into all the bars?

Herbie made a mental note to come back some day. He hoped Gail would feel the same way. In fact, he hoped she would still be in the picture.

It was time to move on, and when they got to Pensacola near the start of the Florida panhandle, Herbie decided to leave I-10. He wanted to see Florida from someplace other than the interstate.

Pensacola Beach was a beautiful spot. Sugar sand beaches visible as far as you could see. They stayed in the Holiday Inn right on the beach. They didn't take dogs normally but there wasn't much going on and for ten bucks, the dog was allowed to check in.

When they decided to go for a walk on the beach, they noticed purple flags every hundred yards or so. Herbie went back into the hotel and asked what they meant.

"It means you'd better keep your shoes on," the clerk said, "because the man-of war-jelly fish have washed onto the beach overnight."

"What do they look like?" Herbie asked.

"They look like a big condom with a three or four foot colored string hanging from them. Don't touch them. They can sting you even when they're dead."

They took a short walk and then dropped Mr. Peabody off at the hotel, and they walked over to a place called Peg Leg Pete's. Someone told them they were known for their oysters. That someone was right. They were the best Herbie had ever eaten. They tried them all. Gail wouldn't eat them raw but loved the Rockefellers.

Herbie thought it might be a good night if what they said about oysters and sexual potency was true.

They weren't wrong.

•   •   •

Panama City was concrete and skyscrapers. Neither liked the place. It was too much of a city for them. Mr. Peabody slept through it, and they headed down highway 98.

When they passed Tallahassee, the terrain started to change. It became more forested. Herbie noticed that his was one of the few out-of-state cars that he saw on the road. There were very few tourists. He liked this part of the state. So did Gail.

When they stopped for gas in a town called Perry, the clerk struck up a conversation.

"Where are you folks headed?" she asked.

"We're not sure. We want to take in the sights but we're kinda small-town folk." Herbie replied.

"Have you ever heard of Cedar Key?"

Herbie said he hadn't, and the clerk told him he needed to go and experience it. She said something about old cracker Florida. When Herbie asked her what it meant, she just smiled and told him to go and find out.

So, it was south from Perry until they got to Cedar Key. After they got there, Herbie wished he could have gone back and thanked the lady for steering them to such a quaint little place.

Gail fell in love with it immediately. They travelled every road on the island and finished on Dock Street in less than forty-five minutes. Right then and there, they decided it was their kind of place.

Herbie parked the Buick on the bridge, and they strolled over to look at the shops and restaurants. Gail bought a tee shirt for herself and pushed Herbie into getting something similar. Herbie smiled at being drawn into the domestic life. He liked it.

They found a restaurant on the second floor of the tee shirt place called Steamers. They decided to do a sampler plate that included clams, mussels, crab and shrimp. As long as they were trying new things, they decided to go with the craft beer sampler, as well. It was two hours well spent.

They decided to leave the car parked and explore the downtown area on foot. It was two blocks to Second Street, which was really the main drag. There were a number of storefronts that sold artwork from local artists. A few were co-ops and Gail was interested. Herbie decided to let her walk around, while he waited on a bench outside taking in the sights. He didn't have much interest in art. He hadn't realized that Gail had the passion.

Herbie noticed a bank up the street and a post office. There was an old hotel that looked interesting. When Gail came out of one of the art shops, she was absolutely bubbling.

"Did you know they take artists' works on consignment?"

Herbie assured her that he didn't.

"Well, they do. Isn't that just fabulous?"

"Are you an artist, Gail?" Herbie asked.

She appeared embarrassed for a moment. "I liked it when I was in school. I haven't had much time to do anything with it since then."

"Would you consider living here?"

"In a heartbeat. It's got everything we would need."

Herbie wondered about that. He decided not to burden Gail with those questions until later.

They wandered over to the Island Hotel and got a history lesson from the bartender in the quaint little bar. It seemed to be a local haunt, and they both felt that maybe they were intruding at first. By the time they left, they had made friends of at least six locals. They agreed to come back for happy hour the following day.

There was one small market located on Third Street, and the couple walked through it, noting that they had about everything they needed for grocery staples. Gail thought they would never have to leave the island. Herbie liked to see her so happy. He knew he would have to get a job, however, and that wouldn't be on the island.

They walked back to the car where Mr. Peabody was waiting, and Herbie suggested they go back to a small motel they saw on the way in. There were four bridges to cross before you could get on the island. There were businesses and campgrounds on the small bits of land between the bridges, however. Herbie had seen the Low-Key Hideaway. It was located between bridge three and four.

It was a great little place. It had five units in the motel and a small adjacent RV park. But the thing that brought Herbie back to the spot was the sign that said "Tiki Bar." Herbie and Gail both went into the office. A tall pretty blonde came to the desk. Herbie thought she looked about their age or maybe younger. He wasn't good at judging age.

When they had booked their room, Herbie asked her about the Tiki Bar. The woman's name was Cindy, and she said her husband's name was Pat. He was tending bar, and it was open if they wanted to join in. Herbie thanked her, and they went back to the car to get their things. They didn't even have to move the car. They were parked directly in front of their room.

The room was a funky collection of Florida. Gail marveled at the furnishings and photographs adorning the walls. After they were settled, they both went out the back door and walked over the lawn to the Tiki Bar, overlooking the bay. They decided to take Mr. Peabody along. It was easier to make new friends when you had a dog.

The Tiki Bar was made from various booze bottles cemented together. It let the light in and made interesting shadows and colored lighting. Herbie thought it looked like a giant prism.

They ordered a drink from Pat and marveled at the beautiful bay.

"This place is absolutely beautiful," Gail said, wistfully.

Pat laughed. "Wait until tomorrow morning when the tide goes out."

"I don't understand."

"We are at the mercy of the Suwannee River to the west. It creates kind of a delta on the bay side. So when the tide is out, all you will see is muck. Some people call it a tidal marsh but it's muck."

"But I've seen people fishing off the docks," Herbie countered.

"Yep. There are fish at high tide, even though it's always quite shallow. They have an uncanny knack of knowing when it's time to leave with the tide."

"What kind of fish?" Herbie asked.

"I think it might be mullet but there might be other varieties as well. I don't have much time for fishing."

He went over to mix someone else a drink, and Herbie picked up a photo album. It looked like Pat was a photographer of some notoriety. Herbie paged through many nature scenes and some from right on the property. He stopped abruptly when he saw a picture of Cindy apparently floating on her back in the ocean, naked. The only thing keeping the picture from being totally revealing were Pat's two feet. One foot covered her breast area, and the other hid her southern region. Herbie couldn't take his eyes off the picture. Finally he showed it to Gail.

"Now, that's what I call art," Herbie said.

Gail reached over and closed the photo album. Pat was watching and started to laugh.

"I get that a lot," he said, and then went about his bartending duty.

Herbie smiled at Pat. He figured he was a lucky guy. Cindy was a beautiful woman and appeared to be uninhibited.

"Would you let me photograph you like that if I asked?" Herbie asked Gail in almost a whisper.

Gail though for a moment, "Yes," was all she said.

Herbie realized he also might be a lucky guy.

24

Zander had no idea how long he would be gone or if he would ever return. He had to put some loose ends together before he could leave.

Fats and Fran had agreed to give up their condo and move into Zander's cabin. All Zander asked was that they treat it like it was theirs and pay for repairs, utilities, and taxes. They agreed immediately.

"Your return will see it in finer condition than when you left it." Fats said.

"If I return, you mean." Zander replied, not thinking.

The comment took Fats by surprise. He hadn't even considered that Zander might not come back. It shook him.

"Of course you'll be back."

"I can't promise it. Life has been passing me by, and I've got some catching up to do."

"So you're just going to leave your T-Bird and boat and never come back for them?"

The comment confused Zander. He hadn't thought about the boat, but it was in storage at Jasper's place. As far as his T-Bird was concerned, he had every intention of driving it to Florida. He was looking forward to heading east on the old Route 66. He remembered watching the television show with his dad every Friday night when he was a kid. Martin Milner and George Maharis would have adventures every week on that old highway. It was the call of the open road that appealed to so many.

"You're not driving that car across country," Fats said simply.

"What am I driving?" Zander wondered.

"You're not driving at all. You're flying. We don't have time for you to wander all over the lower forty-eight."

Fats reached behind the bar and brought out a file folder. He slid it over to Zander. Zander opened it and saw a United Airlines ticket. He looked at it closer and saw it was a one-way ticket to Southwest Florida International Airport. The ticket was for the day after. The flight would leave the Denver airport at 11:00 a.m.

Zander felt like his life was being manipulated, and he had no power to control it. Fats could see frustration in Zander's face. He decided to try and diffuse it as quickly as he could.

"I know this isn't what you had planned, but it's the best choice. You'll have plenty of time to explore the country when we get this Mona thing settled."

"You realize that you singlehandedly caused this whole thing by sticking your nose where it didn't belong." Zander could feel the back of his neck getting hot.

"I know. But I did it with your best interests in the foremost." Fats was contrite.

"Maybe not. Now I've got to pick up the pieces."

"I'll take care of the T-Bird for you. I'll put it on blocks and start it once a week to make sure everything runs properly. I promise I won't even drive it."

Zander thought at least that was something.

"So are you driving me to the airport tomorrow?"

"I'll pick you up at 8:00. We can spend most of the morning together before you fly out."

Zander didn't know if that was what he wanted at the moment.

"I guess I'll go over to Bert and Jo's and say goodbye. When does the plane land at Key West?"

Fats looked at Zander for a moment deciding how to break the next bit of news.

"The plane lands at Fort Myers not Key West."

"Is that far?" Zander asked, showing his lack of geographical knowledge.

"It is quite a distance. But you're not going to fly into Key West. It's too much of a hassle. You'd have to change planes in Miami and fly a puddle jumper to Key West. Not something you'd want to experience."

"So I rent a car and drive?"

"Nah. It would be hassle number two. You're going to take the Key West Express out of Fort Myers Beach. It will get you there in less than four hours, and you won't have to fight traffic."

"You've got it all figured out, don't you?" Zander's tone was sarcastic.

"Listen, I've done the research. It's a huge catamaran. It's air-conditioned and has a galley and full bar or two. It's a jet boat. It's the best way to get there, by far. All you'll need to do is call their number when you get to Fort Myers and book passage. Rent a car and you can leave it in their parking area for ten dollars a day until you return, or you could go to Marco Island. I understand they offer free parking."

"When do I have to return?"

"That's up to you. Stay as long as you like. If I were you, I'd get a one-way ticket and return when you feel the time is right."

Fats thought it was better not to mention Mona or Sara Jane, even though it was why he was pushing Zander to Key West. Sometimes it was just better to leave the obvious unsaid. That was something Fats had extreme difficulty following.

"See you tomorrow at 8:00." Zander walked out of the bar for maybe the last time.

He almost got into the T-Bird, when he remembered Bert and Jo's. When he walked into the office they both were there with smiles.

"Good news, Zander. The former employee of the Coffee Cup has agreed to buy the place."

"That is good news. I'd better call Herbie so he can give Gail the good news." Zander had suddenly forgot all about his irritation with Fats.

Zander went outside and sat on the bench and called Herbie. After a brief conversation, he went back into the office and gave the phone to Bert so they could talk closing. He told Bert to give him the phone back before he hung up so he could talk to Herbie. Then he took Jo by the hand and went back outside to the bench.

"What's up?" Jo asked.

"Your boobs," Zander said, winking.

"As always, but what's up with you?"

"I'm leaving."

"I know that."

"I'm leaving tomorrow."

"What? Why so soon? We were planning a going-away party for you."

"I have no choice. Fats bought me an airplane ticket and it's tomorrow."

"That makes me sad."

"Maybe it's a good thing. I hate long goodbyes anyway."

"Well, this certainly won't be long. I'm going to have a party anyway. I'm going to cook for you. I'll invite some people and we will usher you out with a bit of fanfare, at the very least."

"You don't have to go to all that trouble. We could just go up to Breckenridge for dinner."

"Nonsense. I want this to be special." Jo stood up. The die was cast, and nothing was going to change her mind. "See you at six for cocktails." She went back into the office. Zander followed her to retrieve his phone.

Bert handed the phone over. "We're finished. Herbie is on the line waiting to talk to you." Jo pulled Bert to the back, explaining her new plans.

"Herbie, It's Zander," he said, absent-mindedly.

"I know. I just talked to you, remember?"

"Yeah. Sorry. I've got a lot on my mind suddenly."

"Such as it is." Herbie laughed.

"Where are you?"

"We're in Florida. It's a little place called Cedar Key. You'd love it."

"Well, believe it or not, I'm flying into Florida tomorrow."

"Outstanding. What airport?"

"Southwest International. Fort Myers, they tell me. It that close to you?"

"Not hardly. But I've got some business in Immokalee tomorrow. That's pretty close. I could pick you up at the airport."

"I wasn't expecting that. I thought I'd just rent a car."

"You're crazy. It's way too costly. Anyway, you're not used to driving down here. It's way different."

They talked about when Zander's plane would arrive, and Herbie said it would work out perfectly. When he asked why Zander was coming to Florida, Zander told him he would explain everything when they saw each other the following day. He thought it would take entirely too long trying to explain everything on the phone. Especially when he was paying for the minutes.

It was good talking to Herbie. Zander was almost looking forward to his trip, now that he knew he could hook up with his old friend. It would take the sting out of being forced to go to a place so unfamiliar.

Zander went back to the cabin and packed up his few belongings in his travel bag. It was a bright yellow thing he had purchased at Land's End in the outlet mall in Silverthorne. It was huge, but all his stuff fit into it. He knew he wouldn't be able to carry it on the plane, but he was fine with that. He hated carrying luggage through airports. Besides, he wasn't in any hurry.

He arrived at Bert and Jo's just a bit after six and was surprised to see a number of cars out front. He had thought it was going to be just an intimate little gathering. He was surprised to see Lilly and her husband.

The evening was full of conversation fueled by wine and champagne, and when it was over, Zander was happy to be leaving the next day. He couldn't take too much of this kind of thing. He appreciated the effort, but it just wasn't something he enjoyed. He did find time to forgive Fats sometime before the evening ended. Fats responded by drinking more champagne. It was a good evening.

The next morning, Fats' Cameo was at the cabin right at 8:00. Zander noticed that Fats wasn't driving. It was Fran.

Zander threw his bag in the back and got into the passenger's seat beside Fran.

"Hello Fran. I was expecting Fats to take me to the airport."

She smiled. "So was I. He can't get out of bed. Worst hangover he's ever had."

"I warned him about the champagne, " Zander said.

"So did I. Did you ever try to reason with him when he's on a toot?"

Zander smiled. Of course he had, many times, in fact.

25

Herbie hung up the phone and went out to the patio where Gail was sunning herself. She looked marvelous. The Florida sunshine had restorative powers. Herbie wanted her. He decided to put his hormones on hold for a while and share the good news with this beautiful woman.

He sat next to her. She had her eyes closed and an open book in her lap. Mr. Peabody was asleep on a chair next to her. He waited for a few minutes, taking in the beautiful Florida sunshine himself. He didn't want to disturb her. Just when he thought he might walk over to the Tiki Bar and get a drink, she spoke.

"So, are you going to tell me what the phone call was all about? You were gone for a long time"

"I thought you were asleep. I didn't want to disturb you."

"No, I was just letting the sun fill my spirit and thinking about how cold it is in Colorado about now."

"Iowa would be even worse."

She opened her eyes and looked over at Herbie waiting patiently.

"Tell me about your phone call."

"Great news. Your cook wants to buy the café."

Gail sat up quickly.

"That is great news. Were you talking to the realtors?"

"Yep. Everything is in the works. He signed the purchase agreement and accepted your price."

"He should. I'm almost giving it away."

Herbie looked at her. Then she laughed, because she no longer cared about the Coffee Cup. It was no longer a part of her life, and it was a good thing to be rid of.

She put her hand on Herbie's arm. "Thanks for everything you've done. I couldn't have survived without your help."

"I've always felt it takes two." Herbie blushed.

Gail was happy and excited for what might come next.

"So, now what?"

"Wait. Before we talk about that, I've got some other news. Zander is on his way to Florida. He will be here tomorrow, and I'm going to pick him up at Fort Myers."

"You're going to have a busy day. Weren't you going to Immokalee to see about a job?"

"That was the plan. I can still do it and pick Zander up at the same time."

"So, if you get the job, weren't you going to look for a truck?"

"Yeah. Zander doesn't know it yet, but he's going to help with that little task."

"What time are we leaving tomorrow?"

"I'm leaving at 5:00 in the morning. You are not going along."

She sat straight up in the wooden chair. "We were going together. Why are you changing plans?"

"You asked me "now what," before. Here's what. You sold the business. You love it here. We can't stay in a motel for the rest of our lives. We need a house. It needs to be something we can call home. Something where I can return to charge my batteries."

"I agree."

"So tomorrow, you pick out a realtor and begin looking for homes."

Gail was excited. "What if I find something I really like?"

"Make an offer."

"I couldn't do something like that without you."

"Sure you can. I know that anything you love, I'll feel the same way. But if you're not comfortable, wait until we get back and I'll give you my opinion. Such as it is."

"We?"

Herbie could sense that he needed to tread lightly. After all, Gail had never met Zander. She knew him through what Herbie had told her. Of course that wasn't true at all. She had known him once when he was a child, but she felt that something like that didn't count.

"Well, I'm going to invite Zander here to meet you. But I also want to show him Cedar Key. We're both from a small community, so I know he'll like it."

"How long will he stay?"

"I don't think very long. He's here on some mission, but he wouldn't talk about it over the phone. I suspect it has to do with something from the past, but I'll find out tomorrow."

"Is he going to stay in our room?"

"A three-way. I should think not. I'm not about to share you with anyone, no matter how good a friend he is."

Gail reached over and mussed up Herbie's hair. They decided to go have a few drinks in the Tiki Bar before they went to dinner. Herbie would book Zander a room for the next night, and they would see how many more he thought he might need after that.

26

Zander's plane was on time. When he got back to the Fort Myer's terminal, he phoned Herbie. Herbie was in the cell phone lot waiting for his call.

"We've landed," Zander said, "I'm on my way to baggage claim."

"Good. Call me again when you see your bag on the carousal, and I'll zip right over and pick you up. Which gate will you be at?"

"United." Zander hung up.

When Herbie pulled up to the curbside pick-up, Zander was waiting. Herbie jumped out and gave Zander a huge hug and threw his bag in the back seat.

"Still driving the beast." Zander indicated the big boat Buick.

"Not for long I'm afraid. Gail will need these wheels when I get my truck."

"Back to trucking. Can't keep the man from the open road."

"Not quite. It looks like I'm going to be hauling produce up and down the Florida coast."

"Produce?"

"Fruits and vegetables. I think I'll be dealing mostly with tomatoes. But whatever is in season will be fair game."

"You'll need a refrigerated truck down here." Zander said. He wasn't used to the humidity walking off the air-conditioned plane.

"That's a fact. You're going to help me pick it out."

"I know nothing about trucks." Zander admitted.

"You'll just be there for moral support. It's harder for some salesman to try to buffalo someone when there are two bodies. Even if one of them is ignorant."

It wasn't long before they were heading north on I-75. Zander was so busy talking, that he didn't realize they weren't heading into Fort Myers. Finally he noticed that they were heading away from the population.

"Where are you taking me?"

"We're headed for Ocala. They've got a Freightliner dealer there. I need to get a truck like I told you."

"I'm on a timeline of sorts. I don't think this is going to work out well."

"You'd better tell me what's going on."

Zander did. He left nothing out, from the time they talked about the motorcycle gang, to the phone conversation from yesterday."

Finally Herbie said, "Gees, Zander, you always seem to fall with your ass in the briar patch."

"It is the truth. You told me once that your life seemed to always go sideways just when things seemed to be going great."

Herbie nodded.

"Well, my life has gone completely south lately."

"We're quite a pair, aren't we?" Herbie asked

"We always have been."

"Together we're both 'south of sideways.' An interesting turn of the phrase."

Zander thought about the phrase for a moment and decided he liked it.

"Here we are, both ending up in the south. I suppose it's some sort of irony."

"Maybe so, but I've always thought that it was better not to over-analyze what happens in life. You can't do anything about it anyway."

"I don't know if I agree," Zander said.

"It seems to me, that people are so busy living in the past or anticipating their futures that they fail to live in the moment."

Zander couldn't argue with the statement, so he sat back and looked at the Florida landscape, trying to live in the moment. He was amazed at how the scenery changed as they headed north on I-75.

"This place is amazing. On the left you get glimpses of the gulf and on the right you see trees."

"Have you noticed how they are changing from tropical palms to more forest pines?" Herbie asked.

"Now that you mention it." Zander was impressed.

The trip to Ocala took just over three and a half hours. Herbie found a straight truck with a reefer that he liked. A salesman found and liked Herbie, and together they hammered out a deal. Herbie asked the salesman to hurry the paperwork, because he wanted to get to the Levy County courthouse in Bronson to get the truck registered and change his South Dakota plates for Florida's on the his big boat Buick. He didn't know what time they closed, but he thought it wouldn't be before five. If they hurried, they could make it.

"Zander, you're going to have to drive the Buick."

"I don't know where I'm going."

"You just follow me. It shouldn't be too difficult to spot this truck, even for you."

Zander hit Herbie in the shoulder, and they were off.

It was an easy drive as Herbie had promised. They went northeast out of Ocala on highway 27 right into Bronson. It was just less than forty miles and they made it easily before the courthouse closed.

Zander sat in the car and waited for Herbie to take care of the registration. His mind was far away from Bronson, however. He was thinking about Key West. Then he remembered what Herbie had said about living in the moment. He was one of the biggest offenders. He had lived his entire life resurrecting the past or anticipating the future. He realized it was going to take a conscious effort if he was ever going to change that pattern.

When Herbie finished, they went southeast on Highway 24, which took them right to Cedar Key. In a half hour they were parked at the Low-Key Hideaway. Herbie parked across the road and pointed Zander to the parking spot in front of his motel room.

"I like this place." Zander looked around.

"I knew you would. I booked you the room right next to ours. Let's get you settled and meet later for drinks at the Tiki Bar."

Zander went to the office to pay for his room and get the key. He was surprised that there was no charge. Herbie had taken care of it.

The room was spacious, and everything looked new. There was a seating area and a small kitchen, and the bedroom had a king bed which Zander liked. There was a door that led to the covered patio, and across the lawn was the Tiki Bar.

Zander decided to take a shower and change clothes. It was a long day, and he always felt grimy when he flew. Flying was his least favorite method of transportation. He didn't like the idea of breathing everyone else's germs. The woman next to him on the flight had the sniffles, and he was hoping it was just allergies and not a cold. He didn't want to be under the weather right now.

When he was ready, he walked over to the bar. Herbie was already in attendance. Next to him sat a woman. Zander realized it was Gail from how Herbie had described her. The only thing different was that he hadn't described her nearly as pretty as she looked.

Zander decided to take the lead. "Hi Gail. I'm Zander. I've heard a lot about you from Herbie. He never told me how pretty you were, however."

Gail blushed. She decided she liked this tall man.

"Why would I tell you that? Herbie asked. "Just give you a reason to move in, and here you are, saying sweet things to her."

"Just don't turn your back, my friend."

Gail's face just got redder, and Herbie put his arm around her.

"You're embarrassing her," Herbie said, looking concerned.

"Shut up, Herbie," Gail said, "Let the man talk."

The three had a good laugh. Herbie ordered Zander three fingers of Jack Daniels on the rocks from Pat, and they went out and sat on the dock watching the tide come back into the bay.

When they finished their drinks, it was dark.

"Come on," Herbie said, standing, "let's go to the Island Hotel for dinner."

Zander was tired but didn't want to disappoint his friend, and he thought having dinner with a pretty lady would be better than his usual dining alone.

The hotel was the oldest building in Cedar Key. The dining room was elegant but boasted that it was causal dining at its finest.

Herbie ordered for everyone. They started with crab bisque soup. Zander had never tasted anything so rich and wonderful. He could have stopped with the soup and been quite happy. Herbie had other ideas, he ordered everyone the Crab Imperial. It was baked to a golden finish. It was served with salad, homemade crackers, fresh steamed vegetables, and the starch of the day.

Zander couldn't finish. He was stuffed like the crab. When the server asked if they wanted dessert, the entire table groaned. The server laughed and told them they didn't sell much dessert.

Herbie picked up the tab, much to Zander's objections.

"You are our guest," Herbie said. "What kind of host would I be if I didn't show you every hospitality?"

"You'd be the Herbie I've always known."

Gail liked Zander's response. The three decided to take a stroll down the street to try and walk off dinner. Gail took Zander's arm and talked non-stop. Herbie trailed behind, smiling. He was happy that Gail had taken to his friend.

The next day, he and Gail would take Zander along and look at houses. He would need to deliver Zander to Fort Myers Beach to get on the Key West Express, but that could wait until after the weekend. Monday would also be the day he began delivering produce out of Immokalee. Things seemed to be working out in his life. He was concerned with what Zander would be getting himself into, however.

Herbie didn't realize that Zander was dealing with his own concerns.

27

Avon hadn't been in contact with Fats for a few weeks. She thought it might not be the wisest idea with the Gimp following her every move. But she couldn't call him that anymore could she? Bonnie had forbidden it.

"His name is Fabiano," she had told her. It was such a nice name for such a miserable example of a human being.

Avon had no idea if she had scared Fabiano into not telling Bonnie about using the phone at Rick's bar. She doubted it. She would just play along until something happened. Had she listed the pros and cons about staying, she would have been long gone. She just wasn't the type to let anything go without some type of resolution.

Bonnie was handling the Libertine side of the business, which suited Avon just fine. Things were handled over the phone and the transactions were seldom completed in the shop. Avon didn't know how the escorts got paid, and she didn't care as long as she could stay out of it.

More of the responsibility for the Aphrodisiac fell on Avon's shoulders. She enjoyed talking with the customers and the sales reps, and actually, she was a good salesperson. Many customers walked away with things they never had any intention of buying.

Things seemed to be going along quite smoothly and Avon had even dropped her guard just a bit. She noticed that Fabiano had been hanging around more than usual. Bonnie would call him into the office from time-to-time, and she would shut the door. That was a concern, but she pretended not to notice.

Fabiano's appearance had changed dramatically. His dark hair had been trimmed neatly. It was still long, but Avon had to admit, it looked good. His wardrobe had changed as well. He was wearing cargo shorts with various Hawaiian shirts, and most surprising of all, he was clean. Avon no longer could smell him when he came into the room. She assumed Bonnie had something to do with the transformation.

Bonnie came out of the office and called Avon.

"Would you be a dear and take the deposit to the bank. I've got too much on my plate today."

"Sure. Do you need a receipt?"

"Of course," Avon said, and disappeared back into the office.

Bonnie took the deposit and walked toward the door. Then she had a thought, as long as she was going to the bank, she would take the opportunity to get a safety deposit box. She would put all the items she had in the false bottom of her purse into the box, away from prying eyes.

The bank was a few blocks from the shop. Avon marveled at how many banks there were on such a small island. She wondered how they could all be doing well.

Renting the box took longer than Avon anticipated. She was worried that Bonnie would become suspicious, so she stopped at a clothing store and picked up an outfit as an excuse if Bonnie quizzed her. It was quite sexy. The top was a low-cut, lacey, black camisole. The shorts were white and had a short waist and no legs to speak of. Avon thought she looked quite good in them. She thought Bonnie would think so as well.

She had been keeping her eyes open for Fabiano but hadn't caught even a glimpse of him. She walked back to the Aphrodisiac enjoying the weather noticing how nice it was in December. The oppressive humidity was no longer a bother, the nights were cool, and the days warm. Avon could get used to living in a temperate climate like this.

She walked into the shop and noticed the office door was closed. Fabiano was standing in the doorway that led to the back. He nodded her way. Avon chose to ignore him.

She couldn't ignore the screaming coming from the office, however. She couldn't quite make out what was being screamed. Someone was not happy. She knew it wasn't Bonnie doing the screaming. She never raised her voice. She was cold and calculating.

Suddenly the door flung open and one of the escorts Avon had seen before, immerged in a huff. She went by the name of Bunny

Roberts. Avon had no idea what her real name might be.

Bunny stopped and turned back toward the office.

"This isn't finished. Not by a long shot. I'll be talking to everyone. You won't be in business long after we're finished with you."

With that, she turned quickly and ran out the back door, almost knocking Fabiano over in the process.

Bonnie came out of the office with just the hint of smile on her face. Avon didn't like the look of it.

"What was that all about?"

"Oh, just a dissatisfied co-worker. It always amazes me when people agree to terms of employment and then, suddenly, they are no longer satisfactory."

Bonnie looked over at Fabiano and nodded. He turned around and gimped out of the same door the girl had just used.

Avon handed the deposit slip to Bonnie.

"What's in the bag?" Bonnie asked.

"Oh, I did a little shopping."

"Let's see it."

Avon took out the outfit and held it up for Bonnie to get a look.

"I like that. It's almost ten. Why don't you put that on before we open up?"

"I wasn't thinking of wearing this while I work," Avon protested.

"I don't know why not, you'll sell a lot more wearing that. The guys will love it."

Bonnie went back into the office. It was the end of the discussion.

Avon went up and changed into the outfit. She was hoping Bonnie wanted to see her in the outfit before she wore it for work.

She had to admit, she did look good.

• • •

Two days later, Avon picked up a copy of the *Key West Citizen*. On the front page was a picture of paramedics fishing out a body off Mallory Square. The article said it was a woman, and it looked like she had drowned at least two days before. Her roommate identified the remains as Bunny Roberts.

It was then Avon decided to leave.

28

Zander awoke when he heard a knock on the motel door. It was Herbie.

"Hey, are you trying to sleep the day away?"

"What time is it?" Zander asked, still in a fog.

Herbie looked at his watch. "It's almost 8:00."

Zander groaned.

"Hey, we've got a big day ahead of us. Gail wants to look at houses."

Zander paused. "Don't take this wrong, but I'm not interested in house shopping. Besides, this should be something just the two of you do together."

"What are you going to do?"

"Explore. But first, I'm going to get some breakfast. Where's a good spot?"

"Annie's Café. Just down the road a bit. You want a ride?"

"Nah. I'm going to explore on foot. I need the exercise anyway."

"Suit yourself. See you back here about five for cocktails?"

"It's a date."

Zander shut the door. He turned on the TV to Good Morning America, and went to turn on the shower. The sign on the wall said it took awhile for hot water to make it to the shower and to have patience. Zander felt he had a lot of time to be patient.

A short walk later, he was at Annie's having breakfast. He could tell it was a local place. Everyone knew each other, and they seemed friendly enough. Zander struck up a conversation with a guy in white boots that went up to his knees. He figured the guy was a "clammer".

"Is that your boat parked out front?" Zander asked.

"Yep."

"I noticed that the motor was mounted in the middle of the boat instead of the stern." Zander hoped he would impress the guy with his knowledge of the difference between bow and stern.

"It's a clam boat." He said as if that would answer all questions.

Zander looked puzzled. Maybe his nautical knowledge wasn't so impressive after all.

That clam farmer looked amused. "If we mounted the motors on the stern, they would foul the nets we use to harvest the clams."

Zander shook his head in agreement.

"Maybe you'd like to come along and learn what we do first hand." The clammer stood and stamped his boots leaving a bit of dry muck on the floor.

"Thanks for the invitation, but I'll need to be leaving soon." Zander didn't think it was a good idea to go out in a clam boat with someone he just met. There were too many stories of initiating greenhorns. It looked like extremely hard work, and he was sure the guy would give him all the dirty jobs.

"Suit yourself," the clammer said, "My crab shack is just up the road. When you see my rig parked out front, I'll be there, if you change your mind."

Zander thanked him and asked what he should do first to learn about the island. The guy told him to go to the museum before he did anything else.

It was quite a walk from the café to the museum. Zander thought it would be a good chance to do some thinking while getting some exercise. When he got to the museum, he was impressed with the helpfulness of the workers, and their eagerness to share their love of the place.

The very first thing Zander learned was what the term "cracker" meant in Florida. He thought it was a derogatory term used to label poor rural white people. He found out fast, from a young woman, that it is used in a positive context. In fact, most Floridians used the word self-descriptively with pride. It seems the term came about because of cattle drivers who used whips to herd their cattle. The whips were called "crackers" because of a piece of buckskin on the end. The people who cracked those whips came to be known as "crackers." Some of the residents use the term informally to indicate that their family had lived there for many generations.

Zander didn't know if he believed all of it. But it was a good story. He wandered around the different displays and found some interesting facts about the history of the island. At one time Cedar Key had over 5,000 residents. The timber boom was responsible for the economy and population. Eberhard Faber supplied the cedar trees to his pencil factories, but the trees were harvested with little regard to the future. The timber was gone because of a lack of adequate conservation policies. As the timber declined, so did the population. It dropped to 1,200 in the 1890's. Without timber, the sea life would be exploited. Oyster beds and sponges disappeared. The final blow came on September 29, 1891 with a hurricane that destroyed most of Cedar Key, including the railroad terminus. Over 200 people perished in the storm. Cedar Key had been one of the most important ports in Florida because of the railroad's ability to move goods from the port quickly and cost efficiently. The hurricane ended all that. Zander was surprised to see that the population was around 700. It was a far cry from the bustling 5,000. Zander wondered if the community would have been rebuilt if they hadn't squandered their resources. Shit like that always puzzled him.

When Zander had just about enough history to suit him, he hitched a ride with an older couple in an RV. They were heading for Front Street so Zander offered to buy them a drink. They gladly accepted. They found a large spot in the public parking lot that would accommodate the RV. Zander found the first bar on the street called Sea Breeze On The Dock. It was rustic and made Zander think of the Branchwater. He should remember to call Fats when he got back to the Low-Key.

The couple was from some little town in Northern Michigan. Their names were Mike and Nancy Wonders. They had some banter back and forth over the Iowa Hawkeyes and the Michigan State Spartans. It was basketball season and everyone was in high spirits and had high expectations. Soon enough they all would be saying, "maybe next year."

"What brought you to Cedar Key?" Zander asked.

"We've been wintering in Florida for some time and are always looking for the perfect place," Mike said.

"Well, there has to be better places than this to spend your winters."

"Have you taken the I-75 road?" Nancy asked.

"I've been on it, coming here from Fort Myers."

"Then you know," she said.

Zander was unsure he knew much of anything. Mike could see the questions in his face.

"There are only two places we want to spend anytime down here. One is Cedar Key and the other is Everglade City. We're on our way to Everglade City to spend January and February. We'll spend March and April up here. It's warmer down there this time of year, more tropical. After February it starts to warm up here. We're just stopping through to book a spot in the RV park."

Do you ever stay anyplace in between?" Zander asked.

They both shook their head in the negative.

"Snowbirds and tourists. There's just way too many of them. It's even worse on the Atlantic side."

Zander had to smile, since they were a huge part of the thing they disliked so much. He knew all about tourists. Living in the ski area in the Rockies had taught him one thing. He didn't want to be one.

The afternoon passed by with pleasant conversation, and Zander noticed it was already 4:30. He had to get back to Low-Key to have drinks with Herbie and Gail. He asked for the check and the couple told him they could drop him off. The RV park was almost next-door, and they were staying overnight before they left for the southern region in the morning.

Zander told them to come back to the Tiki Bar after they got settled, when they dropped him off. They agreed, and Zander went to his motel room. Before he could even get his key out, Herbie opened his own door and told Zander to come in. Apparently, he had been watching for Zander.

"What's all the excitement?" Zander asked, as he was ushered through the door.

"Gail and I think we've found a house."

"I'm happy for you." Zander could see they were both excited.

"It's right across the street from the water." Gail said, quickly.

"The water or the muck?" Zander laughed.

"The water!" They both chimed in together.

"We want you to come with us tomorrow and look at the place. An extra set of eyes is always better. We want to make sure we aren't missing anything before we make a decision, " Herbie said.

Zander could see Herbie wanted his opinion, so he agreed. The trio decided to take the rest of the discussion to the Tiki Bar. It wasn't long before Nancy and Mike joined them. It was good to have friends around, Zander thought.

Soon the five of them were on their way to a little pub and restaurant called Pelican Rail-Road. It was a nice little place overlooking some mucky waterway. It was the kind of small-town place they all enjoyed.

Zander hadn't felt this good for quite a while. He wondered if it was the calm before the storm. Cedar Key was a place that knew all about storms.

29

Fats decided to give Zander a call. He wondered where he was and if he had found anything about Mona.

The phone rang while Herbie was talking about friendship over his fourth drink. He was getting syrupy, and Zander was happy for the distraction of the phone. He moved outside to take the call.

"Hello." Zander said, knowing it would be Fats.

"Hey, I haven't heard a thing from you. Is everything all right?"

"I'm in Cedar Key."

"Is that close to Key West?"

"Not really. Probably about as far apart as they could be on the map."

"What the hell?" Fats said, exasperated.

Zander explained what had happened and that he would be heading down to Key West on Monday. It appeased Fats, somewhat.

"You know this whole thing is my fault. If I would just mind my own business, things like this would never happen."

"It's not who you are. If it were, we would never have connected. It is your one redeeming quality, even if it does piss me off most of the time."

"A left-handed compliment if I ever heard one."

"I like to call it south of sideways."

"I like that," Fats said, then got serious again, "You need to help me out on this one. I'll owe you big."

"You always do, but I'll do my best. Just be prepared for the worst. You know who we're dealing with by now."

"Call me as soon as you know anything."

"Will do." Zander had to follow up on that promise. Fats had more guilt over involving Mona than he needed. Zander didn't need to make it any worse.

Zander returned inside the Pelican Rail-Road and sat back down at the table.

"Bad news?" Herbie asked.

"Maybe. Fats is worried." Zander said, not wishing to involve Mike and Nancy. "I need to get down to Key West on Monday. No later."

"I'll have you at the Key West Express right on time."

"Have you made reservations? Mike asked. "It should be pretty safe in December, but you'd better make reservations." He threw down a card with the phone number listed on it.

"It leaves by 7:00 in the morning, so you'll have to go early on Monday morning or Sunday evening and get a place to stay," Nancy said.

Zander looked at Herbie.

"It's up to you, man. If you want to leave at 1:30 Monday morning I can do it. I'd prefer Sunday evening, though, if you're asking me."

"Me too." Zander couldn't imagine leaving at that hour. He would never be able to sleep before that anyway. "What day is it anyway?"

Mike and Nancy started to laugh. "That's what we ask each other every day but we're retired. Every day runs into the next, and soon it doesn't matter."

"It looks like Zander's already fallen into that way of life," Herbie said, slapping him on the back. It's Friday, by the way."

It embarrassed Zander for a moment. It wasn't like him not to know what was happening around him. But now he was going back to work, and he had to be on top of things for the time being.

The fivesome sat around the bar listening to the three-person combo. At 11:00 they stumbled out. Everyone had enough to drink, and Herbie was cautious driving back to Low-Key.

It would be the last night that Zander would experience any real pleasure for quite some time.

30

The week before Zander would make the trip to Key West, Bonnie called in two girls to watch the shop. Avon was puzzled. Bonnie told her they were working so hard that they needed some R & R. The radio said it would be 82 by 2:00, so that made it a perfect day for the beach.

Bonnie decided they would go to the Zachary Taylor Beach. Avon hadn't been there but heard it was the nicest of the beaches in Key West. They loaded a bag with their beachwear and put on their swimsuits under a cover up and were off in Bonnie's car.

The beach wasn't very busy, even though it was a Sunday. They parked the car and began walking until they were on a secluded stretch of sand. They had passed a few couples sunbathing nude. It looked like the more isolated you were on the beach, the less that clothing became mandatory.

Bonnie threw out a blanket and soon they were putting on suntan lotion. Bonnie slipped out of her bikini top and had Avon put the lotion on her back. She did the same for Avon, taking off her top in the process.

Avon was enjoying the warmth of the day lying on her stomach. She glanced over and noticed Bonnie was on her back and had taken off her bottoms as well. Avon liked what she saw, and she moved over to put suntan lotion over Bonnie breasts. Bonnie was enjoying Avon's slow hand movements and lifted her hips just a bit when Avon moved down to her waist.

Soon they were embraced, moving their hips together in rhythm. It was the first time they had sex together in a long time, and it made her forget about her concerns.

Both ended on their stomachs looking at each other.

"That was good." Bonnie stated the obvious.

"It's been awhile."

"We've been too busy, haven't we?"

Avon wasn't quite sure what she meant.

"I guess we need to remind ourselves to slow down now and then."

"I couldn't agree more."

Bonnie got up and when waist deep into the water. She swam a bit and told Avon to join her.

Avon was surprised that the water seemed so warm for December. Coming from the colder climate of Colorado, it was difficult for her to comprehend the tropical climate.

They splashed around for some time. When they were almost finished, Bonnie went over to Avon and put her arms around her and kissed her deeply. Then she held her face close with both her hands.

"I know what you did," Bonnie said, quietly.

Avon pulled away quickly.

"I don't know what you are talking about."

"Oh, I think you do."

"Maybe you'd better explain yourself," Avon said, trying to be on the offensive. She didn't like the conversation and had a knot in the pit of her stomach.

"What's my name?"

"You call yourself Bonnie Marco." Suddenly Avon knew where this was going. Fabiano had informed on her after all.

"But what did you call me when you were on the phone at Rick's?"

"Don't believe everything the Gimp tells you."

"Why do you think I pay him?"

Avon knew she was in trouble, but she knew she could hold her own with Bonnie.

Bonnie grabbed her by the shoulders. She seemed aroused again.

"I don't know why you felt you had to betray me. We had a good thing together. You threw it away for what, money?"

Avon said nothing but looked into her eyes. They were cold even though she was smiling.

"Who was on the other end of that phone call?"

"You'll never know, Sara Jane."

Sara Jane or Bonnie or whoever she was, let go of her shoulders and walked back to the blanket. Avon, or Mona, or whoever she was at the moment, thought for a moment and then turned to look at Sara Jane. She was putting her cover up on, not bothering to get back into her swimsuit. Next to her was Fabiano, the Gimp.

Mona didn't know how he had found them or how he was able to navigate the long walk. She didn't know and didn't care. She began to walk toward the blanket.

Sara Jane had picked up the swimsuits and put them into beach bag. She picked up the blanket and started walking back the way they had come. She never looked back. That pissed Mona off.

"Where are you going, you bitch? Bring back my clothes."

Sara Jane kept walking, and Fabiano just kept looking at Mona. He had a half- smile on his face. That's when Mona realized she was in trouble.

She didn't have many options, so she continued to move toward the beach. The Gimp was just waiting for her. With any luck, she could stomp on his foot again. She didn't even care that she was walking toward him naked.

When Mona was almost knee deep in the water, she stopped, letting him take in the sights.

"Like what you see?"

Fabiano just stared at her.

"Fuck you." Mona said, trying to get him to react.

He did. Fabiano moved into the surf until he was knee deep next to Mona. He ran his hands over her breasts slowly. Mona shuddered, but not because she enjoyed his touch.

Then Fabiano grabbed her around the waist and turned her facing away from him. Mona thought she could feel his arousal through his pants. It sickened her.

She couldn't move. He was strong, and her movements were totally contained. Her legs were free, and when she tried to kick his bad leg, he moved his legs apart. It was his first mistake. Mona took the opportunity to kick back up as hard as she could. She caught him on the bottom of the scrotum pushing his testicles up against his body with a sickening slap.

For moment, Mona thought he was going to throw up. He loosened his grip and grabbed his testicles with one hand, trying to put out the fire that was up in his groin. Mona took that one opportunity to twist out of one of his arms and face him. Then she put both feet on his chest and kicked wildly. He let her go. Mona shot a few feet into the water and then turned her back and started swimming as hard as she could. She could feel that he was trying to follow her.

She hadn't thought that Fabiano's leg might keep him from swimming after her. When she got enough courage to stop and look, she could see him on the beach watching her. She had to think. She was in the ocean without a stitch of clothing. She had to get away from beach and away from the Gimp. She started swimming. She saw the breakwater area, and beyond that she saw the little resort island called Sunset Key. It was just off Mallory Square. It was a long swim but she had no other options. Her biggest fear was that the Gimp would get a boat or wave runner and try to run her down. She had to move fast, so she swam with every ounce of strength she had.

When she looked again, the Gimp was out of sight. She was halfway to the island. She wasn't sure she could make it.

31

The house that Herbie and Gail wanted Zander to see was a three-story box overlooking the ocean on First Street. Right across the street was a rocky beach. It was one of those houses built on stilts to avoid the flooding when the sea surged during hurricanes and some of the lesser storms.

The house was four stories with the open area on the bottom. Zander noticed people used the space as a type of garage and storage area. Every floor had a deck facing the ocean, and the views were spectacular. Zander saw an island where excursion boats stopped and saw kayakers beaching there as well. Herbie told him it was called Atsena Otie Key. Apparently, it had been the original location of the first town called Cedar Key. It was destroyed in a hurricane in the late 1800's. Zander was amazed at the history of the area. It made his hometown of Hospers look youthful by comparison.

Herbie and Gail showed Zander around the house. The main floor had the kitchen, dinning area and living room. The third floor had the master bedroom, an office area and den. The fourth floor had three bedrooms with the one facing the ocean appearing to be almost a second master. There were five bathrooms. It was everything the couple needed and more.

"The second master bedroom will be yours," Herbie said, simply.

Zander looked at Gail.

"We've talked about it, and we want you to stay with us as long as you want."

Zander was uncomfortable with the idea.

"We won't hear any more about it," Herbie stated.

"Oh, I think you will. I'll stay with you for a while but I'll be paying rent and sharing the costs. Don't try to negotiate anything else."

Herbie smiled. "We were counting on it. We've put in an offer and should know early next week."

Zander had seen countless homes for sale on the island. The economy had, like him, gone south. He didn't think there would be much of a problem buying the property. It looked like it was a buyers' market. Zander wasn't so sure he would invest in property in Cedar Key unless he wanted to stay there forever, and that wasn't going to happen.

The weekend moved quickly. Sunday afternoon appeared before Zander realized. Herbie knocked on his motel room door.

"We're going to have to leave soon. We need to get a room in Fort Myers and you need to be at the Key West Express by six in the morning."

"I'm putting my stuff together right now. I'll be ready in a half-hour."

"OK. I'll meet you at the truck." Herbie threw something at Zander.

"It's a backpack. You don't want to lug all your stuff down to Key West. We'll keep it here for you. Just take what you need. Pack light." Herbie shut the door.

Zander figured Herbie needed some time to say goodbye to Gail and Mr. Peabody. He wondered if Herbie and Mr. Peabody had ever been apart before.

He had been ready to go. He had been reading a book by Randy Wayne White that was left in his room. Zander thought somebody ought to say his name quickly five or six times. When he tried, he sounded like Elmer Fudd. The bio said he lived on Pine Island but wrote about Sanibel Island. Zander looked at the map and decided he would like to check out the area when he was finished with the Key West business.

Now he had to rethink what he would take along, some t-shirts, underwear and his shaving kit. Everything else he could buy down there. He was ready in less than the half hour Herbie had allotted. He dropped off his bag in Herbie and Gail's room, said goodbye to Gail and scratched Mr. Peabody between his eyes and they were off.

Neither Herbie nor Zander said much on their trip south. Zander was thinking about his trip on the boat. He was a bit nervous. He had never been on a bigger ship and was hoping he wouldn't get seasick. Herbie was thinking about his new trucking job. Starting anything new always made him nervous. So, he tried to concentrate on Gail and the house.

Five hours later they took the exit to Daniel's Parkway off I-75. There was a convenience store just a half block from the exit and Herbie took the opportunity to fill up. Zander offered to pay, but Herbie told him this would be a business expense, and he needed to start keeping receipts. So Zander bought them two Cokes and some doughnuts that had just come out of the oven. Zander never saw a doughnut he didn't like.

"Any preferences on where we stay tonight?" Herbie asked.

"No. Anything you think would work would be just fine."

"I want to find something close to the boat so we don't get caught in traffic trying to get you there on time."

"Sounds like a plan."

The pair weaved in and out traffic with the big truck. Zander noticed everyone seemed to give them a wide berth. They took a left on Summerlin Road and Herbie took another left onto San Carlos Boulevard. They found a little place called Tip Top Waterfront Resort that looked promising. They had ample parking for Herbie's truck, and the place looked like a charming little Mom and Pop place. They had a couple of rooms left and after they checked in, Herbie suggested they look for the Key West Express. The guy at the desk gave them directions, and they found it was only few blocks farther down the road.

"Turn left before the bridge and it's just a few blocks. If you haven't eaten, I suggest you try the Parrot Key just a few properties past the Express parking lot. It's right next to a place called Salty Sam's," the guy at the desk told them.

Zander thanked him for his help, and they were off. It would be an easy drive in the morning the pair found out.

The Parrot Key was a nice open-air place with a huge bar. They got a table outside overlooking the bay with all the boats in the livery. Herbie ordered them some drinks from a card that said they were their specialties. Almost all of them had rum. They were in the tropics, after all.

Zander ordered the calamari. Herbie turned up his nose.

"That's octopus." Herbie said, pulling an even bigger face.

"Don't judge until you try it, and actually it's squid." Zander knew Herbie had never had calamari just by his reaction.

The appetizer came on a big plate with a bed of lettuce and some stringy things that Zander didn't recognize. Zander dug in. The calamari was superb. Zander told Herbie so and dared him to try it. Herbie wasn't one to back off of a challenge, so he tentatively took a bite.

Zander was lucky to get another piece. Herbie almost inhaled the entire plate.

"I've never tasted anything this good."

Zander smiled. "Well from the little I've had, I would agree. It doesn't always come this good. This place knows how to do it."

They had a few more drinks and ordered poor boys. Zander's was Mahi Mahi and Herbie ordered Shrimp. They drove back to the motel and staggered into their rooms.

Zander fell asleep immediately, and Herbie followed suit after he made a phone call to Gail.

• • •

Zander's wake-up call came at 5:30. He was ready to go by 6:00. When he went to the lobby, Herbie was already waiting with a cup of coffee.

"Let's head out," Herbie said, already making his way to the door.

"Let me at least get a cup of coffee," Zander replied, just a bit irritated.

"We don't want to be late."

"The boat doesn't leave until 8:00." Zander got a coffee.

"But my ship needs to sail now, Zander. My new route starts today, and I don't want to start behind."

Zander felt bad. He was thinking of himself with little regard for what Herbie had going on in his life.

"You're absolutely right. You are doing me a big favor dropping me off like this. Let's go."

In five minutes, Herbie had dropped Zander off at the entrance to the parking lot, and Zander was walking toward the ticketing window. He was glad he didn't have to pay the ten dollars a day parking fee, since he didn't know how long he would be gone.

He got his ticket and walked around until they opened the boat at 7:00. He found a good spot at the back of the boat in an overstuffed chair and pulled out his Randy Wayne White novel, *The Man Who Invented Florida*. By 8:15, his boat was on its way to Key West.

The captain announced that the weather was good, and it would be a smooth ride all the way. Zander wondered if the ride would be as smooth when he reached Key West.

32

Bonnie rode back to the Aphrodisiac in her car alone. She would remember to burn Avon's swimsuit and cover-up later.

It was quiet in the shop and even quieter in the apartment above. Bonnie looked into Avon's room. She would be careful not to disturb anything in case there would be an investigation. She needed to make one more search, however, to make sure she hadn't missed anything.

Bonnie was upset with herself at not getting the truth out of Avon. Her temper had gotten the best of her. She knew better. The identity of the person on the other end of the call Avon made at Rick's became the problem.

By 9:00, Bonnie had searched the entire bedroom, carefully putting everything back in its place. Finding nothing, she went into the kitchen and made herself some mac and cheese. Even as a child, she had always found comfort in that food. Much had changed since she had been a child. Some people mourned their past, Sara Jane tried not to think about it, and it had always worked for her.

She waited for Fabiano Farnum with a Jack Daniels and water. She was on her third when Fabiano walked in at 10:30. She waited for him to speak.

"The last I saw her, she was floating out to sea." He lied

"Was she dead?"

"Face down for as long as I could see." He lied some more

Bonnie looked at him. "Forgive me Fabiano, but I have had some bad luck with people who I thought had drown." It made her think of Lilly back in Colorado.

"No worries here." He smiled.

Bonnie smiled back out of courtesy. She didn't like Fabiano, but he was necessary. She needed someone strong to do what had to be done.

"Did she give you any trouble?"

"She's a fighter. She kicked me in my privates. I didn't like that. I may have broken her neck." The lies were easier now.

"Do you think they'll find her body in the morning?"

"Not if the sharks find her first. She's gone, I think."

"Let's wait and see what happens. I'll pay you when I know she's no longer a problem."

Fabiano didn't like that. He had lied to his employer thinking she would pay him the five thousand she had promised earlier. Then if Avon showed back up, he wouldn't care. This changed things. He would need to go out early and see if anyone had found anything. He would get his money one way or another. Bonnie had been good to him, but a promise was a promise and she would pay. It didn't matter to Fabiano that he hadn't kept his end of the bargain. He didn't think that way.

"That's it for tonight, Fabiano," Bonnie said, breaking into his train of thought, "Come back when you hear something." She didn't want to see anymore of Fabiano for a while.

• • •

The distance from Key West to Sunset Key was a little less than two miles. Maybe it was a little more from Mona's angle. The last she had seen the Gimp he was following her, walking on the breakwater. The next time she looked up, it was dark. She let the lights from the resort on Sunset Key guide her to the island.

There was a little chop on the water but otherwise it was almost perfect for swimming. Mona changed up from an overhand swim to a dogpaddle intermittently. She had thought she was in pretty good shape, but she was tired. A few times she turned around and floated on her back to rest. She hadn't noticed how bright the stars were away from the lights of the island.

It took her over an hour to reach the beach. She let a wave take her into the shallows, and then she paused on all fours to look around. There was a light coming from what looked like a cabana in front of a pool owned by the resort. She pushed herself out of the water and realized that her nakedness made her extremely vulnerable.

The small light coming from the cabana was the only illumination near the beach. She approached the counter from a distance making sure she could see in, and making sure no one could see her. She crouched behind a table and two chairs and looked in.

It looked like a young boy about sixteen or seventeen. He couldn't be any older. Mona thought that was a stroke of luck. She approached the service window from the side and stuck her head around the corner. The cabana boy was folding towels with his back to her. She didn't want to scare him, so quite softly she cleared her throat. The boy jumped anyway. He turned around quickly and looked around until he saw Mona's head at the side of the window.

"I didn't mean to startle you but I need your help," Mona said, almost pleading.

Cabana Boy relaxed. "What do you need?"

"Some of my friends and I were swimming naked after dark, and they thought it would be funny to steal my clothes and run off."

Cabana Boy smiled. "You wouldn't be the first. How can I help?"

"First off, throw me a towel so I can cover up."

He did as he was told. Mona took the opportunity to use the towel to cover all her necessary parts and when she was quite sure everything was tucked away, she leaned into the cabana.

"You wouldn't happen to have something I could put on? I don't want to walk around here with just a towel."

"Let me check the lost and found," Cabana Boy, answered.

For a moment Mona felt heartened. Then Cabana Boy held up a swimsuit.

"How about this?"

It was a true string bikini. Mona thought two Band-Aids and a cork might cover more.

"I was thinking of something a little more substantial," Mona said.

"Well, how about that and this?" He pulled out a sarong someone had left. It was colorful and tied right it would cover most of the bikini.

"Throw them over."

Cabana Boy did as he was told. Mona stepped around the corner back into the darkness and soon had draped herself over the scant swimsuit. She stepped back into the light.

"How do I look?"

Cabana Boy whistled. "I wouldn't kick you out of bed for eating crackers."

Sensing he was harmless, Mona decided to banter a little.

"How about nachos?"

"Depends on what we would use for dip." Cabana Boy was on a roll.

"You are a nasty little thing aren't you?" Mona tried to sound serious but was smiling broadly.

"As much as you might want."

"Have you ever been in bed with an actual woman, or is all this coming from *Penthouse Forum?*"

Mona could see she had pushed him a little too hard. He was looking down, not replying.

"I'm sorry. Here you are helping me get covered up, and I'm being a smart ass. Thank you for everything."

The boy's eyes brightened. "You're welcome. You do look very good."

"Thank you, but I must look a mess with my hair all stringy."

"You make this job worth doing."

Mona was flattered. Suddenly she had an idea. There was an older gentleman who came into the shop every week. Mona thought he was in his mid-to-late sixties. He never bought anything but just wanted to talk. He was a nice guy and had lost his wife a year earlier. Mona had listened to his story a number of times and found out he had a residence on Sunset Key. He had invited her to come over and see him anytime. Of course that had been the furthest thing from her mind, until now.

"Do you know an older gentleman, I think his name is Max something or other. I believe he has a home on the island."

"Oh you mean Mr. Kuhn. Yeah he lives just down the road over there." Cabana Boy pointed in the direction.

"I met him yesterday, and I want to play a joke on my friends. I'll hang out with him until they start to get worried about me."

"Sounds like some good payback."

"It has to be our little secret though. You can't give me away if they come looking."

"Mum's the word, whatever that means."

"Could you be a real dear and show me his place."

Cabana Boy looked at his watch. "Sure. I'm almost finished here. Let me lock up and I'll take you there."

Mona sat down on one of the chaise lounge chairs and realized she was exhausted. She could just put her head back and sleep right here. Just as she was ready to nod off, she heard Cabana Boy slam the door. She startled and got up.

"Ready?"

"Sure. I just want to thank you again."

"I always like a good practical joke but I like paybacks better."

Max's home was a short walk. They were walking on a path. Mona wondered why there were no streets. The she realized that the island was small and cars would be in the way.

Cabana Boy pointed to the Kuhn residence and turned to go. Mona reached out and pulled him close and gave him a huge hug and a kiss on the check. If it hadn't been so dark, she would have seen his face turn stop sign red.

"Thanks again, you are a life saver." Mona meant it.

The Cabana Boy turned around and stumbled off. He would have something to keep in the front of his mind on a lonely night.

Mona found the front door. She hoped Max hadn't already turned in for night. There was a light, and it looked like the glow of a television coming from the rear of the house.

She knocked on the door loudly. Hearing nothing, she tried again. Suddenly an outside light illuminated the entire front entrance almost blinding her.

"Who is it?" Max asked.

Mona almost told him her real name and then stopped herself.

"It's Avon."

There was no reply.

"You remember me. I'm the girl from the *Aphrodisiac*. You come in and visit me every week."

"Oh yes, of course. I wasn't expecting you tonight."

Suddenly Mona thought this might be a bad idea. He seemed

confused. She was hoping that maybe she had awakened him, and he was just a bit disoriented. The other explanation could be he was suffering from the start of dementia. She didn't want to think about that. Luckily, she didn't have to worry.

"Oh where are my manners, come in, come in. I'm afraid I was dozing off, and I wasn't clicking when I answered the door." Max smiled as he ushered her into the house.

"I'm sorry to bother you, but I didn't have anywhere else to go." Mona hoped she hadn't sounded too pathetic.

Max looked at her, puzzled for a moment.

"You'd better sit down and tell me all about it." He led her to the living room and turned off the television. "Do you want some coffee?"

"I'd rather have some tequila."

"Me too. Caffeine keeps me awake. Booze makes me sleep."

He went over and slid open two French doors, which opened up into a bar room with a pub table.

"Come over and sit at the table while I make the drinks. How do you like your tequila?"

Mona did as she was told. "Straight up with lime and salt."

"Nice," was all Max said.

Max set the drinks on the table and brought the tequila bottle over. Mona noticed it was something she had never heard of before, but it said Agave on the label and something else in Spanish.

They both licked the salt off the area between their thumbs and forefingers, tossed back the tequila, and then sucked on the limes.

"That's good stuff. I don't think you need the salt or the lime." Mona was impressed.

"Precisely."

"But you drink it with both those things."

"You are my guest."

Mona was impressed. Here was a true gentleman with all the old world refinements and yet, he was conscious of those people around him. He obviously had more money than he knew what to do with and yet he had a concern for others. He must have been quite a catch in his day.

Mona decided to have the next two tequilas without the

condiments and they sipped them slowly. After the third drink, Max spoke up.

"Do you think it forward of me to ask how you came to be here tonight?"

"No, I think I owe you an explanation."

Mona had decided early on that she would make up some story about her presence and buy some time before she decided what she should do. But now she had a change of heart. She had to start trusting someone besides herself if she had any hope of getting out of her situation.

She started at the beginning with Fats and Lilly. The story continued until she reached that very evening and her experience with the Gimp. It took forty-five minutes because she didn't want to leave anything out. It took two more drinks to explain it all and they were taking their toll on Mona.

Max sat for moment after she finished her story.

"Maybe I've said too much." Mona was worried.

"Nonsense. I'm happy you've trusted me enough to share your story. I'm trying to think what our next step might be."

Suddenly Mona felt relief. Max was planning to help her. She didn't have to go at this all by herself. She sat back and let the tequila have its way with her.

Max could see that the alcohol had ended Mona's power of reason.

"I think we need to sleep on it. I'll show you to the guest room and we'll resume this conversation tomorrow. But we will be drinking coffee so we keep our heads about us." He smiled and took her hand and led her to the spare room.

"Thank you, Max." Mona put her arms around him.

"I should be the one thanking you. There hasn't been this much excitement around here in a very long time. But you already knew that." Mona thought he might be referring to their weekly visits about nothing, but everything was foggy so she wasn't sure.

"Tomorrow I'll take you to the resort and you can do some shopping for clothes. I think you'll need something more than what you are wearing."

Mona looked down and without thinking started taking off the sarong. Max closed the door before she got much further. Mona was very attractive and Max had noticed that he was attracted to her. He knew it wasn't appropriate, however. He wanted her more as a friend and didn't want to risk her considering him a dirty old man.

Mona dropped into the bed naked for the second time that evening. The bed hadn't felt that good in months.

33

No one bothered Zander on his cruise. He got through a good portion of his novel when he heard the captain announce that Key West was in sight. Zander decided to follow the crowd and watch as they came into port.

He couldn't believe the size of the cruise ships that were docked. It made their boat look like a little skiff by comparison. They dwarfed the entire island. Zander was amazed. Then he realized that there weren't any skyscrapers visible anywhere. It would explain why the ships looked so huge next to the island.

When Zander disembarked, he was directed through the terminal. There was a kiosk with information about the island. Zander picked up a map and sat down on one of the benches to plot his course. He decided to call Fats before he got too far ahead of himself.

"Zander. Where are you?" Fats said, without saying hello.

"Good to hear your voice, as well." Zander chided.

"Sorry. I'm always getting ahead of myself."

"I made it to Key West. I'm in the Express terminal. I'm wondering how to proceed."

"The name of the place is the Aphrodisiac. I think it is on Front Street or Greene Street. I can't remember what Mona told me."

"I've got a map." Zander opened it and checked the street names. "It looks like Front Street and Greene Street run right next to each other. I should be able to find it."

"I know that if you cross Duval, you've gone too far. I think it's close to Duval on one of those two streets."

"OK. I'll check it out."

"What are you planning?"

"I have no idea. I guess I'll just see what develops."

"You need to be very careful, my friend. She doesn't want to be found."

"Nothing like stating the obvious."

"It doesn't hurt to remind you of these things. Common sense seems to fly through the window when you deal with her."

"You can say her name."

"I don't want to. She deserves absolutely no credence. She is a user and an abuser. You'd best never forget that."

Zander knew he was right. He didn't feel the same threat that Fats did, however. After all, he had known Sara Jane his entire life. But that wasn't true at all, was it? He knew very little about her.

"I'll call you when I know more."

When Zander walked out of the terminal, he could hardly believe the temperature. It was extremely humid, and it felt like it was almost eighty. Hard to believe December in the U.S. could feel like this. He was overdressed. The blue jeans and the boots would need to be replaced.

As he walked along the boardwalk toward Front Street, he could see a variety of shops and restaurants. He stopped at a little outfitter's clothing store that said it was having a huge sale. Zander wondered if they always had a huge sale.

He looked around the racks of shorts and found something he liked. The brand name was Bimini Bay and they were cargo style. The clerk came and told Zander they were 100 per cent nylon and they wouldn't wrinkle. She scrunched a pair and then showed how they straightened right up. She told him they would also dry almost immediately when they got wet.

Zander found his size and tried on a pair. They had elastic in the waist as well as belt loops. Zander liked the pockets. He needed someplace for his switchblade and stun gun, since he wouldn't be wearing boots any longer. He picked out a light tan and a dark gray pair. He wore the tan, and the clerk put his boots, jeans, and gray shorts into a big bag.

"You'll want to take off those socks, as well," the clerk said, smiling.

"Or, I could be a big dufus." Zander smiled back.

"How about a nice pair of boat shoes? We've got Sperry on sale."

Of course they did, Zander thought. But he went along with the ruse anyway. Soon he was back on the boardwalk with his new sockless boat shoes and shorts. He had a number of tee shirts with him so he would be good for a while at least.

He needed a place to stay and dump his bag and backpack. When he reached Front Street, he found two hotels. He chose the Pier House Resort and Spa and requested an oceanside room. It had a beautiful view of the ocean and the many small islands. Zander thought he would enjoy a few beers on the patio and watch the sun go down later that evening.

When he stepped back onto Front Street, he was surprised to see the Aphrodisiac almost right across the street. On the corner of Front and Duval there was a tour company. They had something called the "Conch Train" that hauled tourists around the island. It reminded him of one of those little trains they pulled kids around at fairs and town celebrations back home in Iowa. It was something he would never have been caught doing. But the train was full, and people looked like they were enjoying it. No accounting for taste, Zander thought.

There was a little café just across from the Aphrodisiac. Zander decided to get a cup of coffee and sit on the open-air patio and watch. There was a local paper on the table, and he paged through it, pretending to be engaged.

He saw some guy with a terrible limp sweeping the sidewalk near the shop. Someone turned the sign around that said, "open." Zander couldn't see who it was. He needed to get a closer look.

Zander walked over to Duval, and then turned back on Front Street, and walked right by the shop. He walked slowly and looked into the window trying to appear to be a window shopper.

He stopped when he saw someone hanging up some clothing. The person had her back to him, but there was no question. It was Sara Jane.

34

Max got up early and went over to the resort's gift store. There was a cute little sundress in the window. He guessed at her size and bought it. When he got back to his house, he put the bag in front of Mona's door and knocked lightly.

"Yes?" Mona answered thickly.

Max was instantly sorry he had knocked. "I'm sorry if I disturbed you."

"No, I was awake. I'm just laying here wondering what I'm going to do."

"Well, first we're going to have breakfast. It will be ready in a half-hour. There should be everything you need in the bathroom. I always keep it stocked for guests. By the way, I've left you a present right here at the door." Max left.

Mona waited for a moment and carefully opened the door. She saw the bag, pulled it into the room, and shut the door. She took out the sundress and tried it on. It fit fairly well. It might have been a little bigger than she would have liked, but she noticed that it showed off her chest quite well. If fact, she thought it made her look bigger than she was. Mona liked that.

In less than the half-hour, Mona was ready, and went out into the kitchen. The table had already been set, and Max was in the process of dishing up two huge omelets.

"I hope you are hungry," he said, putting the plates on the table.

"I am."

"I should think so, with all that has happened to you in the last twenty-four hours."

"Can I help?" Mona asked.

"You may pour the coffee."

Mona did as she was told, and soon they had demolished the omelets and two cups of coffee each.

"I haven't eaten like that in…forever."

"You need to keep your strength up," Max said, clearing the plates. "You look stunning in that dress by the way."

"I haven't thanked you. You must think I'm terrible."

"No, just the opposite. You've had quite a bit to deal with, haven't you?"

"I guess I have."

"Not to worry. I'm going to take care of it for you."

Mona was puzzled. "How do you plan to do that? More importantly, why would you do it?"

"Two part questions, I always like those. It means you are a forward thinker. I'm not quite sure what will happen with the first question, as of right now. But I will be going into Key West and try to get some intel. Secondly, I'm doing this because I like you. You were nice to me when you didn't need to be. I think I owe you the same courtesy."

Mona nodded her head in agreement, but she couldn't help but feel like there was something Max wasn't telling her. She always had a good feel for things like that.

"Well, thank you for everything. I don't think I should be a burden to you any longer. I should go, you don't need the aggravation."

"Let's have the last of the coffee out on the veranda. It's a beautiful day, and we should enjoy it."

Mona couldn't have agreed more. It was almost 11:00 before they decided not to let anymore of the day slip by.

"Why don't you go down to the pool and relax today. If you need a new swimsuit, I'm sure they can accommodate you at the gift shop. Although, from what I saw of what you had on last night, you would be hard-pressed to find anything lovelier." Max hoped he hadn't stepped past the bounds of good taste.

"That was nice of you to say. I think I will use the pool. Will you be coming too?"

"No, I'm going to take the ferry into Key West. There are some things I need to pick up, and I would like you to make a list of the things you need and your sizes."

"Oh, I'll go with you."

"No, it's too dangerous. Don't you think Bonnie and her flunky will have eyes out?"

It made perfect sense to Mona. Besides, she didn't want to go, but thought it was nice to make the offer."

Max gave her a piece of paper and a pencil and told her to write down everything she needed. He would be going to the supermarket, and he would pick up any clothes and personal items she needed.

"I want you to have a few weeks of clothes to wear. You are on one of the most expensive pieces of property on earth; it wouldn't do for you to be seen wearing the same old thing twice. So you'll need things for daytime and also eveningwear. Remember, you are in the tropics so anything goes." He smiled broadly. "I can afford it, so don't hold back."

Mona didn't even know where to start, so they both sat down at the pub table and made a very lengthy list. She decided she was starting to like it here. She also noticed she was attracted to Max. That was the biggest surprise. Sex had always been just a tool she used to further an agenda. Now she felt something for this older man. It wasn't anything she remotely understood. Here was a guy in his sixties, and she was just pushing forty, at least that's what she told everyone. No matter, there were at least twenty plus years between them. How could anything like that make any sense at all? But she had never met anyone like Max before. He was worldly, yet compassionate. He knew how to treat a woman. Maybe that was it. He was in good shape for someone in his sixties, and it didn't hurt that he appeared to be wealthy.

"We will see you late this afternoon. Enjoy yourself. Don't forget the sunscreen, or you'll burn up." Max was out the door and heading for the ferry dock.

Mona watched him go. Suddenly, she didn't care about Bonnie or the Gimp or Fats or anybody. It was time to take care of Mona. She would stay as long as Max would have her. Maybe she'd just follow her heart.

35

Zander decided to wait before he made his presence known. He kept his room at the hotel for a week. He thought that perhaps a week would be what he needed to find out what had happened to Mona.

He did a good job of staying on the edges, always using the cover of the crowds of people. He was interested in the variety of clientele that entered the sex shop. There were the usual customers, but then there were young woman and men who entered and left without any merchandise. Zander decided that nothing he could find out would surprise him in the least. After all, he was dealing with Sara Jane.

Near the end of the week, he saw an older gentleman enter the Aphrodisiac. He decided to risk looking in the window to see what was going on. He talked to Sara Jane briefly, and then turned around and started for the door. Zander turned quickly and walked the other direction and stopped. He pretended to look at a menu posted outside a restaurant.

Zander decided to follow. He followed him all over the island. The guy was apparently on a shopping trip. He had hired one of those three-wheeled tricycles that looked like a rickshaw. The driver took him around at such a slow pace, that it was easy for Zander to follow. He still worked up a sweat in the humidity.

He saw him pick up groceries at the supermarket at the entrance to the island. He saw him buy something in a liquor store. It puzzled him when the guy stopped at a woman's store and emerged with a number of bags.

Zander's tailing ended when the man got on the ferry. Zander watched the ferry go across the bay to an island. He walked over to the ferry's dock and took one of the free maps showing the route. The island was called Sunset Key. Zander thought it looked interesting. It was something he would check out later. He was interested in the man he was watching and the connection to Sara Jane. He would watch for him again, and if he felt the need, he'd follow him to the island.

• • •

Max returned to the island loaded with food, liquor, and women's clothing. He needed help. He left his cache on the pier and walked the short distance to the cabana. The cabana boy was there with a young girl, both helping meet the needs of the guests. Max gave the boy a twenty and told him to take the packages to his home. The cabana boy found a golf cart and was happy to do as he was told.

Max looked out over the sea of bodies around the pool until he spotted Mona. She hadn't purchased a new swimsuit. She was sunning herself in the string bikini she had worn the first night she had knocked on his door. She looked spectacular. Max was attracted to her, even though she could have been his daughter. It was a thought that was somewhat insulated in his mind since he and his wife had never had children.

He made his way over to her lounge chair and sat down on an empty chair.

"You look spectacular."

"You probably say that to all the women here," Mona said, not opening her eyes.

"Of course I do. What's your point?"

She opened her eyes and looked at Max. "Did you have a successful shopping trip?"

"Yes. It was an exhaustive list, but I believe I succeeded in filling the entire thing."

Mona liked the way he talked. "Shall we go and see what you bought?"

"That's why I'm here. I'll walk you back."

"Maybe I'll put on a style show if you're a good boy."

Max noticed she was becoming more playful. He liked her subtle innuendos. Things were heating up. He wondered how long it would be until he would need to tell her the truth. He kept hoping that if everything played out, there would be no need.

The two walked arm in arm back to Max's house. Mona hadn't bothered to put on her cover-up. Max had a hard time concentrating on their conversation. Mona smelled of coconut oil and her skin glistened. Max hadn't had feelings like this for quite some time. He thought that they weren't altogether unpleasant.

When they walked into the house, Mona could not believe her eyes. There were bags everywhere. Most looked like they had clothing in them.

"Why don't you jump in the shower, and get rid of that suntan oil. You don't want to get that on all these new outfits of yours. I'll put away the groceries."

"I will. Maybe you could mix me something to drink?"

"Certainly, what would you like?"

"Surprise me."

Max hated when people did that. He wanted people to be direct and say what they wanted. He found it strange that it didn't bother him when Mona did it. She always seemed to like what he gave her regardless.

Mona went to the bathroom in her bedroom, and Max put away the groceries. Just as he was putting the last of vegetables into the crisper drawer, he heard Mona's voice.

"A person could die of thirst around here."

"I'll be right there." He decided he didn't have time to mix a cocktail, so he opened a bottle of chardonnay and poured two glasses. It was still too hot in the day for a red wine. He brought both glasses to the bedroom and knocked softly.

"Your bartender is here."

"Come in. I'm in the shower. I need some help getting this suntan oil off my back."

Max paused. If he went in, everything would change. Mona had been giving him subtle hints, but he was unsure of himself with such a beautiful young woman. He was still considering his options when Mona spoke again.

"I need my drink, and I need my back soaped. I can't do either of them myself at this moment. Get in here."

Max opened the door and everything changed.

36

Fats was getting nervous. He hadn't heard from Zander and wondered what was going on. He hated to be left in the dark. There was still nothing from Mona, and he had to hold back from calling her cell phone. If something had happened to her, his number would be a dead give-away to Sara Jane.

Fats tried to decide when he began to hate her. It must have been when she left Zander without so much as a goodbye. But he knew it had to be earlier than that. He had never trusted her. He knew Zander still had some deep feelings for her, but she was toxic. Zander didn't want to see it. Lilly had seen it, and so did countless other women she had abused during her Colorado days.

Fats thought about calling Zander, but he knew that would just piss him off. Zander had told him he would call when he found something.

He decided to give Herbie a call. He had to talk to somebody.

Herbie answered on the second ring.

"Hello, Fats."

"Mr. Herbert Schutt, I presume."

"You presume correctly. How are you?"

"Tolerable, my friend. Just tolerable."

"Better than usual then. Is this a social call, or do you have some interesting piece of business you need to share?"

Fats sobered up. "I'm concerned. I have not heard from Zander, and Mona has fallen off the face of the earth."

"I dropped him off at the Key West Express over a week ago. Come to think of it, he hasn't contacted me either."

"I'd like to believe the adage that "no news is good news," but I'm just not feeling it."

"How can I help?" Herbie asked.

"I don't know. Unless you'd be close enough to check in with him."

Herbie wasn't excited with that idea. "Gail and I have purchased a home up in Cedar Key, and all our time is going toward that right now."

"Oh."

Herbie could hear the disappointment in Fats' voice. He hated to disappoint anyone, especially one of Zander's good friends.

"Let me see what I can do. I've got some deliveries slated for Miami next week. Maybe I can pick something up toward the keys as well."

"That would be great, Herbie. I would owe you."

"Big time," Herbie said. He hated driving the keys. It was always a busy road and traffic moved at a turtle's pace.

"Let me know when you get down there." Fats hung up.

Herbie thought about asking Gail to go with him but then dropped the idea. He didn't want to take Mr. Peabody along, so Gail would need to stay with him. He also was just a little afraid of what he might find, and he didn't want Gail involved. He decided to follow through the next week. In the meantime, he would call Zander.

Like Fats, Herbie didn't have much love for Sara Jane. If his buddy wasn't using good judgment, he might have to intervene. Unlike Fats, Herbie had no problem sticking his nose into whatever business Zander might want to keep secret.

He called Zander's number and waited for him to pick up. He would wait a long time. Zander wasn't answering his phone.

37

Max cautiously entered Mona's room. She was in the bathroom.

"I'm in here. Bring my drink."

He could hear the shower running and was hesitant go any further. Maybe he'd just put his arm into the bathroom, holding the drink, and she could take it. He didn't know how to answer. The thought made him excited somehow.

He put his arm into the room, not looking.

"You'll have to do better than that. I'm all the way across the room in the shower."

Max decided to make the move. He wasn't a teenager, after all, and he'd been around more than he would have liked to admit.

When he walked into the bathroom, to his relief, he saw that Mona was in the shower still in her swimsuit.

"Oh, you brought wine. Thank you. Would you bring it over please?"

Max did as he was told. The steam was rising in the bathroom that already seemed hotter than usual to Max. He handed Mona the wine glass. She clinked the glasses together and took a sip. So did Max. It was a nice moment for both of them.

Then Mona handed her glass back to Max.

"Would you be a dear and put that on the sink? I'll drink it after my shower."

Max brought the wine glass to the sink and was ready to leave the room, when she cleared her throat.

"Um, you need to soap up my back, remember?"

How could he forget? "Are you sure that's a good idea?"

"We're both adults. I think it will be all right." Mona winked, and smiled.

Max thought he could possibly escape the uncomfortable situation, if he could just soap up her back with her swimsuit top still on. He walked over and Mona handed him the body wash.

"Put it on thick, and rub it in good. I don't want any oil on my back when I try on all the new clothes."

Max did what he was told. When he felt he was almost finished, he snapped the lid back on. He was about to hand back the bottle, when Mona undid her bikini top.

"You can't get underneath the straps good enough," she said, still with her back to him.

Max didn't see how the strings that held up here bikini were impeding getting rid of the coconut oil. But who was he to argue?

Just as he started putting more body wash on her back, Mona turned around quickly and took his hands and put them on her breasts.

"My front needs some attention as well."

"I can see that it does."

After Max decided that she had enough body wash in all the right places, he made sure to help rinse her off. Then he carried her over to the bed.

He was out of his shorts and tee shirt in record time. He hoped to last a little longer than that when he was naked and lying with her in bed. He wasn't making any promises, however.

When they were finished, Max was lying on his back feeling a little guilty about taking advantage of this pretty young thing. Mona was on her stomach, her arm around him and her head on his chest.

Max hadn't been with a woman in a long time, and the irony was that Mona hadn't been with anyone but a woman. Both were feeling some mixed emotions. Finally, Max felt he needed to say something.

"You know this changes everything."

"I know."

"I didn't mean for this to happen. I want you to know that."

"I did."

Her response came off easily, but it was totally unexpected to Max.

"You are a beautiful young woman. You could be with anyone you'd want."

"How do you think that's worked for me up until now?"

Max was at a loss for words.

"It feels right to be with you. I can't explain it, but the age thing is meaningless. I've never met a kinder and sexier man before in my life."

Max was still mute.

Mona sat right on top of his stomach.

"Do I have to carry on this conversation by myself? It's starting to feel kind of awkward."

Max just looked at her. "You are a beautiful woman."

She arched her back and thrust her pelvis toward him. "How's this?"

Max had never met anyone as uninhibited as this woman. He liked everything about her. He pulled her down and put his arms around her. She looked him right in his eyes.

"If you'd stay with me, you would make me the happiest man alive." Max was serious, but it sounded addlebrained coming from his mouth.

Mona rolled to her side and supported her head with her right arm.

"If you want me to stay, I will. If you ever want me to leave, you'll need to tell me and I'll go."

"Fair enough. Let's shower, and I'll make dinner."

Max finished first, as men generally do, and left the bedroom before Mona. He didn't bother to get dressed but put on a robe and began making dinner. He took out a box of some kind of stir-fry that he had picked up at the grocery store. He loved to cook but there wasn't time to plan an elaborate meal on such short notice. He needed some time after dinner to level with Mona.

He hoped she would still feel the same way about him after the truth came out.

38

Zander saw that Herbie was trying to call him. He decided not to answer. It was difficult, but he didn't have much to share with anyone right now. He didn't need other people's judgments clouding his own. He wanted to give Sara Jane every chance to be able to tell her own story. He knew how his friends felt about her, and he knew they were concerned for his reaction toward her. Zander felt he could handle Sara Jane. He could always tell when she was telling the truth and when she was lying. But that wasn't exactly true. She had been lying to him all along. She was an opportunist, and Zander was what she needed to be rid of the Rooster. But that seemed like a lifetime ago. Much had happened, and life had a mysterious way of going on whether you liked it or not.

Zander had time to think of a lot of things like that, while he kept his eyes on Sara Jane. He wondered where life would be taking him. Here he was sitting in Key West, in December, in just shorts and tee shirts. It was so foreign to him that he was feeling a bit lost. It was probably why he didn't answer the phone. He didn't want to face the problem head on. In the back of his mind, he thought something still might be salvageable with Sara Jane. Common sense said not to pay attention to anything that stupid, but Zander wasn't heeding common sense at the moment.

He thought it might be the weather that made him somewhat complacent. He was surprised by that behavior, because it was so out of character for him. He finished his second cup of coffee and decided it was time for his initial confrontation. He had wasted enough time on the whole thing.

He found a restroom in the café and then casually walked toward the Aphrodisiac. He was in the middle of crossing the street, when he saw the front door open. It was the same guy with the limp he had seen before. He had a broom and began sweeping around the area.

Zander changed his direction and walked toward Duval Street. He stopped close to a women's clothing store, turned and leaned against the wall. It was busy on the corner, and he could keep his eye on Sara's store without anyone noticing. He had decided that when he confronted her, he didn't want any other distractions around.

The guy with the limp was taking his time, and Zander was losing patience. He suddenly felt like himself again. He decided to have a look around the back.

He walked a half-block and found an alley entrance. It exposed all the shops' rear entrances. He stopped short when he saw the blue Camaro. It was Sara Jane's car. He didn't know why it shocked him to see it parked. He knew it was her car, but suddenly this whole thing became more of a reality and not just a job he was fulfilling for someone. The car signaled his past with her in Frisco and Breckenridge. It made Zander realize there was still unfinished business between them. He didn't know how he felt about her anymore. He knew he was confused by her behavior. He had thought that when they reconnected, it would be an ongoing relationship.

He had misjudged that idea completely. Before he had time to analyze anymore of his past, the back door opened and the guy with the limp came out. Zander turned around and left quickly. When he turned at the alley's entrance, he noticed that there was no one behind him. He looked down the alley and saw the guy going the opposite way.

Zander retraced his steps back to the front of the store. He passed the front door casually and didn't see anyone inside. He walked back, and looked in the front door before he opened it. A bell rang, signaling his entrance into the shop.

A voice came from the back. "I'll be out in a minute. If you need me right now, come back to the office."

Zander pretended to look around like he was shopping. He couldn't believe the number of sex toys for sale. He was quite amused, just looking around. He also saw some undergarments he would like to see on some of the women of his past.

He walked around, looking at the items and smiling. He saw a display with dildos of every size and color. There were dozens of the things. Then he spied what had to be the most bizarre thing he had ever seen.

It was a replica of a man's circumcised penis. It looked to be quite realistic with the exception of one thing. It was gigantic. Zander thought it was over a foot long and he couldn't guess the circumference. He couldn't even get his hand around it, even at the head. Zander wondered what kind of woman would be able to take on something like that. He had heard the stories about the women of some areas in Mexico who could take on a horse. He thought this would even be bigger than the horses he had seen. He was still examining the dildo when he heard a voice.

"Generally we have the woman come in here almost drooling over that. Not many men pay much attention because I think it is too intimidating. But I don't judge. To each their own."

Zander kept his back turned toward her.

"Do you suppose you might be able to demonstrate this for me?" Zander asked, trying to lower his voice.

"We're a shop that sells sex toys, not a place to perform any type of sex act. Besides, that particular appliance would take a special type of woman, and I'm not it."

"That's good to hear," Zander said and turned around.

Sara Jane was smiling, but lost her smile when she realized it was Zander.

"You don't appear to be that excited to see me." Zander walked to the counter.

"I'm just surprised to see you here. How did you find me?"

"Let's just say, I've been on your trail since you left Colorado. There I was, in Iowa, burying my parents. You didn't say a word. You just left me.... again."

"Not my finest moment, I agree." Sara Jane looked down.

"So, what's your name these days?"

"Does it matter? You know who I am."

"I always thought I did. Now, I'm not so sure. I'm not even sure you know who you are."

Zander took a small notebook from his cargo pocket in his shorts.

He opened it and looked it over.

"Let's see, you seem to be Bonnie Marco. I'm surprised you didn't land at Marco Island instead of just using its name. I would think it would have more potential for larger monetary rewards. But what do I know; I'm new to Florida. I don't know how everything works."

"I always found you to be a quick learner." Sara Jane wasn't sharing anything besides small talk.

Zander decided to try to bring the conversation toward the reason he was here. He looked at his notebook once more.

"I believe someone called Avon Bartow works here, is that correct?"

Sara Jane's eyes flashed for a moment, and then she got herself back together. It didn't go unnoticed by Zander, however.

"She's my partner. We own this business together."

"I would like to speak to her. She has people who are concerned for her well-being."

"I don't doubt that in the least. She's gone missing. I haven't seen her in over a week. Her things are in her bedroom in the upstairs apartment, just as she left them. Feel free to have a look."

"She's your partner, aren't you concerned?"

"Of course I am. She was acting strangely, and she was making private phone calls. When I asked her about it, she got angry and stormed out. I haven't seen her since."

Zander thought that maybe Sara Jane was telling some part truths and some part lies. He couldn't be sure which were which. She was always good at it. He knew she wasn't being honest.

He took out one of his cards and scrawled his phone number on the back. He handed it to Sara Jane.

"I'll need to talk to her. If you have any information, give me a call."

Sara Jane looked at the card.

"You have a cell phone?" She asked incredulously.

"I don't like it. But sometimes you've got to do things you don't like."

"How well I know."

Zander was sure she knew quite well. He noticed the escort service cards on the counter. He picked one up and looked at Sara

Jane.

"Back in the business?"

"No. This is a legitimate escort business. I put people together for a price. What they do after that is up to them."

"Sounds like call girls."

"We have men escorts as well as woman, so you would be wrong."

"Call boys? I always heard Key West was wide open. Who am I to judge?"

"Where are you staying?" Sara Jane asked, suddenly trying to soften her tone.

"At the hotel across the street."

"Oh, they have a fabulous restaurant. How about I meet you there after work? Let's say around 8:00."

Zander knew he couldn't help but say yes.

39

Fats had been checking his phone to make sure he hadn't missed a call from Zander. He had tried a few more times without any result. Just as he was putting the phone back into his pants pocket, it rang. He pulled it back out and almost dropped it on the floor. He was thinking it was Zander. He was wrong.

He answered and heard Jo's voice. She sounded distraught.

"Hey Jo, what's shaking?"

"We just got a call from the guy who bought the café from the gal in Sterling."

"Is everything all right?"

"No. You need to get to the office right away. We need to know how to proceed."

"I'll be right there."

Fats didn't usually see Jo in a state of panic. But here it was, throwing him off his game. He yelled at one of the regulars to watch the place while he stepped out for a while.

He headed down the street, and in a few minutes he walked into Bert and Jo's office. Jo didn't give him time to say anything.

"They worked him over, and he had to give them our names. He just called to let us know they were coming."

"Who and what. Catch me up."

Bert and Jo took turns reminding Fats about Herbie, Gail, and the biker gang.

"How many are coming?"

"The cook thought that just the three who got beat. Sounds like they are looking to avenge the humiliation they experienced."

"So, are they planning to work you over as well, until you give up

Herbie and Gail?"

"That's the idea."

"We just cannot allow that to happen," Fats said.

"What can we do?"

"You're going on vacation. Make a sign on your computer saying that you'll be gone until February. We want it to look like it wasn't made in haste because of any panic on your part."

Fats grabbed a piece of paper on Bert's desk. As he worked on the sign's wording, Jo was talking.

"Where will we go?"

"It doesn't matter. You can leave or just go home for a bit. When these assholes see the sign, they'll come looking for me."

"How do you know?" Both Jo and Bert asked together.

"Because that's what the sign will say. In your absence, if people need service they can contact me at the bar."

"Do you think it will work?" Jo asked, not convinced.

"Absolutely. I would conjecture that these barbarians are too young to have much patience. They aren't going to wait around for you to return. They want answers and they want them now. I believe I can give them everything they need."

Bert and Jo had confidence that he could do just that.

"Well, we're not going to stay around here. I've got a friend in Glenwood Springs. It is time for a visit. I think we can even take in the hot springs. They should feel pretty good this time of year."

"You just stay put until I call and tell you it's safe to return. You should have a few hours before they get here. I wouldn't waste any time. Get the sign in the window, and get out of here."

"Do we have time to throw some things together for our little trip? I'll need a swimsuit if we're going to do the hot springs," Jo said.

"I was hoping we wouldn't need our suits," Bert said, and winked at Fats.

Jo punched him in the arm, but Fats thought she might like the idea.

"Sounds like a huge shopping experience for me."

"Okay. We can stop home and get our stuff." Unlike Jo, Bert didn't seem as excited to go on a shopping spree.

Fats went back to the bar. He would need to get prepared. He knew he would need more than his pool cue this go-around.

Herbie had told him that these guys packed pistols.

He had an old sawed-off double-barreled shotgun in the back room. He brought it out and laid it on the bar. There was a box of number four shotgun shells that he decided to modify.

Fats took out six shells, pried open the ends, and dumped out the shot into a glass. He could remember hunting as a teenager. He had a 410-gauge shotgun. They had much smaller shells, and he had to be quick to get a shot off at any birds he was hunting. When he changed to the twelve gauge, he was shooting too quickly and not letting the pattern spread. He missed a lot of pheasants, and that's when he decided to saw off the shotgun. His friends all thought he was nuts, but his bird count improved immediately.

He looked at the shot. It was steel now. It was lead in his youth, but the DNR boys decided that eating the lead shot that missed was poisoning too many animals. He wouldn't be using steel or lead shot on this hunting expedition, however.

Fats rummaged under the bar and found a box of rock salt. He had no idea why Jo would stock a box of rock salt in the bar. He thought he should remember to ask her about it sometime.

He filled the shells with the rock salt and closed the ends. He put two of the six shells into the shotgun and lined up the remaining four behind the bar. The gun fit nicely on the cooler below the beer taps. He could reach it easily in one motion, if and when, the time came. He didn't think these assholes would have the nuts to come all the way up to Frisco just to satisfy some stupid payback. He was quite wrong, however.

It was just after the lunch rush, when the three bikers walked into the Branchwater and took a table near the jukebox. Fran was about to go and wait on them, when Fats stopped her. He took her pad and pen and walked over to the table.

"Can I be of service to you boys?" Fats asked, trying to sound pleasant.

"Depends. Are you the guy we need to talk to about the real estate office down the street?"

Fats looked down at the speaker. He figured he was the leader since he was doing the talking. He wondered if he was the one who took the knife up the ass. He had noticed how he walked when he came in, and he thought he appeared to have a cob up his ass. Fats smiled at that visual.

"I'm not a realtor, but if you need help, I might be able to direct you."

"We're looking for a previous owner of a café down in Sterling."

Fats pretended to think about it.

"Sorry. I can't help you there. You'd have to talk to the owners, and I'm afraid they will be gone on vacation for quite a while."

"We know. We saw the sign, you dumbass."

Fats looked at the talker for an uncomfortably long time. He was trying to size him up. He was a big brute, and so were his two flunkies.

"This is my bar, so if you want to order something, I'd be happy to serve you. If your reason for being here is to insult me, then I'm afraid we aren't going to be able to do business together." Fats looked from one biker to the next.

"Well, what have we here? Are you a smartass?"

"I've answered to many things in my life. That may have been the one I could most relate to." Fats smiled.

"Wipe that damn smile off your face."

Fats decided to keep it in place.

"I've been looking at your leather, I can't see what it says on the back."

Once of the bikers turned around to show him their name.

"Los Piss Animas." Fats intentionally mispronounced the second word.

"That's pistoled, you dumbass."

"Dumbass, smartass, I wish you would make up your mind. I can't be both."

The three simply stared at Fats. They didn't seem to know quite what to make of him.

"You know," Fats, continued, "in my day, the bikers had some real names. You know, like Hell's Angels or Devil's Disciples. They wouldn't have been caught dead with anything like piss in their name."

The leader opened his jacket and pulled out a chrome 45 pistol and laid it on the table. Fats turned around and walked to his spot back of the bar.

"Got your attention, asshole?" The other two followed suit and laid their pistols on the table as well.

"I don't know, they look like nice pieces, I guess. I'm not much for handguns. Can't hit shit from over four feet."

"You might be surprised." He took his handgun and pointed it at Fats sideways like they do in the movies.

"I hear tell that you can't hit anything when you hold a handgun like that." Fats reached for his shotgun. "Now this thing in contrast, well, you can hold it any which way and still hit anything you point at."

The three were uncharacteristically quiet.

"I've enjoyed our little chat, but now I believe it might be time for you to move along." He put the remaining four shells on the top of the bar. "I've got two barrels with two triggers. I can take two of you out before the third guy can get his gun up and aimed, and by that time I will have reloaded."

"I don't think you can get all three of us," the leader said weakly.

"Maybe not, but you'd be first anyway. The irony is that you will never know how it turns out. Put your gun on the table."

"No."

Fats yelled at the card players. "You boys better move. I'd hate to have you get hit. I shouldn't miss him at this range, but one never knows."

They moved instantly and headed for the door. Fats saw some hand movement from the leader. He was going to make his play. Fats knew that the biker would want to shoot from a standing position, and that's what he needed. The leather coats the bikers wore would shield them pretty well from the rock salt, but their crotches were vulnerable.

Fats raised his shotgun the moment the prick started to stand and pulled the trigger. He always had been a quick shot but the salt did its job. The biker screamed as the salt blew into his junk.

Fats trained the gun on another biker but neither of them moved. Their guns remained on the table. Fats thought they might have been in shock. He cracked the shotgun open and pulled out the spent shell and inserted a new one.

"Two more shots. Where do you want it?' Fats asked. "Face or balls."

Both of them put up their hands.

"Good boys. Walk over here with your hands in the air."

They did as they were told. Neither of them realized it was salt that their buddy took in the groin. They thought he was dying.

"Fran, duct tape these boys' arms behind their backs." Fran did as she was told. When she was finished, Fats pushed them into chairs and taped their ankles to the legs of the chair. Fran went off to call 911.

"The sheriff should be here soon, and you can all explain what you are doing here."

"What about him? He's going to die if you don't get him some damn help." One of the bikers motioned to the leader with his head.

"He'll be fine. It's just salt. He won't be having any coitus for some time, however." Fats laughed at the joke. The biker seemed to be less of a prick at the moment, literally.

He went over and collected the handguns and looked them over.

"Boy, these things look nice. I might like to keep one of them. I'll bet Zander would like one as well." He put one on the bar top and hid the other two underneath.

"Which one of you got the knife up the breech?" Both just looked at him expressionless. "Up the butt, boys."

They looked over at the leader.

"You know, I thought he looked like he had a cob riding up his ass when he walked in."

The leader was just whimpering now. Fats went over and kicked him in the gut.

"Would you call that a smartass or dumbass move?" The leader wasn't talking.

"So my thought is that you guys are out on bail, and then you come up here and try to push your weight around. Not the smartest move. I'm thinking the sheriff will bring you back and your bail will be revoked. No more riding your bikes, although someone might be riding you. You'd all be young fresh meat."

Fats thought he saw panic in two of their eyes. The leader wasn't in any shape to show much panic. Fats put the shotgun on the bar next to the pistol and sat down to wait for the sheriff.

It didn't take long, and there were sirens and lights flashing in the street outside the bar. Fats got up and looked out. He counted three law enforcement vehicles. He thought it might have been overkill, but Frisco was a pretty quiet place and not much excitement for law enforcement. Fats took his place behind the bar.

The deputies barged into the bar with their guns drawn. Fats raised his hands in the air just in case one of the deputies was trigger-happy.

Fats pointed to the three bikers with his hands still raised.

"The guys you want are over here. I'm Fats, the owner of the bar."

Of course they all knew that. Some of the deputies were regulars. The sheriff walked in almost simultaneously. Fats lowered his hands and began explaining what had happened. He included Bert and Jo's role because he knew they were friends with the sheriff. When he had what he needed, the sheriff spoke:

"A busy day, huh?"

"It gets one's blood flowing, don't you think?" Fats asked back.

"I'll need that pistol for evidence. Was that the only weapon?"

Fats looked at the two taped in the chairs. "Anything else boys?"

The two shook their head "no."

"I ask because this gang is known for their pistols. It seems strange that only one would be carrying."

"It's lucky for them, or they would have been on the floor with their buddy."

The deputies were helping the biker to his feet making sure his hands were handcuffed behind his back.

"Lenny, get him to the hospital and checked out. Then put him in a cell," the sheriff said, and then turned to the other two, "Lock up his buddies here. I'll be right over and make the call to Sterling and have them send over someone to take these idiots back. I don't want to have to deal with them any longer than I need to."

"Sounds reasonable," Fats said.

The sheriff got up and turned to leave, and then he turned back. "I'll need to have your shotgun for a while."

"I understand. I'll feel a bit naked without some protection here, however."

"Well, you've got two nice pistols, I'm thinking. Just keep them out of sight until this whole thing blows over."

Fats smiled and the sheriff walked out the door. Fats knew it was always good maintaining a friendly relationship with law enforcement. It was something he had tried to instill in Zander over the years. Zander had always shown a great deal of mistrust when it came to dealing the law. Fats had always been there to try and diffuse any hard feelings it might have created.

Suddenly, Fats remembered what he had been doing before this big distraction happened. He took out his phone and checked it. No missed calls or messages.

He tried to call Zander again.

40

After dinner, Max and Mona took their wine glasses and sat on the patio. It was cool, so Max started his propane fire pit. They huddled around watching the flames dance. Mona loved watching fire. It had such a mesmerizing effect on her.

Max let the time slip away for a while. He liked the quiet and the fire, but mostly, he liked sharing it with someone for a change.

"What did you do in the day?" Mona asked Max.

Max looked at her, puzzled.

"I mean, what did you do for a living?"

Max looked away. Here it came. He knew he would have to be truthful with Mona if there were to be any kind of relationship.

"I think we're going to need some more wine." He filled their glasses.

"You weren't some kind of criminal, were you?" Mona sounded alarmed.

"I suppose that would depend on who you talked to." He took a long drink from his wine glass.

"Maybe you'd better start from the beginning."

Max nodded his head in agreement.

"I was a military man. Made the Green Berets and saw action in Viet Nam."

"We studied that in history. It was a war that wasn't."

"That's what they said in the media. I think they called it a conflict back then. But, don't let anyone fool you. It was war. We had about ten guys in our division with some special skills. They made us go out into Cambodia and Laos to look for MIAs. We didn't have a name, we just went out and did what needed to be done."

"Do I detect some sadness in your voice?" Mona asked, interested in his story.

"Nobody will ever know the atrocities that were committed in the name of saving the world from communism. We weren't immune either, but you never knew who your enemy was. Our base employed a lot of nationals. One night we had a firefight with a number of Cong that got into the camp. The next morning I saw the base barber in those black pajamas they wore back then. He was dead, and we discovered that he was part of the group that wanted to kill us. He had given me a shave the day before. It shook me up. After that, I just did what we were told and never questioned the orders. Most of us used the excuse that we didn't want to die there for something we didn't even understand."

"How does anyone come back from that?" Mona asked.

"Many of the guys didn't, and those that did were massively screwed up."

"How about you?"

Max sat back and took some more wine. "There were ten of us that had a skill set the military didn't want to lose. After Viet Nam, we were mustered out but became employees of the government. I guess you would have called us a secret organization. Hell, we didn't even know who was giving the orders. Some of the guys thought we were working for the CIA. I think it went deeper than that, but we weren't being paid to ask questions."

"What were you being paid to do?"

"We were off the books. We did what the military wasn't allowed to do. If we were caught, there was no one to help us. We were on our own."

"You are scaring me."

"I scared myself. I won't tell you what we did. I'm not proud of it, but you need to remember that we were trained to carry out orders. We were paid well, and I was able to put away an obscene amount of money."

"Did you have to kill people?"

"Yes. Some of them deserved it. Some of them got in the way. Our job was to keep the peace by taking out our enemies. We were told who our enemies were, and we followed orders. That's how we justified our actions. That's all I'm going to say about it."

"You're not involved now?"

"No. I retired years ago when I met my wife. We had a good life. I had more money than I ever could spend, so life went on."

"I can't believe they just let you walk."

"You need to remember that times were changing, and each branch of the military started training their own secret groups. There was no shortage of private contractors to pick up the jobs the military couldn't or wouldn't do. You've heard of Black Ops?

"Sure. The movies show a lot of that stuff."

"Well, we were the Pre-Black Ops. We didn't have a name. Some of the guys called us Dark Shadows. There was a TV soap opera in the late sixties with that name. It was about a bunch of vampires. It was kind of a joke, but we spilled a great deal of blood just like the show did."

Mona sat quietly for a moment. "Why are you telling me all this?"

"I don't like secrets. My whole life has been a huge secret, and I'm finished with it. If we are to have any kind of relationship, it has to be based on truth and trust. Anything less won't work."

Mona didn't want to say anything. She thought about her own life and realized that Max was right. Secrets wouldn't serve either one of them.

Max looked over at Mona and saw she was struggling with something. He poured her some more wine.

"It looks like you might have something you wish to get off your chest. Before you do, I need to clear up a few more things." He paused and they both drank some wine. "Nobody just gets out of that life, alive at least. Those of us that survived had to agree to help out whenever called upon. Those that didn't agree simply disappeared. We moved down here to get away from the fray and haven't been called on to do much over the years. Now that I'm older, they ask me to do some reconnaissance from time-to-time. That's about it."

Mona looked relieved. "When is the last time?"

Max took her hand. "We wouldn't be having this conversation if I hadn't been watching this Bonnie character."

Mona was confused. "You've been watching us?'

"Not 'us.' You were never part of the assignment."

"What assignment?"

"The Feds have their eye on her for human trafficking in Colorado. I'm supposed to check her out to make sure she's not up to her old tricks. It's coming from the federal marshal's office."

"You know she's running an escort service."

"Yes. It's not illegal I'm afraid."

"I think she killed one of the girls."

Max put down his glass.

"Are you sure?"

"Pretty positive, but I don't have the proof. She tried to kill me, so I'm thinking she had it done to that poor girl. They had words, and the next week they found her face down in the ocean, dead."

"This changes things."

"Maybe it's time for me to get that thing off my chest that you were talking about earlier." Mona smiled.

She told him everything. It was a long story that went back to her chance meeting with Lilly to being hired by Fats to keep track of Sara Jane. Max listened intently and never said anything to disrupt the flow of her story. She finished with her swim to the island.

"I guess we all have our secrets," Max said, putting his arm around Mona.

"I haven't been able to contact Fats. I'm sure he's worried about me," Mona said.

"Let's call him. You need to let him know what's happening."

"Maybe tomorrow. Right now we've got better things to do."

Max smiled. "Like what?"

"We've got to move all my stuff into your bedroom."

That simple statement was enough for Max to realize that their mutual truths had changed nothing.

41

Fats knew he couldn't give up. He had two people trying to find clues on Mona's whereabouts.

He tried calling Herbie. Herbie answered almost immediately.

"What's with you, you have a sixth sense or something? I just now pulled into Stock Island." Herbie was happy to hear Fats' voice.

"Where in this vast planet is Stock Island?" Fats asked.

"Just north of Key West. Most people wouldn't know it isn't part of the island. I'm looking for a place to park the truck."

"I've been trying to call Zander. He's not picking up."

"I know. I've been doing the same with no luck at all."

"Doesn't that send up any red flags? Are you not concerned?" Fats asked.

"Think about it. When has Zander ever behaved the way most people would expect? Besides, you know how he feels about phones. Have you called his answering service?"

"More times than I care to count."

"What do you want me to do?"

"Find the shithead, and call me with any news."

Fats gave Herbie all the information he had on Sara Jane, including the address of her business that Mona had supplied.

"Do you know where he's staying?"

"I think it's a hotel close to the Aphrodisiac. There are only a couple in that area."

"OK. I'll find him and let you know what's happening."

Fats phone beeped. He saw it was a Florida prefix.

"Just a minute, I'm getting a call from down there and I don't recognize the number. Hang on, I'll put you on hold." Fats clicked off.

"This is the Branchwater, how may I help you?"

"Fats, it's Mona."

"Holy shit! Do you know how many people are looking for you?"

"I can only imagine."

"Listen, I'm going to send someone over to talk to you. He just got into Key West. His name is Herbie. Zander is down there as well, but we've lost contact with him."

"You'd better pray that Bonnie hasn't found him."

"That's my concern. I need to know where you are and how Herbie can find you."

Mona gave Fats the information and began telling him the story. Fats stopped her.

"I'm going to put you on hold so I can talk to Herbie. Don't go away, I want to hear everything. Damn, I wish I was there." Fats loved the mystery.

He clicked back on Herbie and explained how he was to find Mona.

"Do you want me to look for Zander first?" Herbie asked.

"No, just get yourself over to Sunset Key and get the details from Mona. You'll have to take the ferry over. She's with a guy named Max. Find his place. She'll be waiting for you." Fats barked out his orders in staccato.

"I'll get back to you as soon as I can. It might take a while. I'll need to find a ride down there. I can't take the truck into Key West. There's just no place to park it."

"I'll wait for your call." Fats hung up on Herbie and switched back to Mona.

"All right my dear. Let's have the story, and don't leave out one detail."

Mona did what she was told.

42

Zander walked down to the bar in his hotel at 7:30. He would have a drink or two and wait for Sara Jane to make good on her dinner date. He didn't know if she would show up, but he thought he noticed something in her demeanor that assured she'd show.

The bar was full. He found the only empty stool near the door. The place was bustling. It reminded Zander of working at The Bridge in Breckenridge. The thought made him sad, somehow. He didn't know why.

The bartender came over and threw down a napkin.

"What can I get you?"

Zander didn't hesitate. "Vodka martini, straight up with Stoli's and three olives. He had decided he needed some liquid courage, and martinis always did the trick.

The bartender left, and Zander took some time to look around. It looked like the place was filled with tourists. Many of them had bright red faces from too much sun. Zander never understood the attraction of getting sunburned and then feeling miserable. Maybe that's why he had been attracted to the Colorado Mountains.

The bartender returned with his drink, and Zander shoved some money at him.

"I'll just be having this one drink. Keep the change."

The bartender smiled and did what he was told.

Zander sipped his drink. He didn't like martinis but he thought it would be better to get a little buzz before talking to Sara Jane. He didn't have much time, so the drink would serve the purpose.

He had almost finished his drink when he caught a glimpse of Sara Jane coming in the front door. His place at the bar was a good vantage point. He stirred the last of the vodka with three olives still on the long toothpick. He caught Sara Jane's eye, and she walked into the bar and stood next to Zander.

"This place is crazy. Might be a while before we can get a table." Zander said, and finished the vodka.

"We've got reservations. It's high season. You can't go anywhere down here for dinner without them."

"Can I get you something to drink?"

"I'll have some wine at the table. They are ready for us." She turned and walked toward the dining room. Zander followed.

The hostess smiled at Sara Jane. It was obvious to Zander that they knew each other. He wondered in what capacity that might be. She was a cute young thing and brought them to a table.

Zander resisted helping Sara Jane with her chair. He sat down quickly and opened the wine list.

"Any preference?" he asked Sara Jane.

"Red and dry."

Zander waited for the server to arrive. He decided not to start the conversation.

"So, why are you here?" Sara Jane was always direct.

"I think we've already had that conversation."

"That's what you told me. But I would like to know why you are here."

Zander hadn't thought about the question previously. Why the hell was he here? Maybe he should ask Fats. He decided to remain mute.

"Was it you that Avon was contacting?" Sara Jane asked.

"No." Zander decided to keep his conversation short but noticed a hint of panic in Sara Jane's eyes.

They both sat looking at each other. Zander was hoping she was feeling uncomfortable. It would be nice to share that feeling with her.

The server arrived with the menus, breaking the silence.

"Bring a bottle of your Dry Creek Poizin." Zander hoped the reference to poison would have unnerved Sara Jane just a bit. It didn't.

"A zinfandel. I usually prefer the cabs," she said, simply.

"You should have said so when I asked. I'm not much for second guessing."

"And yet, here you are." She smiled.

Zander didn't like it, but he looked at the menu to avoid her gaze.

"What do you recommend?" he asked.

"You are in the Keys, so seafood."

"I think I'll have the brisket," he said, and closed the menu with a snap.

Sara Jane stared at him. "Is there something you want to say to me?"

"There's quite a bit I want to say to you, but most of it would be inappropriate in a setting like this. The one thing I will ask, why did you run?"

"I didn't run. I just left."

"You left without saying anything or letting anyone know where you were going." Zander was trying to keep his voice from rising.

"A lot happened. I needed to get away and leave that part of my life behind. You had your own issues to deal with, and I didn't want to add to them."

"I don't believe that for one minute." Zander wasn't buying her explanation.

She stopped and reached for her purse on the floor. After rummaging around in it, she brought out a card.

"I never got rid of this. Why do you suppose that was?" She slid the card over to Zander.

He picked it up and saw it was his card. "I have no idea."

"It's because I was going to contact you, when I felt the time was right," she said.

She pulled out a second card. It was the one Zander had given her in the shop.

"Now, I even have your phone number." She showed Zander the second card.

"All pretty meaningless if one has no intention of using either of them."

"It will remain to be seen, won't it?"

Zander was getting tired of the "cat and mouse" exchange.

"Why did you want to meet me?" Zander asked, taking a swallow of his wine.

"You surprised me. I wanted to know why you were here."

Zander told her the whole story. He felt she needed to hear the truth from him. Maybe some of the truth would rub off on her as well. One could always hope, anyway.

"So you see, Fats meant well. But now he's concerned that his actions may have caused some irreversible harm. Your name keeps coming up. Well, one of your many names."

Sara Jane pretended that she didn't catch the sarcasm in Zander's voice. There was some relief in her own voice, when she responded.

"So it was Fats all along. I was concerned that Avon, or whomever she is, was communicating with someone far more sinister."

"Oh, you mean like the law? You may have a few skeletons they would like to uncover don't you think?"

Sara Jane looked over at him. "You and Fats have a few of your own, I believe."

"Neither one of us have any desire to turn your past over to the law. I'm not proud of everything in my past, but yours repulses me. I'm just here to find Avon." He paused. "Time for more truth. Her name is Mona. She and Lilly are friends. I guess Lilly was responsible for keeping her from Rooster's hooks. That means she kept her safe from you as well."

The conversation, filled with innuendo and accusation, was going nowhere. The server, asking for their order, interrupted the tension.

"I'll have the red snapper, house salad with blue cheese. No potato."

Zander looked at his menu and softened just a bit. "I'll have the same but with the crab bisque and steak fries."

Zander ordered another bottle of wine, and the server left.

"You won't be sorry with the fish. It is excellent."

"I hope not, I've been sorry about so much in the past. This would just be one more thing wouldn't it?"

Can we please try to be civil to each other, at least for the evening?" Sara Jane asked.

Zander thought about it. He decided it would be a good idea. He needed information from her, and he was pretty sure adding too much vinegar wouldn't yield the results he wanted. He would soften his tone, and try to carry on a pleasant conversation.

• • •

As Zander was stumbling to change his tone with Sara Jane, Herbie entered the bar and took a stool with a view into the dining area. He ordered something with rum in it and settled back to keep his eye on Zander.

He had booked a room in the same hotel and was sitting in the lobby with a newspaper, when Zander strolled through and entered the bar.

Herbie had kept his position until he thought it was safe to go to the bar and get just a bit closer without revealing himself. He had watched with some pleasure at a conversation that didn't look very amiable. Herbie didn't have much time for Sara Jane, because she had totally ignored him most of his formative years. He always thought Zander could have done much better.

Herbie couldn't hear what Sara Jane was saying, and Zander had his back to him. He had to be content just to watch. It was a boring job, and soon he was trying to watch what was going on in the bar as well.

He was watching a young couple at a table off to the side. The young man had his hands all over the pretty young woman. Herbie thought they must be newlyweds spending their honeymoon in the Keys. Then he thought they were two lovers having an affair away from their normal lives. He liked that idea. It would be a story worth writing, and Herbie thought he could make it worth reading as well.

He was still watching the couple, when he felt someone sit down near him. There was a bar stool between them, but he could sense his presence as he sat down. The guy pulled up one of his legs with both hands and placed it on the foot ring at the base of the chair.

Herbie thought he must have some disability. He pretended not to be paying attention. He heard the guy order a Canadian Club whiskey with cola. Herbie wondered why people drank whiskey with mixers that masked the taste. Herbie thought it was a waste of good whiskey. He could have just as well have ordered vodka.

Herbie turned toward the guy after he got his drink. "Ever tried that with club soda or just water? It's pretty fair whiskey to waste with cola."

"I drink what I like. I also mind my own business."

Herbie looked at the guy. "Subtle. I was merely trying to carry on a conversation, but I can see that it is wasted on you."

"Now you've got it." The guy sneered.

Herbie didn't like being the subject of a sneer.

"Something wrong with your leg?"

"You don't take a hint very well, do you?" The Gimp took out a knife and unfolded it in front of Herbie.

It was a nice-sized knife, and Herbie admired it as the Gimp pretended to clean his fingernails with it.

"So did your knife slip and cut your hamstring? Is that what's wrong with you?" Herbie smiled.

The Gimp brought the knife down below the bar and pointed it at Herbie. "Maybe you'd like a taste."

Herbie looked at the knife, and then reached down and rolled up his pant leg. His hunting knife looked more like a machete strapped to his leg.

"That's a nice knife, but it's not very big." He motioned to his own knife. "This is a big knife. I always thought having a bigger knife was a distinct advantage. What do you think?" Herbie wasn't asking, just having some fun.

The Gimp looked at Herbie while he rolled his pant leg back down. He decided to fold his own knife and put it away.

"Good move," Herbie said, as Fabiano put the knife back in his pocket.

Herbie decided that a friendly conversation wasn't going to happen. He decided to split his time watching Zander and the couple at the table. He was disappointed however; the couple was gone. Zander and Sara Jane were still in the dining room and seemed to be more amiable. That was somewhat disappointing to Herbie. He was even more disappointed to see the guy with the knife paying attention to Zander and Sara Jane as well. His focus changed immediately.

• • •

Zander and Sara Jane were finishing their dinner. The wine was having the desired effect on both of them. Zander wasn't nearly as upset with her as he had thought. Sara Jane wasn't as guarded as she had planned.

Zander was tired of sitting. He called the server over, and asked for the check. When she brought it over, Sara Jane grabbed it.

"I invited you out for dinner. It's my check," Sara Jane said.

Zander decided not to argue. She threw down some cash and stood. Zander took her arm and they strolled out of the hotel restaurant. It was a typical warm December night for the Keys. Zander liked being able to wear shorts in the middle of winter. He thought about the temps in Frisco and could only smile.

"Let's take a walk," he said, not waiting for an answer.

There weren't many people left on Duval except for the revelers. The bars were full, and music was coming out of all of them. Key West was a pretty good place for people making a living at being musicians. Zander thought it would be fun at first, but he didn't know how long it would take before it became tedious. It was no wonder that drugs became so prevalent. It would hard to get up for performances without them.

They walked for a block or two, and Zander noticed a place where machines distributed slushy drinks into plastic cups. Zander picked out a couple of medium-sized cups and ran two rumrunners into them. He paid the girl and they walked down the street with drinks in hand.

"I can't believe this place. Where else in the US can you walk down the street with a drink and not get into trouble?" Zander asked.

"New Orleans," Sara Jane replied simply.

"Never been there. Thought about stopping off while driving out here, but Fats put me on a plane instead."

"Out of his concern for Avon or Mona?"

The sarcasm wasn't lost on Zander, but he decided to ignore it. They walked back to the Aphrodisiac, enjoying the balmy evening. Zander marveled at the Christmas lights around the island. They seemed out of place in this climate. He hadn't thought much about Christmas at all. It just didn't seem appropriate, and yet it was right around the corner.

Sara Jane broke the quiet. "What are your plans?"

Zander looked at her. "What do you mean?"

"Are you staying around for a while?"

"Yes. I'll need to find out what happened to Mona. I should think you would want that information as well."

"Of course. But you may not find anything. People have a way of evaporating in the Keys. Mostly by design."

"Unless you have something you wish to share concerning her whereabouts, I think I'll just poke around a bit more."

"Suit yourself. It looks like I'm home." She pointed at the front door.

Zander finished his drink and handed the cup to Sara Jane.

"Thanks for the dinner. You were right. The fish was excellent. I'll have to try more of it while I'm here."

"Would you like to come in for a nightcap?" Sara Jane asked.

Zander pointed to the cup in her hand. "I think I just had it. I'm going to call it a night."

Sara Jane shook her head. "I enjoyed your company. Can we do this again?"

"I'll stop in tomorrow and have a look at Mona's things. I'll talk to you then." Zander wasn't about to make any commitments.

"There's no time like the present. I might not be available tomorrow. Why don't you come up and have a look right now?"

Zander thought it might not be a good idea, but he could be strong when needed. He didn't know what Sara Jane had in mind, but everything would be on his terms.

"Fine. Let's go up and have a look."

Sara Jane led the way up to the bedroom and showed Zander

Mona's closet. Zander poked around the room for a few minutes. He wasn't finding much of anything. He walked over to a nightstand and opened the drawer. He saw a book and a tube of some kind of moisturizer. There was nothing here to draw attention to any kind of foul play, but he wasn't expecting to find anything. He knew Sara Jane pretty well.

He was closing the drawer, when he felt Sara Jane's hand on his back. He was aroused instantly. He turned around quickly, and Sara Jane pulled herself close to him and kissed him with an open mouth.

Zander was powerless. He pulled her top over her head ripping one of the seams. He didn't care. He was past caring. Sara Jane was pulling at his belt buckle while wriggling out of her skirt.

Zander didn't bother unhooking her bra, but ripped it off. Her breasts were still beautiful. They were everything he remembered.

He pulled off his shirt and shorts, and soon the only piece of clothing between the two of them was Sara Jane's panties. Zander worked down from her lips to her waist, kissing every inch of her skin. It wasn't slow and sensual, however. It was rough and wild. He pulled down her panties and buried his head.

Sara Jane was lost in the moment, and Zander took her in his arms and threw her on the bed. He was an animal, and she responded in kind. She clawed his back when he entered her. She arched her back and was thrusting just as hard as Zander.

Minutes later, Zander got up and dressed. He hated himself for what just happened. He knew Sara Jane had manipulated him again. He was helpless around her, and it pissed him off. The sex was rough and not something Zander participated in, ever. Yet here he was, looking and acting more like an animal than a human being. If she hadn't been fully participating, it might have been close to rape. Zander wondered who actually would have been the rapist.

What puzzled Zander was the fact that this seemed to be the most engaged Sara Jane had ever been while having sex with him. Zander hated himself for giving in and becoming such an animal. The more he thought about it, he knew the animal was still lying on the bed.

Sara Jane smiled and got up and put on a sheer robe. Her assets were still very visible. She walked to the front door in front of Zander. Neither of them said anything. She unlocked and opened the door in one smooth movement. She smiled at Zander again as he stepped out into the night air. She closed the door and was gone.

Apparently, no words were needed.

•   •   •

When Zander and Sara Jane left the restaurant earlier, Fabiano got up from the bar and followed them. Herbie waited a few minutes and followed. It was easy for Herbie to tail him. His limp was noticeable even in the dark. Fabiano was pulling the almost useless leg behind him. The leg made a sound on the concrete that was unmistakable to anyone's ear, unless they were hard of hearing.

Fabiano kept his distance. He didn't want Sara Jane to know he was following her. Herbie crossed the street and kept in the shadows whenever possible. It was sloppy by both parties, and anyone worth their salt would have noticed either one of them immediately.

When Fabiano figured the couple was heading back to the Aphrodisiac, he shot down an alley and made his way to the shop to wait for them. Herbie decided to keep Zander and Sara Jane in his sight. He didn't know what the guy with the limp was doing, but he felt he would better serve Zander by keeping an eye on him.

The players were all in place…almost.

43

Zander turned to make his way back to the hotel. He hadn't taken five steps, when he saw a shadow to his left coming from the side of the building. He stopped, wondering if he needed to be concerned.

He didn't have to wait long. The shadow emerged, and Zander could see the owner was dragging his left foot. It was the guy with the limp he had seen coming out of the Aphrodisiac. He relaxed a bit. He was sure he worked for Sara Jane in some capacity. It seemed to be more of a charity case judging from the way he looked.

Zander walked on, and just before he met Fabiano, he stopped short. He thought he noticed movement in the store window. He couldn't be sure if it was inside the store a reflection from something on the street.

Suddenly there was a knife at Zander's throat.

"Whoa. What's this all about?" Zander felt for his stun gun in the cargo pocket of his shorts. He realized instantly that he had left both his switchblade and stun gun back at the hotel. Suddenly, he felt very naked.

"You need to leave Miss Bonnie alone."

"She's an old friend. That's all." Zander was trying to lower the guy's anxiety level. He didn't particularly care for the knife at his throat.

"I know why you're here. You're looking for Avon."

Zander realized instantly that Sara Jane was communicating with Mr. Limps.

"Is that a problem?" Zander asked.

"She's dead. You'd be dead right now, but Miss Bonnie won't let me. She says you might have some information she might need down the line."

Zander realized that Limps was saying more than Sara Jane wanted him to. He decided to try and keep him talking, since he had a knife to his throat.

"I think you've made your point. How about you take the knife away from my jugular?"

"I think I might leave you a little something to remember me by." Fabiano put pressure on the knife.

Zander thought he could feel some skin open under the pressure.

"I'd like to keep whatever blood I have left inside my veins." Zander said, trying to remain calm.

"You trying to be a funny guy?"

"Not really. I just need to know what you want from me."

"I want you to go away."

"I'm not planning to stay. I just need to put some things in place, and I'll be gone."

"No. Now. You leave now. Tonight. If you do, I won't kill you."

Zander was becoming angry. He knew it wouldn't do any good pissing Limps off with the knife at his throat. All he could do is wait until he decided what the next move was going to be.

Across the street, Herbie had just stumbled onto Zander's plight. He bent over and pulled up his pant leg. Just as he was ready to remove the knife, he felt a hand on his shoulder.

"Don't move."

Herbie froze. The voice wasn't familiar.

"My friend's in trouble across the street."

"I know. You're Herbie right?"

Herbie nodded his head. "The guy is going to cut Zander's throat. I need to move."

"You don't need to get involved. Let me handle it." The stranger moved and began crossing the street.

"I'm Max, by the way," he said, quietly, "Mona and I were expecting your call. We got worried when we didn't hear from you. Now I'm here."

Max crossed the street and pulled out a pistol. He screwed a suppressor onto the barrel as he walked. Fabiano's back was to the street, and he didn't see Max's approach until it was too late.

Max put the gun to his head. "Drop the knife, or I'll put you down right here."

It took Fabiano a few seconds to realize what was happening. Max could feel Fabiano's muscles tighten; he knew something was about to happen, so he preempted it. Max kicked Fabiano's left leg hard, right behind the knee. Fabiano went down on his back instantly. Max moved his pistol and put it right between his eyes. Fabiano saw the suppressor on the gun. He decided to relent.

Max got up close and personal. "I'm going to say this once, so you'd better listen closely." Fabiano nodded in agreement. "You will leave my friend here, alone. Look across the street. You will leave that guy alone, as well."

Fabiano agreed again by nodding his head. Max bent over and whispered into his ear.

"I know what you tried to do. Avon isn't dead. She's with me. I'm telling you this, so you will know that if I see your face anywhere close to any of us, I will kill you where you stand. The good thing for you is you will never see it coming. I'm a very dangerous man, but I'm giving you this one chance to get out of this alive. There will be no other warnings."

Fabiano just stared at him. Max knew what Fabiano was thinking. Years of dealing with this kind of element had given him the ability to read people.

"One more thing," Max said, standing up.

Max pistol-whipped Fabiano into submission.

Fabiano wasn't completely unconscious, but he wasn't going to be getting up anytime soon. Max took him by the legs and pulled behind a large flower planter. He tucked the gun away, and was wiping his hands on his pants as he crossed the street pulling Zander along as he moved toward Herbie.

"Hell of way to meet someone, don't you think? I'm Max, by the way." He stuck out his hand, and Herbie was the first to grab it.

"Fats told me that Mona was staying with you. Is she all right?" Herbie asked.

"She's fine. At home waiting for the two of you," Max replied, and then turned to Zander. "You must be the Zander I've heard so much about."

The comment took Zander by surprise, and his face showed it.

"Don't look so worried. Mona and I have no secrets, and I know all about you both. But we need to get going before he is able to move. I don't think he's one to take good advice to heart."

"We've both got a room at the hotel," Herbie said.

Zander was surprised again. He wondered what other secrets were bouncing around that he didn't know about. He didn't like surprises.

"You can't go back to the hotel. You have to believe that this character knows all about the two of you." He indicated Fabiano behind the flower planter.

Zander knew what that meant. It meant that Sara Jane knew everything as well.

"I have a friend with a boat, waiting, just down the boardwalk. You two will be staying with us tonight." Max smiled, as he realized he had referred to his home in the plural.

Max led the way to the boat. They made the short trip to Sunset Key. Both Herbie and Zander wondered what would be happening next. Zander felt any control he thought he might have had slipping away. He didn't like it.

Herbie, on the other hand, was just along for the ride. He thought the ride was becoming quite interesting, and he wanted to see it to completion. He just hoped it wouldn't take very long. He was missing Gail and Mr. Peabody immeasurably.

Max talked about the island as the threesome walked the path to his house. Max did most of the talking, giving them the history of the area. There would be time enough to discuss options later. They would have the entire next day.

Max decided he would be going back to Key West alone the next evening. It was something no one else need know about.

44

Mona was waiting for them. She didn't know Herbie, and she had only seen Zander a few times. She decided it would be a good time to make new friends.

"Should I pour some wine?" she asked Max.

"I think we need something stronger. Are you two up for some bourbon?"

Both Zander and Herbie thought it would be a good idea. Max went over to the bar and brought out a bottle of Blantons. He put out four rocks glasses and poured three fingers in each. Zander figured there was fifteen dollars worth of whiskey in each glass. This was the good stuff. Normally he liked ice in his glass when drinking any booze straight, but this was too good to dilute.

Max gave everyone a glass and then raised it up.

"Here's to keeping Mona safe. If the three of us can't do it, it can't be done."

Max had meant the toast to be light, but it didn't sound right. The four drank anyway.

"Man, that's some fine bourbon." Herbie said, and finished off the remainder.

"What are we going to do about Bonnie?" Mona asked, getting right to the point.

"Her name is Sara Jane," Zander said, choking down his swallow.

It sounded harsh, and that hadn't been his intent. "I'm sorry, not used to drinking such a fine drink. I think we all need to be on the same page."

"Here's what I think. We'll have time tomorrow to discuss this. We ought to sleep on it. We can share our information when we've had time to process everything."

Max needed time to decide what to do. He knew he was going to have to go his own way. He couldn't trust anyone else with Mona's safety. He would make a call in the morning, and either he would get permission or not. It didn't matter to him in the least.

"Mona, why don't you show these two to the guest room? You boys can decide who gets the bed and who gets the foldout couch. Unless, of course, you'd rather sleep together in the same bed." He smiled.

"No thanks," Herbie said, "I'll take the bed."

"Like hell you will. I'm the one with long legs. You get the couch." Zander commanded.

"It was worth a try," Herbie said, following Mona toward the room.

Max put his hand on Zander's shoulder, stopping him. "Are we going to have a problem, given your history with this woman?"

Zander considered the question. "Yesterday, I would have said absolutely not, but after today, well, I just don't know how I feel."

"Thanks for being honest. I'll need to keep that in mind when we make decisions tomorrow."

"Do we have to rush into this? Wouldn't it be better to let things play out a little?" Zander asked.

"It has been my experience that once the snow ball starts rolling down the mountain one must get out ahead of it, or it will consume everything and everyone in its path. We're already past the fact-finding part of this."

Zander couldn't argue, and he moved to follow Mona and Herbie to the room. Max looked after him. Zander was going to be a problem. Max knew he would need to take care of everything on his own. He poured himself another drink.

"When you get settled, come back out for a nightcap. I'm going out to the patio and enjoy the night air." Max was moving out of the patio door.

Mona came out of the guest room, and told Max she had enough to drink and was going to bed. She would see him there if he didn't wait too long. Max smiled as she walked to the master bedroom. What a find in his old age. He would do anything to protect this unexpected delight.

Herbie came out to the patio with a filled glass and sat next to Max.

"Zander decided to call it a night. I think he's got a lot on his mind."

Max nodded. "I think you're absolutely right. You'll need to keep an eye on him the next few days, and make sure he doesn't do something to put us all in harm's way."

"He's smarter than that," Herbie said, believing it.

"He's in love with her." Max took a pull on the whiskey.

"I don't think so," Herbie said, weakly.

"Of course he is. You and I both know it. Love is a dangerous thing."

"Like you and Mona?"

"Exactly, so you know there is nothing I wouldn't do to protect her."

Herbie thought about it. He wondered what he would do in the same situation. Of course, he already knew. It had happened at the Sterling café. He would have killed all three of those guys if the situation had called for it. Suddenly, he didn't like being put in the middle of everything.

"What can I do?" Herbie asked.

"Keep him in your sights at all times. He can't be with this woman alone. Let me handle the rest of it. You won't have to worry about that."

Herbie felt a little better.

"What's going to happen to Sara Jane?"

"She's got to go," Max said, without emotion.

Herbie knew he didn't mean she just had to leave. He thought it was odd that he didn't disagree with the notion.

• • •*

Zander woke up the next morning smelling coffee brewing. He always liked the smell in the morning. Herbie was still sleeping on the couch, looking awfully uncomfortable. Zander smiled to himself. He would make it up to him.

Max was at the pub table drinking coffee and reading the paper. When he saw Zander, he got up.

"Good morning. How about some coffee?" He didn't wait for a response but poured him some in a mug with the name Sloppy Joe on it.

Zander wondered if it was lifted or purchased. He was sorry he even considered that idea. Max didn't seem like the type of person that would steal cups from a bar.

"Thanks," was all he said.

"Sleep well?" Max asked.

"Better than Herbie, I think." Zander smiled.

"Mona's in the shower. She wants to do breakfast for everyone. I offered but she wants to be in charge. I think it's her way of thanking you two for being here for her."

"She should go to Frisco and cook for Fats, then. He's the reason we are all here."

"I'll have to thank him in person some day." Max seemed serious.

"So, I might have some time to take a swim."

"Certainly." Max pointed out a good area that he used from time to time.

"One problem," Zander said, "I don't think it is a nude beach, and I don't have a suit."

Max went over to the bedroom and emerged with a flowered set of trunks that still had the tags on it.

"My wife bought these for me once. I never liked them. Keep them."

Zander went back into the bedroom and put on the trunks. Herbie was in the bathroom, and he could hear him singing in the shower. Zander was glad Herbie kept his singing confined to the bathroom.

The swimming area in front of the resort was empty. It was too early for most people. It would be a good time to get his workout in.

The water was cool, but he could tolerate it. He swam toward the pier and made his way back to the beach. On his third pass, there were other swimmers joining him in the water. He watched one woman who he thought was a serious swimmer. She had a number of different strokes and changed them up after every pass.

He was almost ready to call it quits, when he noticed a wave runner coming from Key West. It circled the area, staying out beyond the pier. It was just idling around slowly, which Zander felt was unusual. He kept his eye on it while he swam. As he approached the pier, the watercraft came close to the walkway.

Zander recognized the driver. It was Mr. Limp. He almost choked on a mouthful of water. He didn't think he had been recognized. It looked like he was checking out the shoreline. Zander was sure he looking to find Max or Mona.

Zander swam toward the beach, waited until the wave runner was pointed in the opposite direction, and made his move. He emerged from the water, grabbed a towel, and sprinted behind the cabana. He waited until the wave runner passed again and then he moved toward the path. He made sure he wasn't seen making his way back to the house.

The front door was open, and he burst in. "I just saw this Fabiano character on a wave runner out near the pier. It appears he's doing some recon."

"That's not good news. That means he knows we're on the island."

Mona almost dropped the fork she was using trying to flip the bacon over in a pan. She was visibly shaken up. Zander was sorry he had opened his big mouth.

"I don't think he knows where we are, or he wouldn't be looking during the daylight." Zander offered.

"Did he see you?"

"No, I'm sure he didn't. I was very careful."

"Good. Let's have breakfast," Max said.

Zander could see he was trying to lighten Mona's load.

Breakfast was cordial, and afterwards, Zander excused himself to get ready for the day. When he came back out, Herbie and Mona were sitting on the patio talking. The breakfast dishes were cleared, and the kitchen had been cleaned. Zander didn't see Max.

Mona saw Zander in the kitchen. "About time. You missed helping with the breakfast dishes."

"By design," Zander said, as he joined them. "Where's Max?"

"He had some errands to run. He wanted me to show you around the island. He said he'd be back in an hour."

"Sounds fine. So, when do we begin this little jaunt, Miss Tour Guide?"

"Right now. The island isn't large, so it won't take long. I want you to see the resort though. It is top notch."

The threesome left the house with Mona taking the lead.

Max had gone across the island with his backpack. He had a small storage unit on the commercial side. The unit wasn't much bigger than a walk-in closet. In fact, his closet back at the house was bigger. No matter, it was enough space for what he needed.

He punched in the code, and the door popped open. He flipped on the light and went over to a locked cabinet. There was a combination lock on it, and soon Max had it open. He opened the cabinet, and Max saw his arsenal was intact.

The bottom half contained a rack of various weapons. There were rifles and shotguns of different calibers, all tools of his former trade. The third shelf held handguns and knives. His focus today was on the top two shelves. The second shelf had various blocks of C-4 explosives. The top shelf had the ignition caps that were needed to detonate the C-4. He was careful with the caps. Each was contained in its own sealed plastic bag and then put into separate plastic containers. The C-4 was stacked neatly by size of the blocks. You could use it like modeling clay if there was no detonator, so it was safe enough by itself.

Max selected a small block of C-4, about the size of an aspirin bottle. He wanted a big explosion and some destruction but didn't want to cause any other collateral damage. He didn't want to cause a great deal of structural damage.

He wrapped the explosive in plastic and put it in a zippered compartment in his backpack. After it was secure, he selected a cap, a remote detonator, and put each in a separate area in the pack. He was ready. He wanted to get back home before Mona and the boys. The fewer questions asked, the better.

The pack was safely hidden in the pantry, when the three tourists arrived back at the house. Max was sitting on the patio with his ear to a cell phone. He waved at them through the window and pointed to his phone.

"Looks like Max is busy. Can I get you something to drink?"

"Just water for me," Zander said.

"Ditto," Herbie added.

Mona filled three glasses with ice and water from the refrigerator door. Zander marveled at the decadence. He wondered what his father would have thought about a fridge that was smarter than most of its users. He smiled at the thought. He father would have sold whatever fridge anybody wanted and kept his opinion to himself. Zander decided to do the same.

Max was on the phone to his superiors. He was retired but still had to answer to someone from time to time. He explained the situation. His handler was resistant at first, but changed his way of thinking when Max told him about the dead young woman who had turned up after the altercation with Bonnie or Jane or whatever her name was now.

After some wrangling by both parties, Max got the green light. It wouldn't have mattered one way or another. His mind was already made up.

45

After Sara Jane closed the door, she watched from the darkened shop as Zander moved down the sidewalk. She didn't know how to proceed. Zander's appearance had changed her perspective. She didn't like it.

She was ready to head up to the apartment above the shop when she heard something. She looked back toward the sidewalk and saw Fabiano with a knife at Zander's throat. Her instant reaction should have been to open the door and stop what might have been a tragedy. She didn't follow her instinct.

The scene somehow fascinated her. Fabiano could easily take the fall. After all, she hadn't sanctioned this. Why Fabiano would do something like this, without direction from her, was indeed a puzzle. She decided not to interfere, because Zander could take care of himself. At least that's what she told herself.

It surprised her to see a third man enter the picture. She couldn't quite make out his features in the darkness. She did notice the outline of his handgun, however. Sara Jane watched without much emotion as the shadow pistol-whipped Fabiano. She waited while Zander and the unknown man walked across the street. They were joined by a third person. It looked like a guy, but she couldn't see for sure. She watched as they disappeared down the boardwalk.

Sara Jane decided to wait to make sure they didn't come back. She went upstairs and put together some first aid supplies for Fabiano. She would try to patch him up in the office. He had never been invited to her living quarters, and she planned to keep it that way. Fabiano had repulsed Avon. She had never shared that same feeling, but there was something about him that wasn't quite right.

Fabiano was still lying behind the flower box when she reached him. He was alive and moaning. The shadow had done quite a number on him. Sara Jane put some smelling salts under his nose. He came to immediately. He grabbed her by the throat and then let go when he realized who was kneeling beside him.

"What happened?" He asked, thickly. His tongue wasn't working very well around his swollen lips.

"Looks like you tangled with the wrong person."

"More than one, I think." He spit out some blood on the sidewalk.

"I think you may be right."

She helped him up, and they hobbled into the shop and back to the office. Sara Jane did the best she could at patching him up. He didn't have any cuts deep enough to warrant stitches. That was good, the less people that needed to be involved, the better.

Sara Jane marveled at how most of his wounds seemed superficial, even though Fabiano was hurt quite badly. The guy was good at what he did. That might be a problem. She needed to find out who he was before she did much of anything else. When Fabiano seemed to recover after an hour or so, Sara Jane decided to press him.

"What in God's name did you think you were doing? Did I tell you to go around and hold a knife to someone's throat? You're lucky to be alive."

"He's lucky someone had his back, or he'd be lying on the sidewalk with his throat cut."

"And yet, here you are. All beat to hell."

"I didn't like the way he was treating you," Fabiano said, trying to take some pressure off.

Sara Jane's eyes flashed. "You were following me? Who told you to do that?"

Fabiano just looked away.

It hit Sara Jane right then. Fabiano had feelings for her. The thought made her shudder. Her good deed of making Fabiano an employee and taking him into her confidence would not go unpunished. She decided to ignore the thought.

You are not very smart are you?" Sara Jane said, and moved to sit behind her desk.

Fabiano looked like a whipped pup. He just looked at Sara Jane without blinking. Sara Jane looked back at him not breaking eye contact. She didn't want him to see the repugnance that was slowly creeping over her. Creeping was a good word. The longer she spent time alone with him, the more she could see why Avon had such a loathing for him. His limp didn't help either.

Sara Jane decided to forge ahead. "Don't you suppose people saw us at the restaurant tonight? Fabiano just stared. "So what would happen if the law found his body in front of my shop? Don't you think there would be questions to answer? Don't you think people might remember seeing you following us?"

"I didn't think about it. I just wanted to make sure you were treated with respect."

"I don't pay you to think. I pay you to take orders and do by bidding. That's it, there's nothing else. Do you understand that?"

Fabiano nodded. Sara Jane didn't think he was buying it, however. She decided to try a different tack.

"Who did this to you?" She indicated his beating by pointing to his face.

"The old guy."

"What old guy?"

"The guy that used to come in here and talk to Avon. You know, the guy who lost his wife. Avon said she felt bad for him. He was lonely."

"Didn't look very lonely tonight, did he?" Sara Jane asked, but her mind was already racing.

"He's not so much. I'm going to take care of him." Fabiano said, with some anger in his voice.

"Sara Jane raised her voice, "You'll do no such thing. You will do nothing unless I tell you. This might mean that Avon is alive. If that's true, I'm going to need you to do more than take care of the old guy."

Fabiano smiled. He liked the idea.

"What do you want me to do?" he asked.

"Right now, I want you to go wherever it is you go, and try and get some sleep. When you feel better, come back and we'll talk. I don't want you here until you feel better. I'll need you to be on top of your game."

Fabiano hobbled out of the office. Sara Jane thought he was

favoring his left leg more than usual. It wasn't all that unusual, she supposed, considering the beating he had just taken. She was quite surprised by his resilience. A beating like that would have grounded most people, but here he was, leaving on his own two feet. He was much tougher than she had anticipated.

She watched him walk out the door. Things seemed to be spiraling downward quickly. Just when she felt that she could lead her life in Key West without complications, everything seemed to be destructing all around her.

She turned off the light in the office, and sat in the dark, free from distractions. She needed to put something together. There were far too many loose ends. It angered her that she was thrust into this position. She would try to figure out a way to contain the problem, but she knew it was complex and she would need an exit strategy if everything went south.

46

When he finished with the phone call, Max joined the three in the house. Mona gave him a huge hug. It made Zander and Herbie uncomfortable. There was almost something sexual in that hug.

"Did you have the first class tour of the island?" Max asked.

"She's just an excellent tour guide," Herbie replied.

"Do you think it's time we discussed the situation?" Zander wanted to get right down to business.

"I don't think Bonnie's right-hand man will be doing anything very soon," Max replied. "So, I believe we have a little time to discuss where we go from here."

"Her name is Sara Jane. Now that we know Mona is fine and out of harm's way, I think we can forget the entire thing." Zander was resolute.

"She killed one of her girls," Mona said.

Zander turned toward her, "Was it her, or that Mr. Limp she has hanging around. He almost took me out last night. Maybe he's gone rogue."

"Do you believe that?" Max asked.

"I can't believe the alternative," Zander said, and looked out the window.

"I believe there might be facts about her that aren't in your purview."

Max got up and went into his bedroom and came out almost immediately. He tossed a file to Zander. It was thick, and Zander caught it with both hands. He began to page through it.

"There is quite a bit in there. Take your time and read everything. You should know everything about her."

Zander got up and went out to the patio with the file and began reading. Max went to the bar and poured a full glass of white wine and brought it out to Zander.

Herbie turned to Mona, "Who is this Max guy?"

"I think he's one of those guys who jokes that if you found out, he'd have to kill you. Only I don't think some people think it is a joke."

Herbie whistled. "Well, at least I'm happy he's on our side."

Mona nodded and smiled. "He saved my life."

Max walked back into the room and sat down across from Herbie.

"Tell me the back story concerning this Sara Jane woman," Max demanded.

Herbie told him everything. He even filled in some of what happened in Frisco and Breckenridge, from what Fats had told him. He did preface it by saying it was hearsay. That made Max smile.

"My whole career has been based on hearsay. It's how every situation begins. Sometimes we can use that hearsay to prove some factual data. Sometimes we can't. Sometimes it doesn't matter either way."

Herbie looked at him. "Do you think Sara Jane had anything to do with the attack on Zander last night?"

Max sat back and thought about how he would answer the question.

"You are asking me about something where there is no proof. So, I would have to speculate. If I were to make a guess, I would think this attacker acted alone. What the reason would be, one can't even guess. I just know, that from reading this Sara Jane's background, if she wanted Zander dead, we wouldn't be having this conversation right now."

"That would be a relief for Zander."

"Not so fast. There is no relief here. We've backed her into a corner. We've taken her man out of play. For how long, I just don't know. He was stronger than I anticipated."

"But Zander thinks the pressure is off now that Mona is safe."

"There are too many of her secrets walking around. She isn't sure who I am, but she sure as hell will know about you and Zander. I'm sure she suspects Mona is still alive, so that is another problem for her."

Max decided it would be better not to explain how he had told Zander's attacker that Mona was still alive. One way or another, Sara Jane would know the truth.

"How in the world would she know about Mona?" Herbie asked.

"Fabiano knows who I am. I've spent a lot of time in the Aphrodisiac talking to Avon. He recognized me right away. Sara Jane isn't stupid, she'll put it all together."

"Why do I get myself involved in situations like this?" Herbie asked himself.

"Because you're a good friend," Mona replied.

"We'll let Zander try to process everything. He's reading right now, but my feeling is, we're going to have to try and stick together on this thing. I'm afraid he'll do something to put himself at risk. Fabiano isn't finished. He'll come back for us. He'll do it with or without Sara Jane's blessing. Right now, I would think she'd do everything she can to clean up this mess."

"She isn't going to walk away from everything she's built here," Mona responded.

"Maybe, if she has no other choice," Herbie said.

"Let me worry about what happens next," Max said.

Zander was finished reading and walked back in with the file. He handed it over to Max.

"Can I look at it?" Herbie asked.

"No! You don't need to see what's in there. I can't believe half of it anyway."

Max stuck the file behind his back. "Believe what you want. Just know there is more to this woman than you ever imagined."

"Who are you, really?" Zander asked Max.

"I can't tell you much about me. Just know that I have Mona's best interests at the center of whatever I will do from here on out. Because of that, I'll have you and Herbie's best interests in the forefront as well, even if you don't see it right now."

Zander panicked for a moment. What did that mean?

"It sounds like you wouldn't be opposed to killing her." Zander was upset.

"It's not in the plan," Max lied, "but plans can change whenever warranted.

"I need to go back to the hotel and take a shower. I feel dirty," Zander growled.

"Maybe that would be for the best. I don't think anyone will be in danger for a few days. Just don't let down your guard. Stay vigilant and watch each other's back. When you have time to process everything, we'll decide how to proceed," Max responded.

Zander thought he was being placated, but he didn't care. He just needed to get away and think about things. Max was relieved that the two would be gone soon. He hadn't known how he was going to disappear later that evening without raising their suspicions.

Max looked at his watch. "There should be a ferry leaving in fifteen minutes."

Zander stood, and Herbie followed suit.

"Thanks for everything," Herbie said.

Zander stood for a moment, and then turned to Max and Mona.

"I'm sorry about my behavior today. I'm just not ready to deal with all of this."

"I understand," Mona said, and gave him a little hug. "If it means anything, I really liked her at first. There's just something always boiling below the surface."

Zander nodded. "She's broken, just like me."

"You are nothing like her." Herbie stomped out of the house incensed.

Zander turned to follow, but Max stopped him by putting his hand on his shoulder.

"You're a good man, but your heart is in the way right now. I'm going to ask you to stay away from Sara Jane, until we can sort everything out. You shouldn't try and make any contact whatsoever."

Zander nodded and walked out the door.

"I'm thinking he'll talk to her the first chance he gets," Mona said.

"Without a doubt."

Max knew what had to be done. He hoped Zander could get past it eventually.

47

The following day was bright and sunny. The climate didn't mirror Sara Jane's mood, however. Fabiano had no doubt taken her advice and holed himself up somewhere to recover. She told him not to come back until he felt better, but she was getting restless. She didn't like loose ends, and she wanted this Avon thing taken care of as quickly and quietly as possible. She couldn't do it on her own, and that was making her frustrated.

Sara Jane had been a manipulator all of her life. She was superb at it. She knew how to push the right buttons, and that helped her keep her hands from getting dirty. She had never let herself get into any tight spots, because she always had a strategy. Being two steps ahead of everyone around her had served her well. Maybe that was why she was feeling nervous and a bit angry. Put Zander into the mix, and she wasn't able to stay focused.

She heard the front door chime and almost jumped out of her chair. She looked over toward the door and saw Fabiano dragging his left foot up the carpet toward the office. She met him halfway.

"What are you doing here? I thought I told you to stay away until you healed up." Her voice was stern, but there was some relief there as well.

"I'm fine. My leg hurts where the old guy kicked me, that's all."

"If you say so. I think we need some intelligence on Zander and his friend. We need to find out what happened to Avon and how this old guy is connected." Sara Jane was good at using the word "we" when she actually meant "me".

"I'm way ahead of you. I tossed their hotel rooms after I left here last night. I didn't find much."

"How did you find their rooms?"

"The night desk clerk and I have some history. I gave him descriptions of the two, and he let me in their rooms. They didn't come back last night."

"How do you know?"

"I waited for them outside. They weren't here by 8:00 this morning, anyway. By the way, your friend's buddy goes by the name Herbert Schutt."

An alarm went off in Sara Jane's head. There couldn't be two people with that same name on the face of this earth. She had heard Zander speak of a Herbie Schutt when they were young. She hadn't really known him, but he was a big fat kid and repulsed her somewhat.

"Was he a big fat guy?" She asked Fabiano.

"No. He was taller than me but he was pretty thin. I think I sat next to him in the bar at the hotel."

Sara Jane was puzzled.

● ● ●

Herbie and Zander walked the boardwalk toward the hotel. Zander glanced over at the Aphrodisiac. Herbie stopped.

"You heard what Max said, right?"

Zander shook his head.

"Then don't even think about going over there right now. We need to let Max do whatever he has in mind. When he says it's okay, then you can talk to her."

"You're not my father."

"True, because if I was, I'd kick your ass." He turned and went into the hotel. Zander followed.

Herbie turned toward him in the elevator.

"Another thing, when you go over and see her, I'm going with you. You can't be with her alone."

"I don't need a baby sitter."

"Yes you do. You can't trust yourself with her. You lose all perspective. Fats told me some things about you two. I'm sure there is a lot more he left out, but I think I know enough to worry for your well-being."

"It's over between us. It has been for quite a while."

"Keep telling yourself that. I see things differently."

They were on the same floor, and when the elevator stopped, they both had their keys ready.

"Let's meet in the lobby in an hour. I need to shower and shave," Zander said.

Herbie nodded and decided he would go right down and wait for Zander, so he wouldn't have a chance to slip out without him.

When Zander opened his door, he could see the mess someone had left for him. His bag had been emptied on one of the chairs. The mattress was off the bedframe. Someone had definitely been after something. His phone rang. It was Herbie.

"Someone broke into my room."

"Same here."

"That's not good. We're going to have to change hotels."

"Someone wants us to feel intimidated. I'm not biting."

"Check your clothes," Herbie said and hung up.

Zander went over to the chair where his clothes had been dumped. Every piece of material had been cut. He couldn't wear anything. His shorts had the crotches cut out of them. Mr. Limps had been busy. He'd have to return the favor.

He went over to the small safe in the closet that the hotel provided. He had an envelope filled with bills that came to almost twenty thousand. At the last minute he had decided to put his switchblade and stun gun in the safe as well. Everything was there. The rest of his belongings could be replaced.

He stripped off his clothes from the previous day and hit the shower. He and Herbie would need to do some shopping later.

When Zander was ready, he put on the same cargo shorts and shirt but decided to go commando. It had been twenty minutes since he left Herbie, and he thought he could slip over to the Aphrodisiac without him even noticing.

Zander was disappointed when he reached the lobby. Herbie was waiting for him. Herbie smiled at his long face.

Zander tried to cover. "Good, you're here. I think we need to do a little shopping."

"Agreed." Herbie decided not to ask him why he was early. He knew. He also knew he would have to watch him closely.

They found a small store on Duval that had men's clothing. It was touristy but neither cared. They just needed items to get them by for a while.

"We need to find another hotel," Herbie said, as they left the clothing store.

"Got any suggestions? You seem to be in charge." Zander didn't mean to sound nasty, but that's how it came out.

Herbie ignored his comment. He knew Zander had a lot of things going on in his head.

"Now that you mention it, I did a little research and found something I think will suit us, the Hyatt Key West Resort. It's a bigger place, so we'll be able to be more anonymous. It's just a few blocks north of where we were staying."

"Let's go see if they have any rooms. If we can check in, we can get rid of these packages. Is it expensive?"

"I have no idea. I wasn't worried about that, since you're going to be the one paying." Herbie smiled.

Zander smiled as well. He couldn't help but like his old friend, even when he was pissing him off. They walked toward the hotel.

"Well, since this seems to be your gig, you see if we can get rooms. Here's my credit card. Have them run it. I'll check the place out." He put his packages down on a couch near the front desk and wandered off.

Herbie liked the idea. He decided to ask if they had a two-bedroom suite available. He would be able to keep better track of Zander that way. They had a few to choose from, and Herbie took one that faced the ocean. When he had almost finished registering, Zander walked back into the lobby.

"Nice place. Did you get us rooms?"

"All they had was an ocean suite. It's got two bedrooms, the pictures look nice." Herbie lied.

"Whatever you want. I'm sure it will be fine. They've got a few nice bars."

"Let's dump our packages and check the place out. We need to go back and get our stuff."

"I just need my bag. My clothes are all trash."

"Mine too. I wonder why he didn't cut up our bags?"

"Crazy people do crazy things. I've stopped trying to figure out the whys and wherefores a long time ago," Zander said.

Herbie wondered if that was true when Zander thought about Sara Jane. He thought Zander got just a little crazy when she was around. He was just a bit miffed, when he thought how Fats had talked him into getting involved. But underneath, he knew he would have done most anything to help out Zander.

They picked up their stuff and checked out of the first hotel. Herbie decided to pay for his own room, since Zander was footing the bill at the Hyatt. They decided to take their clothes with them and find a dumpster down the street. It was Herbie's idea because he thought the cut-up clothing might draw attention to them, and he didn't think they needed anymore of that.

The Hyatt bars were beautiful. They chose the Blue Mojito pool bar. The attitude adjustment hour provided the necessary medicine Zander needed. So, from 4:00 to 6:00, Herbie and Zander enjoyed themselves and made some new friends who wanted to enjoy their company as well. Herbie thought it was what Key West should be, and Zander just needed to think about something other than Sara Jane.

• • •

Sara Jane needed to push Fabiano, even though he might not be healed as much as she would have liked.

"You need to nose around and find out where Avon is hiding. Ask your friends to help. I'll pay."

Fabiano looked at her. "The old guy lives on Sunset Key. I think she might be there with him."

"How do you know that?"

"I followed him once. He got on the ferry with some bags of groceries. Looked like more than one person would need."

"Why haven't you done anything?"

"I took a wave runner over one day, hoping to see him or Avon, but I didn't have any luck. There are a lot of houses on the island, and maybe he even lives at the resort. It's a small island but a lot of properties to cover."

"Then you'd better get started. Go over at night when you can't be seen so easily."

"I need to keep my eyes on this Zander and Herbert."

"Sara Jane gave him an icy stare. "You let me take care of them. You do what I asked you to do. These loose ends will come back to haunt us if we aren't careful. Attempted murder is nothing to take lightly."

Fabiano knew there was a veiled threat in there someplace.

"When you hire someone to kill someone, it's not something to take lightly either."

He didn't want her to forget about the other dead girl. He also wanted her to know that if she were thinking about throwing him under the bus, he would be happy to retaliate. This wasn't going the way he had planned. Maybe this relationship was only one-way.

He realized he needed to protect his backside, because she had no intention of doing it.

"Go to the island. Find Avon and get rid of her. If the old man gets in the way, kill him. They should just disappear. I don't want to read about any bodies washing up on the beach."

"That's going to cost you more." His voice was cold.

"That's not a problem. Just take care of it."

The conversation ended. Sara Jane went back into her office to brood. Fabiano went out to make arrangements. He would make the trip over in a boat with a quiet outboard motor as soon as he could find what he needed. It wouldn't be that evening. He knew that for sure. He would do this on his own terms. She wasn't going to push him into anything unprepared.

Sara Jane watched him leave the building. She had to get rid of him as soon as he took care of Avon. Then she had another thought. She hadn't come grips with how to deal with Zander and Herbie. She might need Fabiano for them as well. He was a loose cannon, and she didn't want him around any longer than necessary.

Sara Jane buried her head into her hands, and knew she needed to come up with something. How it had come to this?

Maybe she should leave. She did it before. In her mind, she knew she just couldn't leave without putting all the loose ends together. What had Zander always said? "A dog with a sock."

She might be one as well.

48

After dinner at the resort, Max retrieved his backpack that contained the C-4. He told Mona to stay in the house the rest of the evening. When she asked where he was going, he told her it was time to make a permanent solution to this temporary problem.

"You shouldn't ask me any more questions until this is all over. Then I may tell you everything. Maybe it will be something you'd rather not know. You'll need to be the judge, but I'll never keep anything from you if you want to know details. That includes everything I do."

The explanation satisfied Mona, and she agreed to stay in for the evening.

"I don't think I'll be gone very long, but it's no guarantee."

"All I ask is that you be careful, and come back to me."

Max liked her response and kissed her gently on the lips. He didn't know if someone like Mona could love him, but there was an attraction and that was enough.

Max stopped at the storage shed next to the house and picked up a few items he would need later. There was a half-gallon of white gas he used in his portable lantern and stove, if the power was lost. He threw in few alligator clips and some speaker wire he thought would be of use. He cut off about ten feet. He found a pocketknife that had a Queen Steel label. He liked it because it had a very sharp blade that he could use for the speaker wire. It also had a few other foldouts that included both a Phillips and regular screwdriver. There was a packet that looked like it contained dental tools, and he put it together with the knife. Looking everything over, he decided it would be enough.

He was careful as he walked down to the beach in the dark. He didn't want to draw any attention. He found the rack that held the kayaks, and he selected a two-man model. The double oars were leaning against the cabana. He had no trouble pulling the kayak and oar to the beach even with his backpack over his shoulder.

He had thought long and hard about how he would get himself to Key West. He decided that the less people involved in his whereabouts, the better. The kayak was an easy way to get himself and his load to the island without being noticed.

He reached the Mallory Square beach just after ten. He pulled the kayak onto some rocks and turned it over making sure the oar was underneath. When he was satisfied that it was somewhat hidden from causal view, he turned and headed toward Front Street and the Aphrodisiac.

There were a few revelers still active on the streets, but he fit in just fine with his backpack slung over his shoulder. Most people would have thought he was a tourist heading to a hotel. He was in no hurry and walked right past the front of the Aphrodisiac. It was closed and dark inside. He paused and looked into the shop and saw no movement. He moved down the sidewalk until he came to the alley entrance. He paused and looked around. There was no one in the alley, and he made a quick exit from the sidewalk into the darkness. He made his way down the alley quietly, until he came to the back of the shop. He was relieved to see his target was in place. The blue Camaro sat next to the building.

Max went right to work. Once his eyes got used to the darkness, he found he could find things in his backpack without even rummaging around in it. He realized that it wasn't completely dark. There was some very dim light coming from the streetlights on Front Street.

He had the package of picks and selected the two that he thought he needed. The trunk popped open on his first try. He hadn't lost his touch.

Max was wary of his surroundings and made sure no one was coming down the alley. Nothing he had done signaled anyone inside the Aphrodisiac. Satisfied, he continued.

He stripped the end of the speaker wire and attached the alligator clip. He cut off a strip of insulation from the wire that led to the left backup light. He attached the alligator clip to the bare spot. Carefully, he took out the cap with the electrical detonator. He cut off two feet of the speaker wire and attached the wire to the detonator.

He paused to look around and was pleased with the quiet. He took out another detonator. This one went off by pressure. He attached an end of the remaining wire to the pressure ring. He worked fast and the worst was over. Now he needed to bind the detonators to the block of C-4.

He put the block into the trunk. It didn't matter where he placed it. It would do the job in any position. Carefully he pushed the electrical detonator into the putty-like material. Then he closed the trunk lid until he could just get his hands and arms into the trunk. He measured how much wire would be needed and cut it off. He fastened the wire with a series of knots to the lid of the trunk. He pulled on it to make sure it was secure, and then he lowered the trunk lid with one hand and pushed the pressure detonator into the putty next to the other one.

He closed the trunk. It would be a good backup. If she got into the car and put it in reverse, it would blow. If she decided to open the trunk for any reason, it would blow. Max thought it was foolproof.

He moved around to the driver's door and was ready to pick the lock. It surprised him that the lock was open. The dome light was a concern. He decided there was no way around it. He would need to open the door quickly and find the switch. He decided to hit the switch with his foot. Max was skilled and extinguished the light immediately.

He took the can of white gas from his backpack. He opened the lid and threw it back into the pack. He put the can behind the passenger's seat. He did all this with his foot on the light switch.

Max figured the fumes from the gas would continue to fill the car and give some lovely fire to the explosion. The subtle thing about white gas was that it didn't smell like regular gasoline. It had a peculiar odor, and it was hard to recognize unless you were an outdoorsman. She would merely think there was some kind of unusual smell. It wouldn't summon any cautionary reaction. He had seen it before.

He got up out of the driver's seat, and pulled off his foot off the light switch, while closing the door. He closed it just enough for the light to extinguish. Then he looked into the car making sure nothing was out of place. He gently pushed the door closed, until he heard the lock click quietly. He was satisfied that no one had heard it.

Making sure everything was in his backpack; he stepped back into the alley and made his way back to the kayak. Waiting was always the hard part.

●   ●   ●

Sara Jane was still wrestling with she was going to do. She had closed the shop and remained in her office. It was a place she did business. This was business. This business with Avon had to be reconciled. She needed to pay for her betrayal. That's all she had known when she was with Martin, and it was all she knew now. If you didn't live by a certain set of standards, then your life lost any meaning. You had to be true to yourself, because no one else would. She knew that to be true from her life's experiences. There was disloyalty everywhere. The biggest Judas had been Martin in the end. There was no one to trust. She thought about Zander but tried to put him out of her mind. She wasn't ready to deal with that right now.

Then she thought she heard something from behind the store. She got up, making sure she didn't put on any lights. There was nothing moving, and it took a little time for her eyes to adjust.

She looked over toward the alley and there was nothing. Just before she sat back down, her gaze caught something out of place. The truck lid on her Camaro was open. She stopped and looked out of the side of her eyes. You could see better at night when you didn't look directly at something. Something was moving behind the trunk lid. She waited, patiently, and wondered if someone was trying to steal her car. A thought struck her; she could turn on the floodlights and catch the bastard in the act. She decided against it.

It was more of a fascination just watching to see what would come next. It didn't take long, and she saw a shadow move toward the driver's seat. Shortly after, the dome light came on for just an instant. It wasn't long enough for Sara Jane to make out any facial features. She saw the figure reach into a bag and put something in the car.

Finally, she saw the shadow move to the alley and disappear.

Sara Jane wondered if the shadow got cold feet and left. Something in the back of her mind said this was more than an attempted robbery. She wasn't going to check it out in the dark. This someone might be hanging around waiting for her. Tomorrow was another day, and she had other things on her mind right now.

49

Zander and Herbie spent more time in the Hyatt bar than they should have. Both were slow to get up the next morning. It was after nine when Herbie hit the shower. He had looked out and noticed Zander's door was still closed. He was hoping he hadn't slipped out, while he had overslept. He didn't think it was likely. Herbie had taken it easy on the drinks, while Zander had tried to be somebody.

When Herbie was ready, he knocked on Zander's adjoining door. It was after ten.

"Go away," Zander moaned.

"I'm going down and get a paper and some coffee. Can I get you anything?"

"Go away," Zander repeated.

Herbie smiled and left the room. This was going to work out better than he had anticipated.

Zander was sitting on his bed listening for Herbie's room door to close. He had been ready at eight and just waiting for Herbie to get up. He figured Herbie would feel safe leaving the room thinking he was still in bed with a bad hangover.

Zander waited another ten minutes and then decided it was safe to venture out. He made sure his door was closed in case Herbie came back before he did. He took the stairs down the three flights and came out close to the elevators in the lobby. He looked around wondering where Herbie had gone. Seeing nothing, he made a move toward the front door. People were coming into the lobby, so he didn't even have to wait for the automatic doors to open.

He crossed the street and made his way directly to the Aphrodisiac.

• • •

Herbie had decided to take advantage of Zander's hangover and speak with Sara Jane privately. He felt the preemptive move was his only choice. He knew what Max had said about contact, but he felt the order was aimed at Zander. He needed to try and talk some sense into her, before it was too late.

It was after ten, and the place was open. Herbie walked directly to the office and looked in. The office was empty. Suddenly he felt something behind him. He turned around.

"Can I help you with something?"

"I think maybe I'm the one to help you."

"Really? I suppose you better sit down if this is business." She slid past him with her cup of coffee and sat in her chair.

"I'm here hoping I can talk some sense into you," Herbie replied.

"Why don't you tell me who you are and what this is about?"

That stopped Herbie for a moment. He had assumed that she knew who he was. This changed things. It might be to his advantage.

"I'm Herbie Schutt. Zander's friend."

If she was shocked, she didn't show it. Sara Jane was good at masking her emotions.

"I heard you were around. Quite frankly, I would never have recognized you. You looked much different back in the day." She tried to be pleasant.

"I'm almost positive you wouldn't have recognized me if I had looked the same. You never paid much attention to me, even though I was Zander's friend."

"So, I would imagine there is a reason for your visit." Sara Jane frowned.

"It is a courtesy call. I'm here to warn you," Herbie said.

"About what?" Sara Jane was interested.

"You need to leave this place. Your life is in danger."

"What's that supposed to mean?'

"It means there is someone set on killing you. I think the wheels are in motion, and if you don't pay attention, you'll be dead by the end of the week."

Sara Jane stared at him. Suddenly the action with her Camaro the previous evening was blinking in her head like a red light.

"You'd better listen to him. He's telling you the truth." It was Zander's voice coming from behind Herbie. Both Herbie and Sara Jane jumped.

Zander had slipped into the Aphrodisiac quietly. He had grabbed the bell above the door, so neither Sara Jane nor Herbie heard him come in. He had listened to most of the conversation, and he was amazed that his friend would try and help a woman that he seemed to hate. In spite of everything, Herbie still had Zander's back. It was nothing short of amazing.

"You're not supposed to be here," Herbie said, forcefully.

"Do you think it matters now? It appears you just did what I was going to do."

Herbie just looked at him.

"Do you suppose one of you two could pause, and let me know what the hell is going on?"

Zander put his hand on Herbie's shoulder. "Why don't you let me talk to her alone. Go out and look at the stuff in the store. Maybe there's something you can find to take back to Gail. Might spice up your life just a bit." Zander smiled.

Herbie got up. "Just be careful, my friend."

"I will."

Herbie left the office to become lost in the world of sex toys. Zander closed the office door.

Before he could say anything, Sara Jane spoke:

"Are you two afraid of me?"

Zander thought about it. "Sure, what did you expect?"

"I've learned to expect nothing. You never are disappointed that way."

"So, does that mean you're happy with your life?"

Sara Jane turned and looked out the window. It was quiet for an uncomfortably long time, but Zander decided to let her respond before he said anything.

"What is happiness anyway?" she asked, "are you happy?"

"No, I am not happy. I haven't been happy for a long time. I think it's your fault."

"Oh, don't blame me for your unhappiness." Sara Jane was hot.

"Why not? Every time I think that maybe my life has turned around, you show up somehow. You need to let go, and let me go my own way."

"You're the one who found me, remember?"

Zander nodded, "I do, but then I find out you're carrying around my card. What am I supposed to make of that?"

It was quiet in the room for a time.

"Maybe you should realize that I still have feelings for you."

"You have a damn funny way of showing it."

"I'm toxic. It would never work. I can't have anyone close to me. It's who I am. I hurt everyone in my life. You know that. You've seen it first hand."

"And now you want to hurt Mona."

"She betrayed me."

"Look in the mirror. How many times have you betrayed me? Should I satisfy my anger by killing you?"

"I wouldn't blame you."

"That's not how it works. There has to be a line that none of us cross."

"Did you feel the same way about...Rooster?" She used the nickname Zander had given him for effect.

"That was self defense. He would have killed us if we hadn't acted."

"It's easy to accept anything if you think you're justified."

"We're not talking about your inability to let something go even after it no longer has meaning."

"I have no idea what you are talking about."

"I think you do. Your little secret life was discovered. There are a number of us who know all about it. There is no longer a reason to pursue Mona. You need to tell your man to back off," Zander said, and then thought for a minute, "Unless you are planning to get rid of all of us."

"Don't think I haven't thought about it."

"Good luck with that." Zander was pissed.

"Oh, get off your high horse. I could never hurt you."

"No, you'd just get someone else to do it."

Zander got up.

"You've been warned. Why Herbie would go out of his way to help you defies all logic."

"Well, maybe if I call off my man, you can call off yours."

"He's not my man. I could never hurt you. But he knows Mona will never be safe as long as you're around. If you're not here, then you're not a threat. That's why we're giving you the heads up. But you would need to get out immediately. I'm just afraid it may already be too late."

Zander opened the door, and Herbie almost fell into the office.

"Did you get all that?" Zander asked.

"Close enough."

Zander turned to Sara Jane.

"I believe this is goodbye, one way or another. I hope you're smart enough to take the option that keeps you alive. Unfortunately, you are already dead to me."

Zander's long legs took him out the front door with Herbie trying hard to keep up.

Jeff Zwagerman

50

Sara Jane sat in her chair. She knew she needed to get out of that chair and do something. For the first time in her life, she was unsure of herself. She needed to find Fabiano and tie up loose ends.

Then she remembered her Camaro. Her keys were in the desk drawer. She needed to find out what had been going on the night before. She would be careful. If someone was trying to kill her, this could be the vehicle. She smiled at the joke. But there really wasn't any joke about what was happening to her.

She looked into the car. The front seat looked clear. She put the key into the lock, and then realized she hadn't locked the door the last time she used the car.

She looked at the lock. It was up. She opened the door. Nothing looked out of place. She looked under both seats and saw nothing but some dust bunnies. She closed the door and headed for the trunk. She stopped abruptly. Something in the back seat caught her eye. It was a square silver can with red lettering over it. She saw the word Coleman written on the can. It was some type of fuel and the cap was off.

Sara Jane had an inner alarm going off in her head. She knew right then that the trunk was trouble. She turned around and went back into the Aphrodisiac. It was time to change plans.

• • •

Fabiano made plans for the following evening. He rented a boat to do some "night fishing." He had an acquaintance that had worked the resort on Sunset Key, but had been fired for banging a teenage girl on the beach. The parents were incensed and wanted to get the law

243

involved. He took the opportunity, in the confusion, to become quite scarce.

There was no love lost, and he was happy to help Fabiano with the exact location of Max Kuhn. He even drew a map.

Fabiano was happy to only have to make one trip to the island. He would need some items to make sure the bodies wouldn't be discovered. He would be happy to let Bonnie, or whatever her name was, pay for the items. When this was all over, she would be paying him much more than she realized.

Fabiano made his way over to the Aphrodisiac and explained his plan to Bonnie. Leaving out the part how he was planning to deal with her. He still had his honor, and she would not be taking it away. He would be taking hers. Fabiano smiled as he drug his left leg over the boardwalk.

•   •   •

Max finished washing the breakfast dishes. He liked to wash dishes by hand when he had the time. It always had been an enjoyable task. Mona was finishing her coffee while reading the paper.

"Sounds like it's going to be 85 and sunny today."

"Maybe some pool time for you?" Max asked.

She stopped and looked at him. "What are you planning?"

"I thought I'd spend some time at Key West today."

"Then I'm going with you."

"I don't think that's such a good idea."

Mona was hot. "You've kept me prisoner here long enough. I need to get off this island for a while. I also need to know what's happening with Sara Jane and the Gimp."

Max didn't say anything but folded his towel and hung it over the dishwasher handle. He walked slowly over to Mona, took her face into his hands and looked at her.

"You know I'm doing all this to keep you safe. I know it is frustrating, but humor me."

Mona wasn't backing down. "No. I'm going with you. I'm safe with you at my side. Don't you think she realizes I'm alive by now?"

Max knew she was serious and decided not to fight it any longer.

He knew she was going a bit stir-crazy.

"All right. But you need to stay close. Don't go wandering off without me."

Her mood brightened. "Of course. I just need to feel like I can move again. I hate being so confined."

"You wouldn't do well in prison would you?" Max joked.

Mona shuddered. "I never gave that much thought. I've done some things in the past that might have warranted some prison time. I don't think I could do it."

"Don't be so sure. The human being is a complex machine that seems to adapt to most outside stimuli. Look what you've dealt with over the past few weeks. You probably didn't think you could have done it, until it was thrust upon you."

"I'm a survivor. Is that what you're saying?"

"I don't know, am I?"

She reached over and messed up his hair.

It always amazed Max at the restlessness of the human spirit. He had seen it time and time again. People could stay at home for days on end and never give it much thought. Throw in a blizzard, or flood, and people couldn't stand to be confined to their homes. It was just their spirit trying to take flight. It was knowing they could leave at anytime that kept their spirit from becoming restless, but take away that ability to leave and everything would fall apart. That's why prison was such a great punishment for the bulk of the population. Just the threat of imprisonment kept most people from doing something that would put them in jeopardy.

"I'll get ready and we can go over for lunch."

"It will have to be at the Hog's Breath."

"I don't care, as long as it's not here."

Max watched her go into the bedroom. He was a lucky guy.

• • •

Zander and Herbie left the Aphrodisiac. Zander was two steps ahead of Herbie as they made the turn on Duval Street.

"Hey, slow it down. We're in Key West. No rush, mon." Herbie tried to sound like an islander.

"We're not in Jamaica, mon." Zander slowed his pace. "Never say 'mon' again."

"Okay. Now what?"

"I've got to forget about all this shit."

"Why don't we look around the island? There's a lot to see, I'm told."

"Like what?"

"I just read about the Mel Fisher Maritime Museum. He's the guy who found that huge Spanish treasure worth millions. It's on display at the museum."

Zander didn't care what he saw. He just wanted to stop thinking about Sara Jane. He agreed to tag along. It would be good to let Herbie be in charge. Then he could focus on other things.

It was almost noon when they came out of the Key West Butterfly Nature Boutique. Zander was surprised that the place had such a calming effect on him. He loved it when the butterflies landed on his head and shoulders. They were so gentle and beautiful, and the colors were amazing. There were many varieties that he had no idea even existed. Back home, the only butterflies he ever saw as a kid were monarchs.

Zander was in a good mood as they walked down Front Street. Then Herbie spied Mona and Max, and everything came rushing back.

• • •

Sara Jane made up her mind. She was leaving. She thought about going to the Cayman Islands to be near her money. It would be too difficult, on short notice, to get the proper clearance. She knew she couldn't travel by anything commercial. She had a client who had made several offers to take her on a cruise any time she wanted. She had done him a few favors with some of the girls on the Libertine side of the business.

After a phone call, it was set. They would leave by three from the docks. He gave her his slip number. Sara Jane had asked to go to Marco Island. He balked at that idea. He told her he would take her anywhere in the keys but he wouldn't go anywhere past Flamingo.

Sara Jane found out that it was the southernmost headquarters of the Everglades National Park. She had never heard of it, but she needed to get as far away from Key West as possible.

She looked at a map and noticed there was one road out of Flamingo that led to Homestead. Miami was just north, and she could get lost there for a while until she could decide her next move. It sounded like her only option.

There was a medium-sized suitcase, with wheels, that she could manage. It was open and lying on her bed. She wouldn't be able to take much with her. Mechanically, she went about packing what she could fit into the case. She sandwiched an envelope filled with cash along the edge. She hadn't counted the money, but she knew there was more than a hundred thousand. It was enough to get her by until she felt safe enough to find a bank.

She zippered the suitcase and put it on the floor. It was heavy, but after she pulled out the handle and rolled it across the floor, it was manageable. It rolled down the stairs easily, and she put it close to the front door behind a rack of sleepwear. There wasn't much she could do until Fabiano showed up.

Sara Jane sat back down in her office to wait. She hadn't planned on such a quick exit, but circumstances had changed. Now it was a destiny almost beyond her control. It frightened her not having total control, but this appeared to be her best, and actually, only choice.

She hated to leave the Aphrodisiac without some closure. Since she was leaving so abruptly, she decided to leave Avon a letter. She could have the business and do whatever she wanted with it. Maybe that would be enough for Max to stop his pursuit. She wanted some reassurance.

Dear Avon or Mona,

Much has happened as you are reading this letter. I have left the island, or I have been killed. Either way, you are free. I can no longer be a threat to you. Fabiano is no longer a threat to you, either. Quite honestly, I'm tired of the whole game.

The business is yours. It was always in your name anyway. At least, the name you gave me. Do whatever you want with it. You never liked the Libertine side, so I would suggest you give it to one of the girls. Someone will want it to continue. There's too much money to be made.

I'm sorry that things turned out the way they did. We had a good thing going for a while. There were just too many secrets that we couldn't share. It was sad, really.

Enjoy your life. You've been given a reprieve. Don't make a mistake and pursue me. It wouldn't turn out well for anyone.

Sara Jane

It had pissed her off to write a letter like this. It showed weakness. But after further examination of her situation, Sara Jane realized she had no other choice. Still, she didn't have to like it.

Sara Jane folded the letter, put into an envelope, and wrote Mona's name on the front. She stood, put the letter on her chair seat, and pushed the chair under the desk.

She heard the front door bell and saw it was Fabiano. Suddenly she felt some relief. Maybe this was going to work out after all.

She went out to meet him.

51

Max invited Zander and Herbie to join them for lunch at the Hog's Breath. He had reserved a table streetside. The Aphrodisiac was a half block down. The front was visible from their table, and Zander wondered if that was by design. He wondered if Sara Jane had decided to take their recommendation, but maybe it was too late. The worst part of the whole thing was that he didn't know how he felt about any of it.

Max ordered Key West Sunset Ales. It was a local brew, and a red ale that Zander liked. They were on their second when the server came for their orders. Everyone ordered burgers but Zander. He decided he wasn't hungry and wanted to enjoy the beers instead. In fact, he thought he might like to enjoy a lot of them.

He was on his fourth when he decided to get some information from Max.

"So, what do you have planned for Sara Jane?"

Max looked at him. "Better if you don't know."

Zander didn't know if he should be angry or relieved. He knew that he had done what he could and was resigned with whatever happened. But that wasn't true at all. He knew it, and everyone at the table knew it also.

He ordered another beer.

• • •

Sara Jane listened, as Fabiano told her what he was planning to do later that evening. He had a boat, and he had body bags that he would weigh down with cinder blocks. Everything was in place.

"What kind of weapon do you have?" Sara Jane asked, playing along.

Fabiano didn't say anything but showed her his knife.

"You can't go after this Max guy with a knife. He's got firepower, and he'll take you out. That would lead to me."

"I don't have anything else. Guns are hard to come by down here."

Sara Jane handed him her keys.

"There's a package in my trunk that I think you'll be wanting."

Fabiano's eyes lit up. "Tell me it's a pistol."

"Colt 45. Six shot. No shell casings to worry about."

"I might need to find a place to practice before tonight," Fabiano said, and twirled the keys around his index finger.

Sara Jane could see he was excited. She still could play the game.

"One more thing. There is a suppressor in the package. Don't forget to use it. We don't need someone stumbling onto the scene because they heard something."

Fabiano nodded, smiling. This was going to be better than he had first thought. His attitude was softening toward Bonnie. Maybe this was all going to work out. He would deal with Zander and Herbie later.

Sara Jane watched Fabiano limp out the back door. She looked after him sadly— collateral damage. There was always collateral damage in life. The trick was avoiding it on a personal level, and she decided she had done a good job so far.

Fabiano approached the Camaro and went right to the trunk.

He put the key into the lock. He was thinking about the colt 45 with the suppressor, but the last thing he saw was a gold-covered wire with a ring hanging loose from the trunk lid.

Sara Jane had watched Fabiano go out to the Camaro. When he had reached the trunk, she closed the office door and walked over to her bag. She was waiting for an explosion. She wasn't disappointed. The entire building shook.

Sara Jane looked at her watch. She would wait exactly two minutes before she moved out the front door. That would be enough time for most everyone to focus on the explosion, masking her exit.

Time ticked by slowly. She had all she could do not to burst out of the Aphrodisiac on a dead run. Finally, it was time. She opened the door and looked out of the doorway. No one was coming toward the door. She looked both ways and then pushed her suitcase in front of her while pulling the door shut. She checked to make sure it was locked before she left. She wondered why she would do something like that.

Keeping her pace as normal as possible, she crossed the street toward the boardwalk. Soon she would be on her way to Flamingo. It couldn't be too soon. She tried not to think about Fabiano. He was just collateral damage.

• • •

The group in the Hog's Breath had finished their lunch. Zander was finishing his fifth beer when the Camaro blew. Everyone just sat and watched the fireball rise above the buildings. It looked like the fourth of July, not two days before Christmas. Everything stopped around them. Zander thought it looked like a freeze frame in a movie.

Max was the first to move. He got up and turned to Mona.

"Stay here. I mean it. Don't you move." Max was demanding, and Mona was not about to argue. She just nodded.

Max sprinted toward the alley entrance. Two beats later, Zander and Herbie followed. Herbie realized what had happened. Zander was just going through the motions. He didn't understand anything.

When they got to the alley, they saw what was left of the Camaro. The trunk lid was gone and so was the top. Glass was all over the ground in chunks. The can of white gas had done its job.

There was a body smoldering about twenty feet from the car. It was close to where the three stood. The limbs were all there but there appeared to be no face. Max went over and crouched next to the body. He didn't like what he saw. It wasn't Sara Jane.

"Looks like your Mr. Limps has just had a very bad day." Max sounded disappointed.

"I think we should get out of here." Herbie looked around.

"I think you're right," Max said.

Zander was staring at the car blankly.

Herbie wrapped his arm through Zander's and pulled him away.

"It wasn't Sara Jane," he told Zander.

"I know." It was all Zander could say.

Max had moved ahead and was almost back to the Hog's Breath. Mona had run out to meet him. Mona was animated, and Max ran off toward the marina. Herbie wondered what was going on.

"Was there another body in the car?" Zander asked Herbie.

"I don't know. I didn't get that close. I don't think so. It looked just like that Fabiano guy."

Zander tried to turn around. "I've got to know."

"You're not going anywhere. That place will be swarming with cops in a minute or two. You don't want to be anywhere near that. What would be your explanation?"

Mona walked over and took Zander's other arm.

"We're supposed to wait for Max at Sloppy Joes. We're supposed to mix with the crowd."

"Where did he go?" Herbie asked.

"I don't know," she lied," he just said he had something that needed his immediate attention."

Mona had caught some movement, out of the corner of her eye, when the three had moved toward the alley. It came from the front of the Aphrodisiac. If she hadn't sensed something, she might very easily have missed seeing Sara Jane emerge from the shop. She had moved very fast, pulling a suitcase behind her. Mona watched with fascination. She knew all she could do was watch. She wanted to go after her but she had promised Max she wouldn't move. That was the prudent thing to do at this moment.

Zander didn't want to go to Sloppy Joe's, but his mind wasn't in sync with his body. All he could do was follow Mona and Herbie.

• • •

Max ran down the boardwalk toward the boat slips. He was in good shape for someone 70 years old. It was good, because Sara Jane had a good head start on him. Most of the boats were charter-fishing skiffs. He couldn't see Sara Jane on any of those. He would need to go farther and check out the bigger cruisers. He was near the last of the slips, when he caught sight of her blonde hair. She was boarding a yacht. It was a big thing and must have cost a mint.

"Figures," Max said, out loud.

There was some dock guy pulling the ropes from the cleats. Max saw him give the boat a push, and they were running backward away from the docks. He was too late.

He walked to end of the dock, and Sara Jane saw him. The boat was loud, and she wouldn't hear him. So he mouthed the words:

"Don't come back."

She nodded and turned away.

Max watched them move into the bay, and then he moved over to the dock guy.

"Where is that boat headed?" he asked.

"I don't think that would be any of your business, buddy."

Max reached behind him and pulled out his pistol. He took out his suppressor and began to screw it together. The dock guy's eyes got big.

"I'm about to make it my business, unless you don't want to live that much longer." He smiled, but kept screwing the suppressor to the barrel.

"Listen, I don't want any trouble. They didn't share their destination with me, but I heard the woman ask how long it would take to get to Flamingo."

"There, that was easy." Max was taking the pistol back apart.

The dock guy let out a deep breath.

"You aren't planning to visit with anyone about our little conversation are you?" Max looked up.

"No, man. I never heard a thing." He was moving down the dock quickly.

Max decided he wasn't going to be a problem. He just had to go and change his underwear. He tucked the pistol in the back of his pants and took out his cell phone. If the boat were going north to Flamingo, it would be a good thing.

Max decided to make two calls. The first was to an associate based in Marathon. He had been one of the finest shots in his unit. They had used him as a sniper until he decided he was finished. He had gone on his own, and now they used him as a gun for hire when they needed something done off the books. It was all perfectly legal by government standards.

He and Max had done favors for each other over the years. Max knew he could count on him. He answered on the first ring, and Max gave him the details of the hit. He described the boat and gave him the name. His sniper had all the necessary surveillance equipment in his fast boat. Max had always kidded him that he stole it from the TV show *Miami Vice*.

Max was assured that it wouldn't be a problem.

The second call was to one of his handlers. It was a courtesy call to let him know he was going off protocol and sanctioning a hit. The handler asked for the details and Max explained who it was, and who would be completing the assassination. The handler approved and Max hung up.

He walked back to the Sloppy Joes. He would need to amend the story for his three friends. He could always level with Mona later.

• • •

For a moment, Sara Jane had been concerned when she saw Max. She could read his lips and decided just to nod in the affirmative. Her first impulse was to give him the finger, but things were too tense, and she needed to leave. It looked like that was going to happen.

She watched as Key West became smaller and smaller. It saddened her a bit. She sat on one of the couches at the stern of the second deck. The air was still warm, and the sun felt good on her skin.

She reached for her purse and dug around, until she came up with the two cards with Zander's information. She looked at them for quite a long time, turning the one over with his phone number on the back.

Then she threw them both in the air, and watched as they fell down to the boat's wake below and disappeared into the white water.

She wouldn't need them any longer.

52

Max's handler made a call to Marathon and amended the kill order. He had decided the woman could be an asset. If nothing else, the US Marshal's office wanted to debrief her. Max didn't need to know the details. She wouldn't be doing much of anything for quite a while. When they got finished with her, she wouldn't be worrying about Max or anyone close to him. It was a win-win situation for everyone. Marathon agreed to stand down. The handler called the coast guard to stop and secure the asset, before she reached Flamingo.

Max was somewhat relieved that Sara Jane hadn't been killed in the blast. He knew Mona wouldn't be worrying about Mr. Limps any longer. She wouldn't even care that Max took out the bastard.

Max joined the threesome at Sloppy Joe's. All eyes were on him. An explanation would be in order. He was happy to share part of the news and did so before he sat down.

"Zander, I think you'll be happy to know that Sara Jane is alive and well. She's on the run. I watched her leave the island on a yacht the size of my house. It looks like she'll get out of everything unscathed."

Max could see relief rush into Zander's face.

"I don't know how I feel about it," Zander said, truthfully.

"She won't be bothering you any longer, you can bank on that. In fact, she won't be bothering anyone here. She got my message." Max decided to stop talking before he shared too much.

"Where do you think she's going?" Herbie asked.

"I don't know, and frankly, don't care," Max responded.

"So this whole crazy thing is over?" Mona asked.

"I hope so," Max said, "but I think you should go over to the

Aphrodisiac and talk to the investigators. We need to be proactive on this thing. They will want to talk to you since you are a partner in the business."

"What will I say?"

"Just tell them the truth. You don't know anything about Sara Jane's whereabouts and if they identify the body, you can say he worked for you doing odd jobs." Max was thinking out loud.

"Let's get this over with," Mona said, standing.

Max turned to Zander and Herbie. "So what are your plans now?"

"I need to call Fats and give him the details. I'll need to apologize to him for not being very forthcoming." Zander still was trying to process everything.

"I need to get back to work, but more importantly, I need to get back to Cedar Key. Gail will be wondering what's happened to me," Herbie said.

Max took Herbie's hand and shook it. "If you ever get back this way, stop in and visit us."

He turned to Zander. "What are your plans?"

"I haven't thought about it at all."

"Why don't you check out of your hotel and spend some time with us until you decide."

Max could see that Zander needed to have some time to himself, and he would need people around him who could answer his questions and offer support.

Zander was about to decline, when Mona spoke up:

"And we won't take no for an answer, either. Go check out, and meet us at the Aphrodisiac."

It was settled, Max and Mona went off to face the music at the Aphrodisiac, and Herbie and Zander went back to the hotel.

• • •

Mona and Max went over to the front of the Aphrodisiac and found the front door locked. Max said that it was a good thing. It meant that the sheriff hadn't been inside looking around.

Mona had taken her purse along and was happy she had. The keys to the shop were at the bottom of the bag, and she unlocked the door. She and Max wasted little time and went right to the office to see if anything looked suspicious. Mona spotted the letter on the office chair. They read it together. When they finished, Max spoke:

"This changes a few things. If your name is on the business, they may not know about Sara Jane."

Her name is Bonnie Marco. Let's not forget that," Mona said.

"And your name is Avon Bartow, at least until we get through the investigation."

"So, what do we tell them about Bonnie?" Mona wondered.

"She went on an extended vacation. She took off with some guy on a big yacht."

"I get it, mix in a little truth."

"Always," Max said.

"What about the car?"

"It was hers. She left it for you to run errands," Max said.

"You think they'll buy it?" Mona asked.

"I don't know, let's go find out. Just remember to act stunned about everything. Can you shed some tears when they tell you about the body they found?"

"I can give it a try. Damn, I'm going to have to be a great actor to pull this off."

"I'll give you an Academy Award later." Max smiled, and pinched her lightly on her butt.

They went out the back door looking for the sheriff.

• • •

Zander and Herbie checked out of their suite. Zander paid.

"Let me buy you a drink before I shove off," Herbie offered.

"It's the least you could do after sticking me with the bill."

Herbie smiled. He knew Zander was going to be all right. He was starting to give him his usual shit.

They sat at the cabana bar and looked out toward the bay. They both had a light beer. It was too early to drink anything else. Zander put a few olives in his beer glass and Herbie looked over.

"A South Dakota martini. I haven't seen anyone do that in a long time."

"Sometimes, I even put tomato juice in it," Zander said, easily.

"I like that. We shouldn't lose some of the things from our past." Herbie drank his beer.

Zander thought about Sara Jane. She was one thing from his past that he needed to lose.

"Why don't you ride with me back to Cedar Key? You could spend Christmas with Gail and me in the new house."

"Thanks for the offer, but I need some time alone to work this out in my head."

Herbie looked at him. "She's gone, Zander. Let her go. We've all got to move on. What sign did our old history teacher have on the wall? I think it said, "Stagnation Is Regression." I never knew what that meant, back then. I do now. I lived it for most of my life. I'm done with it now. You need to be as well."

"I know you're right, Herbie. It just takes me longer to make the changes in my mind. I'll get there. When I do, I'll look you up in Cedar Key."

"Well, you'd better. All your stuff is there, remember?"

Zander had forgotten about his bag. He smiled. Herbie handed him a slip of paper with the address of his new digs on it, proudly.

"I guess it's a plan then."

When they finished their beers, Herbie decided it was past time to leave.

"I guess I'll find a ride to the truck and be on my way," he said, standing.

Zander had an idea. "Hey why don't you walk with me to the airport? It isn't that far, and it will give us some time to reminisce."

"How far is it?' Herbie asked, a bit hesitant.

"Not so far that we can't walk it. We can take the Smathers Beach Road. I hear it's a beautiful view. Maybe we should enjoy some of the island before we both leave."

Herbie couldn't argue, but he wondered why they needed to go to the airport?

"Are you planning to fly somewhere?"

Zander laughed. "I just want to rent a car. It looks like the only reasonably priced place is the airport."

It was a great walk. Zander and Herbie connected once again.

Zander chose Budget Rental, and soon they were headed for Herbie's truck in a bright red Mustang convertible. Zander drove back down Duval Street, and then after they felt they had turned enough heads, he went up Roosevelt Drive back to Stock Island and Herbie's truck. It was a nice ride, and Zander was sad as he watched Herbie wave from his truck. Herbie wasn't excited to head up Highway 1 to leave the Keys. He had made the trip a few times, and it was a slow go.

Zander hadn't seen any of the other Keys, so unlike Herbie, he was excited to make the trip. It was all he could do to not to follow Herbie's truck, but he knew he had to go back and say goodbye to both Mona and Max. He wanted to make sure everything was going good with the sheriff. He thought that maybe he could be of some help there.

The ride back to the Aphrodisiac was pleasant, and Zander was enjoying everything about driving on the island. He had been so focused on Sara Jane; he hadn't noticed what the island had to offer.

Everyone was in a festive mood. Maybe it was because Christmas was three days away, but Zander thought it must feel that way most of the time. Key West was considered to be in the tropic zone and therefore had sunshine most days. Zander knew that sunshine usually made everything better.

He had to park in a parking garage a few blocks from the Aphrodisiac. Parking seemed to be at a premium on the small island. When he reached the shop, the door was locked. He peered in and saw Mona and Max talking. He rapped on the window and Mona came and unlocked the door.

"You can't come in. The cops are combing the place for clues," Mona said.

"Let's sit outside," Max countered. "They're upstairs looking through the residence right now."

"Are they buying the story?" Zander asked.

"I think so. It helped that Bonnie kept some hate mail we received from some religious nuts. It's giving them a motive. That takes the heat off us."

The three sat on the top step that led to the shop.

"What now?" Zander asked.

"We've been talking. Mona is going to stay with me. She wants to turn this place into an island clothing store for women."

"Are you kidding, you want to get rid of all this good stuff?" Zander indicated the items in the Aphrodisiac.

The three laughed.

"Well, maybe we could keep a few items for our personal use," Max said, and winked at Zander. Mona slugged him in the shoulder.

"I have an idea. Would you pick out a bunch of stuff, and send it to Herbie as a housewarming gift?" Zander asked, reaching into his billfold.

He handed Mona Herbie's address, along with a hundred dollar bill.

Mona took the address and threw the hundred back to Zander.

"I would be happy to do it, and you can keep your money. This one's on the house. Besides, it's going to be fun putting together some crazy stuff for him."

"What are you going to do with all of the sex stuff?" Zander asked.

"As soon as the police let us re-open, we're going to have a big Christmas sale. We'll make some customers very happy." Mona's eyes twinkled.

Max changed the subject.

"Are you going to spend the holidays with us? We would like that."

"Thanks for the generous offer, but I need to move on. I'm going to take my time and explore Florida. I've never been here before, and the place interests me. It's so much older and has so much more history than Iowa. I want to take it all in and forget all about Sara Jane."

Max figured he wouldn't have a problem with that any longer. Of course, it wouldn't be for the reason Zander thought.

Zander said his goodbyes and gave both Mona and Max a hug. They told him to come back for a visit when he had his fill of being a tourist. Zander said he would, but he doubted it very much.

He wanted to move on, and this place reminded him too much of Sara Jane.

53

Zander left Key West and noticed it was after five. It was dark, and it would never do to explore the keys when he couldn't see anything. He drove up Highway One for fifteen miles, until he came to Sugarloaf Key. There was a hotel there called Sugarloaf Lodge. The sign said they had a tiki bar. It might be a good place to spend the night. He pulled into the driveway and parked near the office. He decided to make a phone call to Fats. Fats answered on the first ring.

"It's high time, my friend."

"You are right, I apologize for being such a dick."

"How is that different from your normal day-to-day self?"

"I deserve that. I just wanted to call and tell you what happened."

"No need. Mona has filled in all the details."

Zander was relieved. He didn't want to relive the events again. They talked for five minutes about the bar, friends, and plans. Zander told him he had no plans but thought he would hang out in Florida until he got tired of it.

"You won't be able to get in touch with me by phone anymore," Zander told Fats.

"Why would that be?" Fats asked.

"Sara Jane has the number. I'm getting rid of it."

"Sounds like a good idea. Why don't you just go to Wal-Mart a get a new one? It won't be the same number."

"I don't think so. I'm going dark for a while. If there is some kind of emergency, you can always call my answering service."

"Always and forever, old school. I'm going to tell you one thing: *Get back to where you once belonged.*" Fats quoted the Beatles' tune and hung up.

Maybe Fats was right. Only time would tell.

Sugarloaf Lodge had vacant rooms and soon Zander was enjoying the bar with other revelers. It was a fun place, and everyone was in good spirits both figuratively and physically. The sign said "attitude adjustment," and Zander decided it was time.

There was a guy playing guitar and singing. He encouraged people to sing with him and after a few drinks, Zander did just that. It was a great night, and when everyone began to call it quits, Zander decided to go back to his room. He wanted to take off early. His goal was to be on Sanibel Island, off Fort Myers Beach, by Christmas day. If he didn't make that goal, it didn't matter. He thought it was important to get some routine back in his life and organizing his schedule was something he could control. But if something more interesting came along, he would be able to amend the schedule. It was a new tactic for Zander, but he thought he needed to make some changes in his life. Herbie's comment about stagnation had made an impression.

He was up by six the next morning. After a light breakfast, he was back on the road by seven. Zander put the top down on the Mustang even though it was cool. He had purchased a sweatshirt the night before, at a little roadside shop, that had all the Florida Keys listed on the back. He liked that. It would remind him of his trip. He pulled it over his tee shirt and enjoyed the scenery.

Most of the smaller keys looked alike, and it didn't take him long to drive past. He spent a little time in Marathon, because it was bigger and he wanted to make sure he didn't miss something important. Marathon was ten miles long but maybe a mile at its widest. Zander could see it was a great place for boating and fishing. There were all kinds of charter boats for hire. There were also quite a few waterfront restaurants featuring the catch of the day. Zander decided that if he ever got back this way, he wouldn't mind doing a charter-fishing excursion. It was something that he needed to add to his to-do list.

Heading north out of Marathon, Zander crossed the seven-mile bridge. It was nothing short of amazing. It was one of those human marvels that almost took one's breath away. The other man-made structure that had impressed Zander was the Eisenhower Tunnel in Colorado. This was better, however. The tunnel was amazing considering whoever built it, went through solid rock through an entire mountain, but once inside, all you saw were walls. Here you saw both the gulf and the ocean separated by a bridge that lasted for seven miles. Zander was thankful for the slow speed limit of 45 miles per hour. He was able to look around and enjoy everything the keys had to offer. The best it had to offer was the huge expanse of water, and about halfway over the bridge, Zander took the opportunity to throw his phone into the Atlantic. It lifted his spirits and a huge weight from his shoulders. This was going to turn out just fine.

Zander felt that Islamorada would be a good place to stop for lunch. He found a nice resort with a tiki bar that served food. It was a real find. He enjoyed himself for over an hour. The Mahi Mahi po'boy was the best he ever had. When he told his server that, she asked:

"How many have you experienced before this one?"

Zander had to admit it was his first. They both laughed, but she told him he was right. It was their specialty.

Zander left feeling like he had experienced the best of the keys. Now he needed to move on. He drove right through Key Largo without stopping. He wanted to find a place to stay down the road. In fact, he decided he wanted to find a small community to spend Christmas Eve and Christmas day. He thought it might make him feel better. He had spent every Christmas in the small community of Hospers, Iowa with his parents until he was twenty-one. Small communities were the best at Christmas time. He didn't know about spending it in such warm weather, however. It just didn't seem like Christmas, even with the decorations.

He decided not to hook up with I-75 but turned off on Highway 41 and headed west. This was the first road that hooked Miami with Tampa and was labeled the Tamiami Trail. It had quite a history as Zander learned when he pulled off and read one of the historical markers at a visitor's center.

The highway was lined with signs that told drivers to turn on headlights at all times. He thought that was strange, until he travelled a few miles. The road was so flat and lined with trees, that it was almost impossible to see oncoming traffic. It was even worse when he tried to pass a slow-moving vehicle. He decided to slow down and enjoy the drive. He even saw some alligators sunning themselves on the bank of the ditches that ran parallel with the road. It was a nice drive and, it took Zander's mind off other things.

It was 2:30 when Zander saw the sign pointing to Everglade City. It was just a few miles off Highway 41, so he decided to check it out. He went south and soon came to a sprawling little community that boasted 400 souls. It would be perfect.

He drove through the town looking at whatever caught his eye. He decided to stop at a place called the Rod And Gun Club. It looked like a bar and eatery and the sign said, "open to the public."

Zander parked the Mustang and entered the building. It was a beautiful old structure with various dark woods lining the walls, floors and ceilings. Someone had spent a great deal of money here during the late 1800's.

A server welcomed him, and Zander explained he was just there to have a drink and maybe get some information. She smiled and pointed to the bar and told him if he had any questions, she would be available until 5:00.

He walked into the bar. It was old and beautiful. Zander always loved old bars especially ones that had been done in such gorgeous old woods. There was a woman behind the bar busy washing some glasses in the back sink. She didn't hear him come in.

Zander cleared his throat. She turned around.

"Oh sorry. I didn't hear you come in. What can I get you?" she asked, as she dried her hands on a bar towel.

Zander couldn't believe his eyes. The woman looked exactly like Natalie Wood. She had been one of his favorite actresses growing up. In 1969 he went to see *Bob & Carol & Ted & Alice,* and he literally fell in love with her. He mourned her death in 1981, and he never believed that Robert Wagner was innocent. Her sister Lana Wood was also in the movies, but Zander never had a thing for her like he did Natalie. He was still thinking about her, when he heard her speak.

"Hello. Anybody home?"

Zander snapped out of his stupor.

"Oh, I'm so sorry. You took me by surprise. Has anyone ever told you that you look like Natalie Wood?"

She laughed. "You and about a hundred other people in here."

"I didn't mean to come off like an idiot, but ever since I was young I had a thing for Natalie."

"Not your best pick-up line, I'm thinking," the bartender muttered.

"Sorry, I wasn't thinking along those lines. I was just so surprised."

"Well, now that you're over it, what can I make for you?"

"Since it's Christmas Eve, why don't you make me a vodka martini? Straight up, three olives, shaken not stirred."

"Coming right up, Mr. Bond."

Zander liked her. She had spirit, and she was beautiful. The dark hair was a welcome change from the blondes of his past. He wondered if she was available. He didn't see a ring on her finger, but that didn't mean she wasn't committed.

She brought over his drink and placed it on a bar napkin.

"You aren't from around here. Where do you call home?"

"I'm in transit right now. Looking for a place to land."

She looked him over. "I'd say you are a Midwest boy."

"What gave it away?"

"Your accent."

"I don't have an accent."

"Everyone has an accent. There's a difference between the panhandle and southern Florida in the way we speak. That is, if you were born here. Not some tourist or transplant from the Midwest." She smiled.

Zander liked her smile. He liked everything about her.

"So, where in the Midwest do I come from?"

"I can't quite place it. Certainly not from Wisconsin or Michigan. I'm thinking west of there."

"You've got a good ear. I'm from Iowa."

"Oh, the potatoes state."

Zander started laughing.

"What's so funny?"

"Sorry, but everyone always confuses Iowa with Idaho and Ohio, mostly because they haven't been east of the Mississippi. You know, Idaho is a western state anyway."

"Guilty as charged. I've been up and down the East Coast but never been to any state in the Central Time Zone."

"I've been west but never past Chicago in the east." Zander said.

"It looks like we've got the beginnings of an interesting conversation. Will you be staying around Everglade City long?"

"Depends on how I like it here."

"What do you think so far?"

"I like what I see." Zander thought he saw her cheek turn a bit red as she turned around to stack some glasses.

"It's Christmas Eve. Where are you staying?"

"I was wondering if you could point me in the right direction. I noticed a few small motels when I drove in. Any suggestions?"

"Let me do some checking for you."

She reached under the bar and brought out a rotary phone. She dialed some numbers, and someone answered on the other end.

"Les, this is Aubrey at the Rod and Gun. I got a guy here who needs a room for at least a few nights. Anything available?" She waited for a few moments and then responded. "Great, why don't you hold it for him?" She put down the receiver. "What's your name?"

"Sander Van Zee, but everyone calls me Zander."

"How you gonna pay?"

"Cash."

"Les, his name is Zander and he's paying cash. Don't you go ripping him off now, he's a friend of mine." Aubrey hung up.

Zander liked the sound of that.

"You let me know what he charges you, and if it's too much I'll let him have it. You've got to watch people around the holidays. They think it's a license to steal. They've got free Wi-Fi, so you don't have to pay for that, either."

"What's that?" Zander asked.

"You don't know about Wi-Fi? Wow. Tell me you have a cell phone."

"Well, I used to have one, but I got rid of it," Zander said, almost apologizing.

Aubrey looked at him. "I think I kinda like you."

Zander felt his own cheeks flush just a bit. He tried to find something to say.

"You have a nice name, Aubrey. Did your parents name you after that 'Bread' song?"

"'Bread' song?"

"Well, David Gates wrote it, but he was performing with the group *Bread*."

"Never heard of it."

"You've got to be kidding me. You never heard of the song, 'Aubrey'?"

"Nope, never heard of it. I doubt my parents did either."

She started wiping down the top of the bar and began whistling the song. Zander did a double take, and she caught his expression.

"Aw, I'm just messing with you," she said, laughing.

"I thought you might be old enough to know that song."

"What's that supposed to mean," Aubrey snapped back.

"Just messing with you." Zander smiled back.

"I think I really do like you. Do you have dinner plans?"

"Well no, I just got here and still need to check into my room. Why are you asking?"

"I have to work here tonight. But they have a fabulous Christmas Eve dinner. People around here never miss it. I could get you in, if you didn't mind eating at the bar. You'd have to look at me instead of the dining area."

"That's the only way I would agree," Zander said, and didn't even mind that it sounded cheesy.

Aubrey smiled, and Zander forgot about everything else.

"You should check into your room. It's called the Ivy House and the only thing they had left was their cottage. It's a two bedroom nice little Florida-style cabin. I think you'll like it, Midwestern Boy."

"Thanks for all your help, Aubrey. You've made my day absolutely spectacular." Zander meant it.

"Do you have anything besides that sweatshirt and shorts to wear? This is Christmas Eve, and it's semi-dressy."

"A collared shirt and blue jeans?"

She shook her head no. "What color is the shirt?"

"It's a pale yellow."

"Well, that's good, but not the blue jeans. Go down to the general store at the edge of town. They are open until five today. Get some pants that are dressy, and pick up a tie to match. Let's get you looking good tonight."

Zander did as he was told. He was hoping he wouldn't have to spend the night by himself, and he would do what it took to make this girl like him.

"What time is appropriate for arrival this evening?" Zander asked, and tried to sound as gallant as possible.

"Come as early as you like. I've decided I like the way your face looks. It brightens up the place."

Zander smiled and turned to go look for his accommodations. He decided that he wouldn't be leaving this place anytime soon.

Epilogue

Bij Nacht Zijn Alle Kats Grau
At night all cats are gray.
— Dutch Proverb

About twelve hours before Zander passed through Key Largo, Sara Jane was being transported in handcuffs from the coast guard cutter to an unmarked black SUV.

When they hailed the yacht, the coast guard said it was a routine stop. Since the stop came just before they had reached Flamingo, Sara Jane knew it wasn't a routine stop at all. It was heartbreaking. She thought she had been in the clear. The boat captain was pretty shaken up, but they told him he was free to go. He wasted no time heading back to Key West.

Sara Jane was alone once more. She was used to being alone. There had been no one else to take care of her needs her entire adult life. There was peace in being self-reliant. This was something else.

She had never been in a position of weakness like she was right now. She decided that she would be as honest and forthcoming as possible. She had no idea who she was dealing with, but she knew it was some government entity just by the secrecy surrounding the men in their suits.

She was taken to some government installation in Miami. It was a cinder block bunker without any windows. The steel door clanked behind her when she entered. A woman behind a desk stood up and moved toward her. She was a humorless ugly woman with horn-rimmed glasses. She looked like something out of the cold war. Maybe she came from some Communist bloc country. It made Sara Jane shudder just to look at her.

The woman took off Sara Jane's handcuffs and showed her to a room with a cot, sink, and stool. The walls were black, and they absorbed the single light in the center of the room. The place was dark, dank, and humorless, like the woman.

Sara Jane wondered how this was going to turn out. She wasn't frightened, but she was curious. Everything reminded her of some spy movie. Maybe she was a threat to national security. That made her smile.

Her belongings had been taken, and she was sure they were going through every item with careful scrutiny. She was happy that she had thrown away Zander's cards. There would be no reason to involve him. She had caused enough hurt in his life, and it was time to let him go.

The commie woman came back into the room and told her to follow. They walked down a hallway and into a larger room with a table and three chairs. The woman sat Sara Jane on the single chair facing the other two and left the room.

Sara Jane looked around the room. There were black walls and flickering florescence lighting. Who did they possibly think she was anyway?

It didn't take long and two men, both in dark suits, walked in and sat in the remaining two chairs.

Mutt and Jeff, Andy and Barney Fife, Boris and Natasha, Sara Jane didn't care. She just wanted this all over with.

One of the men stared at her over his glasses, and the other cleared his throat.

"Can we get you anything?"

Sara realized this was going to be a good cop/bad cop scenario.

"I would take some coffee, and I haven't eaten for a while."

"You'll eat soon enough," the bad cop muttered.

"I'll get you some coffee." The good cop got up and went out the door. He returned with a stainless steel mug.

Sara Jane figured the coffee was ready before they came in the room, but this was part of their little show. She took a sip of the coffee.

It was strong and hot.

"So, you must be wondering why you are here." It came from the good cop.

"I suppose you are looking for information. I assume it's about my past."

"What about your past?" the other one growled.

"Why don't you tell me what you want? I want to cooperate and get out of here as soon as possible."

"That's good to hear. Why don't you tell us about Colorado and…" He checked his notes. "Martin Van Vugt."

Sara Jane told them everything about Martin. She even explained what her role was as business manager. She even told them about his trips to Mexico to get the young girls, but that's where her truth ended.

They asked her where he was, and she told them she didn't know. He had left suddenly, and all the money was gone with him. The only thing left was the business and the little money from the legal side of things.

"I suppose we could turn this over to the IRS, and let them deal with you," the bad cop said.

"I believe you've already examined the tax returns and found them to be in order, or you would have them here right now." Sara Jane didn't like the guy.

"Let me be very honest with you," the good cop said, "we're just looking for information from you concerning Van Vugt's human trafficking business. Your involvement has already been vetted."

Sara Jane was relieved. "You're probably wondering why everything is in my name."

"Please tell us."

"Martin was paranoid. He was AWOL from the military and was always afraid they would be coming after him."

"We know all that."

"We didn't own any property other than Marty's estate out at Cripple Creek and an apartment complex for some of the workers. I sold all that stuff, including his automobile collection, to pay the taxes and have some money left over for me to come down here to Florida."

The explanations she was giving seemed to be satisfying the pair, and Sara Jane could feel the tension starting to lift. She didn't know how much more she could tell them without involving Zander, or Lilly, for that matter.

"So, where did he go?" asked the bad cop.

"I don't know," she lied, "If I had to guess, I'd say Mexico. He knows the place, and he knows how to disappear."

She drank her coffee, and they kept asking her questions. Sara Jane kept her wits, even though she was tired and hungry. It went on until almost 10:00 p.m.

Finally, the good cop spoke.

"I think we've heard enough. We're going to let you go."

"Go? Go where? What time is it anyway?" Sara Jane was now on the offensive

"We've booked you a room in South Beach. It's a funky little old Florida hotel. I think you'll like it," the good cop said.

"But we're not paying. It looks like you've got quite a bit of money you're transporting." The bad cop was still playing.

"It's everything that I have. It better all be there," Sara Jane said.

The guy stood up and got right in Sara Jane's face. "Or what? I don't think you're telling us everything. I think you're hiding things, and we will be watching you closely."

Sara Jane decided it time to back off. She was ahead of the game so far. No sense screwing it up.

"Sorry, I'm a little tired."

"I'll give you a ride," the good cop said.

They drove to South Beach in silence. Sara Jane saw a liquor store and convinced the good cop to stop so she could get some wine. When they arrived at the hotel, Sara Jane asked him if he wanted to come up for a drink. He declined, as she knew he would.

When she reached her room, she was pleasantly surprised. It was beachside and tastefully decorated. She thought about dinner but found that she was no longer hungry. It was just fine sitting on her veranda with a glass of wine and watch the nightlife below her.

She poured herself a large glass of merlot and took a sip. She grimaced. It didn't taste right. She knew the second sip was always better. The taste buds would have time to adjust. She took another sip. It wasn't any better. Was the wine bad, or had the events of the last twelve hours gotten to her? She didn't know but she put the wine aside and leaned back in the chair. She was lucky. Things could have gone much worse. She would find a travel agent after Christmas and book a cruise that would include the Grand Caymans. Maybe she would land next to her money after all. Things might just work out for everyone concerned.

In another month she would be noticing some subtle changes in her body. There would be decisions to make.

She had never given pregnancy much of a thought.

Tin Roof Rusted

Prologue

De waarheid wilniet altijd gezegd zijn
All truths are not to be told.
---Dutch Proverb

The rabbit died.

It seemed like an archaic way to announce a pregnancy.

Sara Jane's childhood experiences in Iowa should have been the first clue. Nobody ever used the word pregnant. It might be whispered among woman, but no one with any upbringing said the word out loud, and certainly not in mixed company.

She had heard all of the clichés: "bun in the oven," "knocked up," "in the pudding club," "up the duff," "pea in the pod," "eating for two," "slipped one past the goal line," "ate a watermelon seed," "bat in the cave," "up the sprout," "preggers," and "she's glowing." Sara Jane wondered what she was.

Her mother had been more discrete and mostly just said: in the family way or with child. Later, it would be acceptable to say PG.

The strangest phrase, Sara Jane had encountered, however, was from the eighties song, "Love Shack." Near the end of the song, the female singer cries out "tin roof rusted." It meant she got pregnant in their little love shack. Maybe it should have happened that way with Zander when they were younger. It might have changed both of their lives back then.

There was always a great deal of baggage connected with an unmarried pregnancy. Things weren't like they were in the 50's, but there still seemed to be that same old stigma among many.

She wasn't going to let that bother her. What did bother her was that she got herself into the situation in the first place.

Her little affair with Avon didn't require birth control, so she went off the pill. Zander hadn't even entered her mind. After all, he wasn't in Florida, until he was.

That little ill advised tryst would end up costing her much more than it was worth. It wasn't even satisfying in the end for either of them.

It wouldn't do much good to relive this mistake. It couldn't be changed. Now the only thing to decide was where to go from this moment on.

It was only two months, but Sara Jane could feel her body changing. She had never considered childbirth. She wasn't opposed to it. It just never entered into any of her schemes or plans. She had been too busy trying to wring out the most in her life.

Now she would have to decide if this were one of those things that would be value-added or if it would hinder her future.

The thoughts were ponderous, as she sat on the beach of her hotel in the Grand Caymans. It was at least a pleasant place to ponder all the considerations.

Where would she go? Who should she tell? The more questions she asked herself, the more confused she became. One thing was painfully apparent; she had very few people in this world that she could actually trust.

One of those people was her sister back in Iowa. The other one was her childhood friend, part-time lover and father of this future child, Zander. But he made it quite clear that he didn't want to continue the relationship. If that's what you could call it. It was never really much of a relationship from her perspective.

Sara Jane supposed it was mostly her fault. Her selfish decisions had come home to roost.

She pushed her drink glass off the armrest of her beach chair. Her drink, "Sex on the Beach" ran into the sand and disappeared immediately. Certainly there was a life lesson there, but she was too preoccupied to consider it.

With that one simple act, she had made her first decision. She was going to quit drinking, because it made her sick to her stomach.

That was the surface decision, but it also sparked the deeper predetermination. A conclusion she wouldn't even comprehend until later.

She was going to keep the baby.

1

Zander had every intention of finding his way to Cedar Key, so he could spend the holidays with his friends Gail and Herbie. That was the plan anyway.

But his travels through the Keys slowed him down. Mostly it was by design. He wanted to take in as much of the area as he could. Traveling the country had been something missing in his life, and he was bound to make up for it.

Everything might still have worked out, but he made the decision to turn off Highway 41 and explore Everglade City. That's when he met Aubrey Moreno. She looked like his favorite actress, Natalie Wood. He just couldn't get himself to leave after that.

Aubrey had told him that she was of Cuban descent. She had the dark hair and eyes to be certain, but her first name didn't seem to fit.

"Where did you get the name Aubrey?" he wondered.

"My parents wanted to name me something more American. I think the name is English. I read somewhere that it means "fair ruler of little people.""

"Sounds about right," Zander said. "You could rule people with just your smile."

"You are so cheesy, makes me want to urp."

"I just can't help myself around you."

"Try to get a grip," she said, gruffly, but her eyes were twinkling.

"So, did you start your life in Cuba, or have you always lived here?" Zander asked.

"My parents emigrated from Cuba when Baptiste was overthrown. There was too much unrest to suit them. I guess they wanted a better life. I was born in Miami. My father and mother worked all their lives trying to bring Cubans to this country. They both worked as translators for the government."

"What did they do in Cuba?" Zander had always been fascinated with the little island only ninety miles off Key West.

"They both worked for the university. My father was a professor of natural history and my mother worked in the business office. That's where they met. Of course here in the states, his degree didn't mean anything, and he couldn't get a job teaching."

"That's just not right." Zander meant it.

"They didn't seem to mind. They were free. They loved this country and they hated Castro, so their government jobs were a good fit."

"Do you see them often?"

"They're both gone now. That's why I left Miami and came here. I wanted to start over and make some new memories. Those had become too painful." Aubrey's voice never wavered, but there was something in her eyes that told Zander she wasn't telling the whole truth.

"Have you ever been to Cuba?" Zander said, trying to change the subject.

"No I haven't. My parents said it would be too dangerous. I guess I never had much of an interest in going there."

"I think it would be fascinating. Everything I've read points to a country stuck back in the 50's. It amazes me how they can keep all the old cars running."

"Cars are just a way to get around." Aubrey didn't seem interested in old cars.

"But old cars from the 50's and 60's have so much style. They are things of beauty. Besides, you drive a '68 Opal Olympia. That's almost a one-of-a-kind work of art. How do you keep that old German vintage running?"

"It's not mine. It belongs to someone else. I'm just using it to get around. I don't even like the looks of it."

"It is peculiar looking, I'd agree. It's probably why they didn't catch on much in the US."

"This conversation is boring me."

Zander decided to worm his way into another subject.

"If I could find a way to get to Cuba, I would love to make a visit. Would you be interested in coming along?"

Aubrey thought about the proposal for a moment. "Possibly. I do have some interest about where my parents came from, and I want to know more about any relatives I might have."

"Let me do some research. Maybe there is a way for us to visit educationally."

"I said, possibly. If I did agree, there would be no discussing of cars."

"Agreed." Zander said.

He didn't have the slightest idea of how he could accomplish getting permission. He had some contacts in the educational world. Maybe he could start there. It would be no easy task.

"If we went, would you smoke a Cuban cigar with me?" Zander asked, trying to lighten the mood.

"Only if you bought me their best rum. I'm told they have some good stuff."

"Deal."

Zander didn't really like cigars. He remembered smoking a few on Jasper's deck in Omaha. He never really saw what the big draw seemed to be for Cuban cigars. They all tasted like a camel took a shit in your mouth the next day. He decided not to share that thought with Aubrey.

• • •

After the holidays were over, Zander decided to get rid of his Mustang rental car. He didn't really need wheels in Everglade City. Most places were within walking distance and if he did need to go somewhere else, he could always use Aubrey's Opal. The fact that it wasn't hers bothered him just a little.

The closest Hertz rental car agency was located on Marco Island. One Sunday in January, the two went to the island. Aubrey followed in the Opal and once they dropped off the Mustang, they were free to make a day of it.

Aubrey wanted to go to the beach, and it was fine with Zander.

When they found a spot, Aubrey pulled into a parking space. She got out of the car and began taking off her clothes.

Zander was a little disappointed, when he saw she had on a two-piece swimsuit underneath. He was wearing his cargo shorts, so that would be just fine. He could take off his tee shirt if it got too hot. It was a pleasant day but not overly warm. It didn't seem to bother Aubrey in her skimpy suit. It certainly didn't bother Zander, and he made sure to get his fill of looking at her. If his gawking bothered Aubrey, she never let on.

Aubrey went to the trunk, pulled out two short beach chairs, and handled them to Zander. She reached in again and pulled out a cooler. She was prepared. Zander liked that immediately.

"What's in the cooler?"

"A few beers, some water, and two ham and cheese on rye."

"Perfect."

The day sailed by. Zander got a terrible sunburn, and he cried about it all the way back to Everglade City. Aubrey told him to shut up. She would rub aloe all over his body when they got back.

Zander thought that might be quite satisfying, and he shut up immediately.

View other Black Rose Writing titles at www.blackrosewriting.com/books and use promo code PRINT to receive a 20% discount when purchasing.

BLACK ROSE writing™

CPSIA information can be obtained
at www.ICGtesting.com
Printed in the USA
LVOW12s1407010217
522878LV00001B/65/P

9 781612 968117